BL(

ROSEMARY A JOHNS

Ruby and I swaggered through the shadowed streets, towards the promenade and Palace Pier - her in crimson silk, me in military Great Coat - two creatures from another world and time, unnoticed by these petty First Lifers because we weren't painted in the colours of their tribe. We twirled each other round, dancing in the carnage and the flames.

FANTASY REBEL

FANTASY REBEL

For A.

'There's nothing but snowflake patterns.'

King James Bible – Leviticus 17:14

'For it is the life of all flesh; the blood of it is for the life thereof; therefore I said unto the children of Israel, Ye shall eat the blood of no manner of flesh; for the life of all flesh *is* the blood thereof; whosoever eateth it shall be cutoff.'

1

You know those vampire myths? Holy water, entry by invitation only and sodding crucifixes?

Bollocks to them.

Because you know what? There are no monsters and no immortals. There's just us: the Lost.

Somewhere deep inside, you know it's true.

I can see a glimmer Kathy - give me something - the slightest flicker in those glazed blue peepers.

You remember me today, don't you, love? At least you *used* to and wouldn't need me raking it up. If I can just get this down, or if you can just remember, I won't lose my last thread of humanity. Sanity. Otherwise there's no one with the pretty pictures in their mind but me. Of what I've seen. Or what I've done.

Do you even remember my name? *Your Light*?

You laughed when we first met and said my parents must be *right hippies*. You were direct like that: I loved it. But I couldn't explain. Not then.

How many months since you've looked at me and said my name? Looked at me and known me?

After all these decades, you're lost. And I'm alone.

Ilkley Moor's bleak when you look out at it under the crisp snow of winter; sod it, it's bleak when the sun beats down in the broiling heat of summer too.

Not that I've seen more than photos of the daytime. I don't fancy bubbling to a stinking pool.

Yet now, when I can't even see the heather, just rolling mounds of snow, which cast blue shadows and make burial mounds of the hills (the boulders the gravestones), it's bloody bleak. So the tourists, dog walkers, day-trippers and climbers, don't come out here in the freeze of the dead months.

Except we're here because I wanted to bring you somewhere familiar, which you'd recognize: for the end. For *your* end.

The docs say – oh, you know, so much bollocks. They're wankers, the quackmongering lot of them.

This last decade, as you've slipped, and I've had to watch, useless as a...

Dementia they call it. They always have a pretty label, don't they?

Dementia.

Box it in. Mask the nasties with their lists and tick boxes. I reckon the physicians of this age figure themselves dead brainy fellows.

So I brought you back here to Ilkley Moor, in the howling wind roar of December, because I wanted you to feel at home. I hoped you'd remember one last time.

Only now I realise all it's done is haunt. And we've a hell of a lot of ghosts clamouring on our backs.

I've a Soul to haunt, the same as you. Of course I died (hollering, I don't mind admitting). Yet when I was reborn into my second life, my Soul was stuck to me. They're fat, mewling consciences, until we choose to carve them away, slice by crimson slice, with every First Lifer we slaughter. But others? We tend to our Souls' shreds, chaining the pulsing migraine hunger.

We're individuals, get what I'm fixing at? More so, because after election, every emotion is amplified: the good, along with the bad.

It's not as if freewill is your headline act alone. We Blood Lifers decide the body count, how fast the tune plays and how deep the darkness bites. Because little by little – year by year – it consumes us all eventually.

It was you who taught me that.

I stand most nights in the damp of our whitewashed stone farmhouse, where everything has been changed from when it was first our home. The shell, however, remains. No one can gut the core of a house. Its beams. Walls.

Soul.

I can taste our life still throbbing warm.

I stare out at the rugged wilderness, which is shrouded in the haze of mists that threaten to swallow us, because I don't have the balls to turn and watch you.

To see you rock backwards and forwards in the crumpled mess of our bed, wringing your hands until the nails rip the skin, like there's something dirty you can't clean off.

That should be me, love. It's all on my hands. Not yours.

On those nights, I know you're lost in the past - not with me - when you say one word, like a bloody mantra: 'Advance, Advance, Advance...'

Why can't I wash it clean for you? And I'm too much of a coward to turn round.

So this – here - is me turning round. This. Here. Now.

I can't change the past. I never thought much about it before. I never had to. I was always the one, who lived in each fleeting second, high on its intoxicating splendour.

You never got that. Not like Ruby.

Sorry, that's a jinx just there. The blood talking. Calling to me. But now I see the tracks left behind are more than the picture perfect moments in my brain; not clinically still, but blurred bloody lines.

I want to share them with you. Fully, unabridged and unedited. All the nasties and wankery. The truth (as far as that exists), before you no longer understand me. I'm writing it down because then I can cut it straight. How I want you to hear it.

If these are the last words I ever say to you, then I need them to be right, so let me get it in at the start: I love you.

From the moment I saw you...no scratch that...from the moment I *heard* you, I loved you.

All right, there was awhile I reckoned I hated you, and *you* thought I was a pillock and a bad boy Rocker too, let's not leave that out. Have you forgotten what a hard time you gave me? But these last five decades..? Although of course to you our love was forever. Yet to me? It flamed brighter than the bloody sun, but it's not forever because that's so much longer than you'll ever know.

Your First Lifer world doesn't get that theirs is only the starter, not the main. None of us know what's for dessert. I fear I haven't been a good enough boy for that and I wager I'm most like to be sent to bed without any.

We tell ourselves lies, however, to maintain the pretence of safety, as if the folks in our civilized country wouldn't burn the world around their ears if they missed just three square meals.

So you see, if anyone but you reads this book, then that instinct for self-deceiving self-preservation (along with every other fib in the web of status quo that bind First Lifers), will kick in.

Still reckon they'll believe? Think this more than fiction?

You lived it. Breathed it. Bled it. I want this to bite to your Soul. But to them?

It'll appear merely ink stains on a page. Not the howling of a vast new world opening up in the shadows.

2

Rough leather motorcycle jacket, studded and faded, decorated with a worn gold *Ace of Spades*, collar firmly turned up, over a black t-shirt, jeans and tall motorcycle boots, topped by a light brown pompadour, tamed with Brylcreem.

'That's what you kids are wearing now, is it?' Your new carer for Wednesdays was studying me, like she'd just revealed a manky specimen in your bedpan. 'Latest fashion?' Her gaze curdled; you could tell it would've done, even when she was half a lifetime younger and not dried up with defeated dreams.

Karen the little thingy on her blue overall read. But after years of an endless parade of day to night handovers, these birds blurred into a day of the week, rather than a name.

I grinned, as I slouched against the wall. 'No, luv, these've been around awhile.'

Wednesday flinched at the *luv*. Babes to this world, you First Lifers bristle at words, which are deemed outdated, as if they had more power than echoes. I'm too old, however, to change more than I already have (and that's more than most).

How about a bit of bloody appreciation?

Wednesday was shuffling around your bed, as if checking for hospital corners. Now I knew she was pissed because no carer ever does that. They stick to checking your pills, pressure sores and signing timesheets, before dashing out of the piss stink of this room as fast as they can.

I try to cover the old woman smell with your Chanel No. 5. You'd have bit my bloody head off for spraying that around mist-like, back when you could speak. But the sweet scent of you darling, it's faded, as if you're withering. I can't even smell the blood in your veins. It's like you're being fossilised inside out, every day one drop less.

Are you still inside there?

As I watched Wednesday's disapproving rearrangement of the sheets, I dragged out my pack of ciggies, clenching a fag between my teeth. Then I rummaged in my jean's pocket, pulling out my gold lighter. I snapped open the smooth lid, flicking on the heady orange surge of flame: I've got to get my kicks somewhere and there's nothing like looking into the fire.

When I lit the fag, Wednesday emitted a squeal, as if I'd sacrificed her newborn to a Druid god (and yeah, I've seen that done a few times, although it's not my cup of tea).

I raised my eyebrow. 'Sorry,' I proffered the lit fag to Wednesday, 'want one?' She drew back, her lips pursed. Wednesday's peepers were puffy with exhaustion; little burst blood vessels threaded her cheeks. You looked dead small in the middle of that big, white bed without me. I wanted to climb in with you and hold you against the emptiness of that white but I didn't reckon Wednesday would've got it. 'Suit yourself,' I withdrew the ciggie, rubbing the tumbling ash between my fingers and thumb, as I took a deep drag. Wednesday looked significantly down at you. 'Oh right,' I wedged the fag between my lips, shrugging. 'Pretty sure she's not gonna want a puff.'

'Second-hand smoke,' Wednesday hissed.

'Christ, reckon she could die from..? Wait, she's already snuffing it. And I can honestly say - hand on heart - smoking's not gonna kill me.' When Wednesday swung her bag onto her shoulder, slamming towards the door, I sighed. Then I flicked the stub to the wooden floorboards, before stamping it out. 'The world's now safe one more night.'

That's the thing about you First Lifers: you're burnt up so fast, like fire consumes oxygen, that every second's precious. Yet your bodies with their fragile cells are open to attack by mutation. Bacteria. Decay.

The worst of it, is that you understand enough of the threat to fight your own desires, impulses and urges. The joys of life, see what I'm fixing at? Smoking. Drinking. Sex...

Life is fear.

Just the act of living for the whole bloody lot of you. And yeah, you're right to fear.

Us Blood Lifers? We died already. We evolved past all that.

At least, that's what we've conned ourselves.

The butcher's delivery service had left the box in the cold of the stone porch, as per monthly instructions. They're good like that - dead efficient.

As always, I'd waited until I'd heard the roar of their van struggling away down the snowy track, skidding on sheets of black ice, which were treacherous underneath. One year, when the winter bites too deep, maybe they'll not be able to make it with their bloody titbits. Then we'll see how well I've chained the hunger: or whether I'm the one in chains. Either way, Wednesday would be top of my nosh list.

Oh yeah, there's a list.

As soon as Wednesday had stomped down the stairs, huddling like a malting owl in her coat, and then out into the smudge of shadows, I snatched up the box.

Bugger me it felt blinding: warm in the cold, beating and pulsing. Alive even in its death. I slammed the door shut against the frost of the night air. You were asleep up in the bedroom, shrivelled in that vast white bed, and I held red life in my hands.

I panted, wiping my knuckles across my lips. I hugged the box to my chest, as I darted across the hallway towards the dark of the connected garage. Your light-proofing's still holding up for the glass panels above the shelves.

I clicked on the over-head. It was fetid; mould seeped across the far wall in black blossoms behind the empty jam jars, which you were going to use six summers ago before...

So many sodding *befores*. Like before this thing got its teeth in you, munching through your mind, piece by bleeding piece. Before it took you away from me. Before it took you away from yourself.

I dived further into the garage, dropping the box, so I could start dinner preparations.

It'd been a long wait; the hunger had become a part of me. This isn't sodding milk we're talking about. It can't be left in the fridge for later: this is kill or be killed. Basic predator 101. You hunt and then you feast. Want to recreate that artificially?

Eat fresh.

I pressed by my Triton motorbike - a slash of crimson in the drear. She was nudging me to take her out. She hates the winter slumber as much as I do. It makes her restless trapped inside.

I selected a latex glove, stretching it out – it'd do.

The blood from the butchers was thick, fresh pigs' blood. I must be their most regular customer: I'm one for *black pudding* me. It was your idea to drop that in, when we set up the order. You still knew what was what back then, at least for some of the time. You always got how to cover, well, you know, *what I am*. You First Lifers act like blood drinking's manky but you still nosh it with your fry ups, don't you..?

I heated the blood in the microwave, which was stowed behind the broken plant pots, waiting for the *ping*. When I poured it into the glove, it bulged out each finger: a fat blood hand waving. Then I tied up the top tight.

Here comes the best bit, when I hold back, anticipating and letting the thirst build: that blinding, intoxicating thrill. How could a First Lifer understand the rush?

You never got it - how all life is laid bare in a moment - no matter how many times I tried to explain. Even though I'd see this look, as if you were laying yourself open, exposed to anything I gave you. Yet it didn't matter: you weren't one of the Lost. You'd never tasted the gush of blood. Words are simply the shadow. The memory of our real lives. But what else do we have?

So right, the glove? It's the closest thing I've found to human skin. Then I can mimic the glorious sensation of violation, when the fangs sink in deep. It's about more than the blood, you see.

Slowly, I extended my fangs: two thin canine needle points. As I closed my peepers, I imagined...

Said I'd tell you all the *nasties and wankery*, didn't I? Flay myself bloody?

I imagined it was *your* neck, as my mouth closed on that glove. I always have done. I imagine, as my teeth pierce the latex in dual sharp points, it's your skin I'm breaking. Your blood I'm sucking. Faster and faster. Harder and harder. That the warm coating the back of my throat is your life drawn into mine.

There's a dizzying buzz, like the world's exploded into multi-coloured connectedness, after a month of monotone loneliness. Then the glove's empty, and you're in me - all in me - completely. Then I climax.

It was over. My fangs retracted, as my peepers snapped open. I dropped the sucked dry glove into the bin, wiping the blood away with the back of my hand.

Now, don't get narked. You're to blame (or to be thanked, I don't know bleeding which), that I have to drink this animal piss to start with.

For my abstinence.

It was an ultimatum - yeah, *yours*. Give up First Lifer blood or lose you. I reckoned you were barmy.

Not bloody likely, I said.

Then we rowed. I swore. Bargained. Begged...

Of course you didn't get it (you never did), what First Lifer blood truly is to us Blood Lifers: it's our very breath. No drug blows your mind to such a high. And the dead sweet part? There's no down.

When it hits, you actually feel each chamber of your heart pumping, as every cell, nerve and synapse sparks. The atoms of the world unite in flowing motion, as if you're part of something infinitely bigger than you or the world. You could touch the face of sodding...god, nature, the universe because you're truly alive. In that moment more than when you slithered from your mama's bloody womb.

But here's the thing - animal blood? Not the same bleeding deal. It's like pretending sugar free can give you the same rush as the sugar laden, delicious original. The spark and life is only just there. It singes but it doesn't burn.

And I hunger for the burn.

Look, a pig's not exactly as high up on the evolutionary chain. It doesn't have the same DNA to ignite the match.

But you'll survive, you'd insisted, *you'll live*.

Yeah, a half-life. A shadow.

Still I'd done it for you: a half-life with you was better than a full one alone.

There was no choice between loving you, or loving the blood, after what we went through to be together. After the corpses we left behind.

Real hearts and cupid me, aren't I?

Still, I deserved the ultimatum. Don't think I'm wriggling out of the blame. After all, you found me with that skanky donor.

You must've followed me, when I was too drunk on the call of the blood to smell you.

This punk rocker had invited me up. She had piercings in her mush, lower down too, but I didn't have a shufti because with that much metal, she'd have stuck holes in me if I'd got too intimate. She must've dressed for the occasion: pink tutu and combat boots, with eyeliner drawn on like battle paint.

The punk kept stroking the *Ace of Spades* motif on my jacket, like it was a religious symbol she'd sworn to memorise; it made me wonder if she was writing a text for a band of deluded Blood Life worshippers. But the smell, Christ in heaven, the *smell*. Pot wafted in mushroom clouds, choking me, as I swaggered after her inside. My peepers watered.

The bint had already drained her blood into a chipped *I Love My Mum* mug. It balanced on a dressing table that overflowed with spiked bracelets, ripped fishnet stockings, razorblades and a bowler hat, which jauntily hung off one edge, as if it'd dropped out of the pages of *A Clockwork Orange*.

The bird smiled when she passed me the mug, just a hesitant twitch of her mouth's acned corners. Her fingers drifted over mine. I'd already offered cash, but she'd refused. I'd suddenly realised I wasn't bloody well offering what this bird - in her crush daydreams or death wish fantasies - reckoned either.

The blood was warm, swimming; I watched it dancing round and round in beautiful circles, singing to me to *drink*...

Then came hammering on the door downstairs and your voice, hollering loud enough to wake the dead, 'Get out here Light right quick, before I come up and belt you one.'

I never did get that last drink.

I was pacing around the garage, my shoulders hunched, clenching my fists up, as if for a barney or a bonk, with the blood bobbing through me, when I noticed the board over the window was rotted.

It was flaking snowy splinters in dust showers. The rusted nail was bent out of shape, like a deformed spine. As I tested the board with my thumb, the wood suddenly crashed from the glass panel in a decaying mist, flooding the garage with the orange glare of the dying sun.

'Buggering hell.'

I leapt backwards, as my cheek smouldered like the tip of a ciggie, my eyeballs melting ice-cream at the bleeding beach. I hissed with the agony of it, the nitwit braindeadery of it, the indignity of the one sodding vampire myth that holds true – night walking.

A sharp shaft of sun burnt across the garage, over the Triton and between me and the door out to the hallway.

I was trapped.

What if you needed me?

I strained to listen. But the house was silent. You were either sleeping or were...

Bloody morbid I was nowadays - death catches you like that. I'd forgotten. Not because Blood Lifers are immortal, in fact we simply decay more slowly because the blood replenishes us. We still have a shelf life: this whole planet does. I've never seen one of us much older than half a Millennium.

I leant against the damp wall, exploring my tender mug. I couldn't make out anything but dim shapes in the garage with my burnt peepers, except that blinding spear of light. The blood would fix that, give it time. It heals, restores and resurrects, even pigs' piss poor substitute for the good stuff. The new skin cells were already tight where they were knitting themselves into place, grafting my mush back to its never changing contours.

That bursting into fire in the cruel light of day?

See here's the thing, it's more like wax reacting to a flame. Us Blood Lifers are candles: we burn bright.

But there's always a cost.

If you want the science and not the poetry (you used to say that, and I'd nark you by merely grinning), it's to do with how our cells synthesise the blood to repair themselves.

What gives life, takes it away. The world's big on irony. Or would be if it cared enough. And it doesn't.

Our clever thinkers know the formulas.

Me? It's enough to know the sun and me don't mix. But I walked in the day once and now I have the night: 50:50 seems a fair split.

I tried to edge around the strip of light, but the sun was still too high. My boot protected my foot for the second test, but by the intense heat in my toes, wouldn't for long. I didn't want to have to get out the stink of skin fused to leather because that's nasty. And not something you ever forget.

I slunk to the trapdoor in the far corner, swinging it open, before I slid down into the belly of the basement. The basement is a tiny cave-like room, with nothing in it but a truckle bed, wireless music system and my tatty editions of Mojo.

I sprawled on the blankets, letting the door slam shut and entomb me in a familiar blackness, as I waited for my eyesight to return and my cheek to mend.

I slipped in headphones, moving by touch alone in my private refuge. I hoped the haunting melancholy of The Stones' "Ruby Tuesday" would sear the pain away; the driving piano, plucked bass and recorder were part of the permanent soundtrack of my life. Memories of my own Author

- lost to me - were brought to life in the black. My own Ruby.

This is where I retreat - my underground hole - when the daytime carers come.

In the early hours, when the sun's still pausing for breath over the hills, I hand over your breakfast (toast and honey), your wash things and make-up because you deserve to look...yourself and your mountains of multi-coloured pills, to the whichever day of the week it is carer.

Then I pretend to head for work through the garage. I don't know what the carers reckon I do, or how I get there, but they don't bother to ask, and I don't bother to tell. It's a game we play. We all do that. Not that I *can* work, not even cash in hand, no questions asked stuff, with you to look after. Other avenues aren't much better. Not since you knocked the nicking stuff on the head.

When I was first elected into Blood Life, there was nothing I couldn't take, if I fancied. Now I have to budget your pension between the two of us.

Talk about being bloody defanged.

At least pensions are one less thing *I'll* have to plan for: silver linings in the dark, right?

But when you... When I'm left behind, there'll be no more pension or house. No more you.

What shred of the First Life, which we've built for nearly fifty years, will I have to hold onto then?

What part of it's been *real*?

The terror rises - sticks in my throat, darling - chokes me...when I think that.

The past, it's like this series of photos. But the future's just this expanse of black. What if I slip back into those shadows with nothing to hold onto? But I don't want to because I've already seen what's in them.

I know what's waiting for me.

I always lock the garage, once I've left for my pretend work because I see those women's looks, suspicion like spiders in their peepers. Big bloody double padlock on the basement once inside. I'd dug this hidey-hole the first year we came back here. *Overkill,* you'd called it. *Security,* I'd said.

Because they know: the carers, delivery boys and all the other gormless First Lifers, who stumble across us. Not *what* exactly but they still pick up the prickling sense that something's dodgy. *Different.* But do they say anything? Of course not. That'd be too simple and straightforward. The truth without artifice.

No, I get the *smile* instead. You know the one. We get any more repressed in this great country of ours, we'll implode with all the crap we're *not* saying.

It's always been a problem. First I was your husband. Then toy boy, son, grandson...to strangers. To you I've simply been *your Light.* But we've had to keep moving, Christ, so many places, because of those labels. Also because of *me*, in the bible of you.

'Why won't you register with the Blood Life Council? Things could've changed? They'd sort it.'

Sort it? Those nasty bastards? The Blood Lifers, who give other Blood Lifers the willies?

We'd have got sod all from them. Apart from maybe done in.

At least, they'd have given it their best shot.

Let's say they were reasonable for once. Reckon I want my balls crushed in the sweaty hands of Westminster? Just another dog to be leashed and tagged? Those wankering bureaucrats are no more than petty shadows of the First Lifer Parliament. And you know what I think of *them*.

Except we don't even have the vote. There's no democracy in our world, only a bunch of brats no more than decades old, wielding their power like their dicks, in the way only blokes can, who are excited to discover how to use them: by buggering the rest of us.

'Stop playing the rebel,' you'd said.

Know what? I'm not playing, love. I tried conforming once, didn't fit.

I won't be what the First or Blood Lifers want. But I've tried - for you. My blindside. My wonderful weakness, for whom my blood hums.

The sun had finally bled behind the moors. My new skin was tight and pale. I could see as sharp as a night owl again.

I switched off The Stones, swinging out of the trapdoor into the shadowy garage.

When the rotten board crumbled in my hand, as I tested it, I ached for you; I'm a creature of the night, but you were the creature of the toolbox. I ripped what was left of the wood from the nails, hurling it against the far wall, where it shattered with a satisfying *bang*. When I heard you startle awake, I instantly regretted it.

You were crying. A low animal wail.

I legged it into the hallway and then up the stairs into our room. You were thrashing side to side in the bed, agitated. Your gaze wandered to me in confusion, as I dived towards you. But there was no recognition. Only fear.

'Just me, luv.'

'No, no, no...' Your fingernails were scrabbling at me, as I soothed, scratching deep gouges.

'All right,' I backed away, the blood trickling down the backs of my hands, 'you're safe. It's night. Sleep time, yeah?'

You quietened. For a moment. These bursts of violence burn you out. And scar me.

I tried to smile. 'Kathy...'

A low moan. Your mouth hung open and then twisted into a snarl. You clawed at the covers, raking them up and down, as if you were trying to escape.

It was your white wisps of hair - more fragile than even the bones in your thinning body - which got to me. Sometimes it's the little things, which you could never guess at, rather than the big stress or drama, which boots you in the gut. It made me march to the door, without looking round again, as I mumbled, 'I'll make us a cuppa.'

Only once I'd clicked on the kettle in the dark of the kitchen, resting my forehead against the exposed stone of the open hearth, did I realise we were out of mugs. That cheeky bitch Wednesday had slurped tea into her mush all day, without sodding well cleaning up after herself. Instead, she'd stacked the slimed mugs, with grainy rims, in haphazard piles in the Belfast sink. Sighing, I threw off my jacket, ran the water and started bloody rinsing.

The image of your white hair on that white pillow, forced itself on me: no escape this time. Look, I've seen enough corpses in white coffins. Morbid, right?

I concentrated on drying your special Union Jack mug: the one I'd filched from "I was Lord Kitchener's Valet" on Carnaby Street in the 1960s.

We're both still here.

The mug's colours were faded and there was a hairline crack under the handle. Me? I'm smart as ever - not that I ever *was* smart.

I dropped the teabag in but as I turned for the kettle, I heard your shriek, 'Advance...'

I swung round, catching your mug tottering off the edge. I saw the danger but bugger me if I could do anything to stop it. Not this time.

Everything was in slow motion: the Union Jack mug tumbling arse over elbow to the flagged floor, red and blue smashing in a spectacular *bang* Mr Firework. Great Britain shattering. Yet all I could do was watch.

I stared down at the now still pieces. Your mug. Broken.

Then I was bawling out my nancy little heart, balled up under the oak table, because it was like the world was falling and I'd better find somewhere to hide. Except I'd forgotten how to feel like that because Blood Lifers'll tell you that we don't fear. Yet we do, when we're motivated. And love's the greatest motivator of all.

So I kept on bawling, until it felt like there was nothing of me left - I'd salted it out in tears. Then I cleared away that old broken mug, before brewing you a new cuppa.

You studied me dead close as you supped your tea.

I experienced one of those moments, when I reckon you know me - not for long - just for a second or two.

I snuggled down next to you, massaging your palm, in the way you always like: round and round, anti-clockwise. You smiled.

'We'd lie like this out on the moors, remember Kathy? That first night we did it, on the hilltop by the Twelve Apostles? Buggered your dress with stains, but you'd stripped me down to the skin, so *my* clothes were all right.'

Was that another smile? Your blue peepers were wide.

'Your hair was...' How could I go on, when I could see the dandelion fluff puffed over the pillow beside me? '...bloody gorgeous. Just growing long again. It'd tickle me when you did that thing you liked to...' It didn't feel right going into details. Not if you weren't with me. Not truly with me. Christ I ached for you. 'Well, yeah, that thing you love. Of course there was the danger and the thrill. You told me I was a junkie for it. You were right. There's nothing like the hunt. Also nothing like being the prey. I grew out of it. Or maybe I did.' I looked down.

You were whining again. Your gaze was unsteady.

'But it was a rush. What they'd do if they ever... It heightened those moonlit shags. Ranks them in our top ever and we're, well, thoroughbreds, at least in that department. But you know what I never told you? It was the moments after, when we were starkers, yet in no hurry to dress, when I'd share the night and the beauty of the stars with you, whilst you'd share the day and the sun with me, all those details of your life that I couldn't live with you, which I loved the most. Did you ever get how sodding jealous I was of every daylight hour? You'd say how tasty the blackberries were, or how yellow the spikes of the Bog Asphodel. Or you'd tell me about the flutter of the Green Harstreak butterflies, the loud bark of frogs, or whirr of Red Grouse over the low heather. You brought a world to life that I'd died to. Day and night united, darlin', that's us.'

I grinned, but you snatched your hand away from me with a deep growl.

You were lost in the darkness again, and I was lost to you.

You didn't know who I was; I frightened you, some kid in a studded leather jacket yakking about day and night.

Just leave out the poetry? Well, all right then.

3

Sometimes Blood Lifers come back wrong.

We never talk about it, as if pretending it doesn't happen makes the nasties of the world *puff* in a cloud of bleeding smoke. But it does, all right?

During the Cuban Revolution, I had a run in with this one berk, who didn't like me much on his territory. Not to mention he was a bite at cards. He drained a dozen chicks a night but he was touched. Because after? He washed, not only his hands but also his whole body, head-to-toe - *scrub, scrub, scrub* - with these stiff wire brushes and bleach, until he scraped the skin from his muscles. But then he killed and washed and healed and killed and...

See what I'm fixing at? *Touched*.

Blessing for him really when I staked the poor sod.

Disappointing bollocks vampire myth two: we can be staked.

In this particular tosser's case, I shanked him. Anything pointy, however, does the trick. Wood doesn't figure: sword, knife, spoon (if you're twisted), it just has to stop the heart. Everything comes down to the heart. It always does.

Here's the thing, this geezer was always tooled up, apart from when he was starkers in the bath awashing away his bloody sins: that's what gave me my chance to do him, before he indulged in all the nasties, which he spent his nights bragging round town he intended to visit on me. It's kill or be killed in this world.

There used to be these blokes, Order of Electors, who made sure no one came back addled. You'd cop it at the end of a sharp sword, if you failed their tests - doggy jumps through bloody hoops to prove you weren't off your trolley. Ruby told me about them. I reckon she had to go through those trials back in the day. But now? They're long gone.

So we come back any old how.

Then we whisper behind closed doors about whether a fragment of Soul's been screwed up in the transmutation, or the wiring's simply different, as if in some buggered up universe we're experts in mental health. But know what I reckon? The problem was already there, deep inside that person's Soul. In the dark places folks don't talk about. The hidden demons we don't admit to.

Blood Life simply lets them come out and play.

The thing is, we're not big on self-control. It's not like we give in-depth interviews, or decide we'll move in together for a year first, in case things don't work out, before we choose who we're going to elect.

We go on heart and gut alone, you know? A few months of stalking, or nowadays maybe throw in a search engine or two. There's no psychological screening.

Not even a pop quiz.

Psychopaths? Sociopaths? The mentally unstable? That worm was already eating the apple from the inside out, but the Author only saw the fruit's glossy red surface, until after they'd gorged.

Every emotion amplified, remember? The bad right along with the good. Even love curdles into obsession.

All right then, here's a thought: maybe none of us come back right. Maybe *I* didn't. But then maybe there's no such thing as *right*. Who gets to sodding judge?

It used to drive you wild, me not knowing things, which seemed bright as day clear to you, yet were dark as dirt to me.

It's you First Lifers, who divide and categorise.

Abnormal, normal. Sane, insane. Gay, straight. The in-crowd and the out. Good and bloody bad... So many labels I can't keep them sticky in my mind.

Even when you shade to grey, you call things *spectrums*: rainbow arcs that everyone's to be charted on. Sharp pins along a curve to mark our bleeding place.

The Lost? So there's something wrong with us? But there's nothing wrong with *that* because I slashed the chart up to confetti, fluttering pieces like paper snowflakes. No one pattern the same. And there's nothing so pure as snow.

What First Lifer can see the snowflake patterns and not the black and white divides or the rainbow?

You could. And you loved me because of it...eventually.

Yeah, maybe I did come back wrong. But buggered if I'd go back to how I was.

I prefer the pretty patterns in my brain.

Your snowy hair laced eerie beauty across my fingers, as I lay with you in the cold of dawn. The sun was peeping around the blind, searing brands to mark me.

You were stroking your ivory silk scarf again - that *sexy little thing* as I call it - up and down. It was as if the sensory touch of it could snap you back to me and wake you up to yourself. I'd sprayed it with Chanel No. 5 and now your scent clouded the air at each caress.

I breathed in deeply - breathed you in - bloody well wanted to devour you.

My Kathy.

But you weren't here this morning.

Where'd you gone gadding about to again? A point back in your timeline, with me? Or when you were some tyke and I was..?

All right, the same as I am now, of course. Different coat though.

You'd have bleeding loved my coat.

You were so still this morning, corpse-like (and I should know). Your peepers were wide open but there was no response in them. Not a glimmer.

If you were really dead - not Blood Life and not this living death - but six feet under, worm-food dead, I'd understand, grieve and move into the blackness, which I can see even now on the horizon. But this twilight? One foot in both camps? The body lives on but the mind..?

It's like you're being sucked into an oblivion, which is obliterating everything you are. I'm not going to sodding well let that happen. Not to you. So I remind you, in the only way left to me, when I'm now a stranger in your eyes.

'How about some music, luv?'

I slipped off the bed, dragging my vinyl collection out from underneath it. I flicked through the jackets: Johnny Kidd and the Pirates, Marty Wilde, Eddie Cochrane, Chuck Berry, The Animals, Them and Billy Fury and THE FOUR JAYS – now *that's* my man.

I bowed "The Sound of Fury" open, holding it against my chest and letting the LP slip first out of its inner sleeve and then slide between my fingers. You never truly appreciated the first wave of rock 'n' roll pioneers. Instead, you developed a taste for the wild electric magic of Hendrix and the later anarchy of The Sex Pistols. But this song? It brings back memories of 1968.

The year we met and the first time we danced.

The Dansette record player was out of shape but the old girl's done us good service. I placed the needle down midway: it still played.

"Since You've Been Gone" crackled to life. As soon as the first bluesy piano chords riffed, shivers trembled through me - the same as always.

When that raw voice started up, with its ravenous caged passion and the hunger under the surface - the one we'd listened to at night under the covers and swayed to in this house, when you'd been young but not innocent - I was suddenly back there... I never wanted to surface: my arms tight around you, your fingers curling in mine... Then the fast, slapped bass kicked in, igniting the song *bam*.

I strutted towards you, grasping your hand and swinging it in time to the rhythm.

Still not a flicker. But maybe deep under the layers, beneath the crust and the magma in that red hot core, you knew.

Something stirred and all of a sudden, *you did*.

Your fingers twitched and then clutched mine. Bloody hell, I could've burst and never stopped dancing.

I laughed. 'Now you're getting it.' A spark in your peepers. Your brow furrowed. Then your back jerked. 'All right, darlin'; don't get too excited.' But now you entire body was thrashing in a paroxysm. I couldn't tear my hand away without hurting you. Your nails were digging in; blood was dripping onto the white covers, staining them in fat blossoming drops. The core was now awakened, exploding in fiery volcano. 'It's me...it's only... I'm not gonna...'

Then you screamed - a high-pitched terror - your peepers were wide with it, as you let go of me to claw at them, like you wanted to put them out.

I trapped your bird-like body under me.

Christ, what were the carers going to write in their bloody paperwork, when they saw the bruises?

'You're all right. You're safe.'

But you weren't seeing me. When did you now?

You were hallucinating some past horror and thanks to sodding me, you had more real horrors in that beautiful mind of yours than most. You were weeping, quivering like a cornered animal.

Then you said, clear as day, 'Ruby.' I stared down at you, pretending – wishing – I hadn't heard. Those lies we tell ourselves, right? Because I was a total wanker. I'd conjured up that nasty from your murky memory, with my own selfish wander down memory lane. When I'd been trying to remind you of love, I'd invited the devil in, instead. 'Ruby,' you repeated and then screeched, over and over, 'Ruby, Ruby, Ruby, Ruby, Ruby...'

'It has been many weeks, my darling Light, you have grown weak.' Ruby drew me further down the London Docks, by the low lodging houses, lusheries and bordellos, through streets still swarming with labourers, sack-makers and all the poor, who clung onto the stinking river, which swept away both the City's filth and delivered up the world's riches.

Rats those First Lifers seemed to me now in the dark.

I was shaking but I struggled hard to hide it.

Ruby's red hair swung loose, like a bawd. She dressed, however, as if a queen. Although not one this Victorian age had ever seen. She floated above humanity in her own world, where she was without question, sovereign.

Here's the thing, Blood Lifers don't follow trends. When you live as long as us, it'd be a sodding waste of our second life. Instead we choose our favourite and we stick (at least for a century or so), until something new comes along, which takes our fancy. Then we add it in, eclectic-like.

It's all dressing up, isn't it, the whole bloody thing?

The birds don't go in for makeup because they don't need it; night lighting's not exactly harsh on the skin. And the blood? It gives us a glow. Ruby shone brighter than anyone – or anything – I'd ever laid eyes on.

Ruby was still a bleeding mystery to me though because all she'd told me, since she'd elected me into this Blood Life, was that she'd been Authored in the reign of Elizabeth the First, which made her one of the powerful Long-liveds. There was something about the crimson silk of her dress and the way she moved, as if she was an aristocrat and I was a servant on her Estate, which whispered of the world she'd died to.

'Dearest prince, if you do not eat, you will not live.'

'Then I won't live.'

The back of my nut banged against the sail maker's window. Ruby's long-nailed fingers were hard against my chest, crushing me, as she twisted the choker at my neck, until it bit.

The tar from the lines stank. I couldn't control it, these new nocturnal senses: seeing in the dark, smelling the stench, hearing the cacophony of sailors' shanties, goats bleating from some ship's hold in the basin, a rope splashing in the water and the *feel*...like my skin was being grated down to the eyeballs. It was as if I'd been surrounded by a bubble, which had separated me from the real world, and now everything was touching me for the first time. And all at once.

'You will live. You will obey me. And you will feast most heartily.' Ruby's lips were close to mine. I couldn't move. Ruby stroked my mush, with a tenderness I'd never experienced in my First Life.

I remembered waking only a couple of hours before in our crib, tumbling naked in white sheets with Ruby and without a word, making the beast with two backs. Ruby had done things to me, which I'd never known had even existed.

When Ruby released the pressure on my chest, I gulped for air. 'I can't do this.'

'I am your Author, muse and liberator. Put away First Lifer thoughts. Death is a human companion. We are simply the agents, no different to smallpox or a tempest. God created those too, did he not?'

Ruby nibbled my lower lip; her bite was hard enough to draw blood. When she pulled back, she stroked the hair out of my peepers in careful, moulding motions.

'God created us?'

Ruby smiled. It was child-like, yet so very ancient at the same time. 'In that he created the world, and we're of it. Should a wolf be begrudged its hunt, or its kill, because it too has to feed? There's no sin in your new blood hunger; it's as natural as the moon.' Ruby tipped my chin back, and we stared up together at the bloated satellite, which was suspended in the fug of black. *Blood.* The word had triggered cruel clawing pangs, which hollowed me, driving me half barmy with the pain. 'Let us play a little game.'

Raising her eyebrow, Ruby pointed out into the bustling street, with her beringed finger, at a satin-waistcoated mate, who was clasping a green paraquet that was trapped inside a cage.

The bloke was scrutinizing a shop window, which was stocked with quadrants, bright brass sextants and mariners' compasses: he must be about to set off on one of those huge ships. Soon he'd be swept far away from these stinking shores. Just like I'd always dreamt of, when I'd watched the ships sailing up and down the Thames. In one bite I could end his journey...forever. I knew exactly why Ruby had chosen him.

Bugger this.

But still...I could smell the bloke's blood from here, *all* their blood and its pulsating heat: he looked like a sodding feast.

I breathed deeply, as I shook my nut. I wasn't yet ready: for what I was, or what I could no longer be.

'That one?' Ruby whispered close in my ear, as she singled out a sailor, who despite the heat, had a large fur cap pulled low.

There was something off about the sailor's aroma, however, like it'd curdled. He was glancing at a covey of whores, who were already worn out with grinding the lads for pennies - fire ships, every last one of them. And that bitter scent? I reckoned he'd been sent out a sacrifice and had come back a burnt offering. I could taste the clap even at that distance

I shook my nut hurriedly again.

Next was a smart custom-house officer in brass-buttoned jacket, who was shoving his way through the little people, his piggy eyes sparking with contempt.

'Come now,' Ruby nuzzled down my cheek, 'a customs officer? Who will weep for him?'

'No.'

I thought Ruby was going to belt me then.

Instead she slipped her arm around my waist, dragging me close. 'I'll not let you die, when I have tasted your Soul. This...shyness is not curious for one so young to Blood Life but it must be mastered. See it for what it is: the dying of your old life. I have a gift, something to ease your too human guilt. The crossing from day to night.'

Hushing my questions, Ruby dragged me by the hand further into the labyrinthine docks. The ships on the jetties, which reached out into the four basins, were a forest of masts; flags hung dead without the breeze, between the fingers of chimneys. And the stench...

Every warehouse we passed, as we drew further away from the crowds, I was hit by a different wave: first pungent tobacco, next sickening hides and bins of horns, then fragrant coffee and spices and finally overpowering rum. That last one I didn't mind so much.

Ruby hauled me into the shadow of a titanic warehouse, snapping open the door as easily as if it'd been sugarcane. Inside the floor was sticky, like it'd been newly tarred.

Now I got real quiet because I could smell something mixed in with the rest... *Blood*... But there was a fast thud to it. A surge of some extra ingredient.

Then I realised it was *fear*, which was making it so delicious.

Yeah, so I'm a bastard, right?

But is it a First Lifer's fault the lamb tastes better than its mama, or did nature choose to make it that way?

I could hardly stand for the hunger now; Ruby had to wind her arms around me, heaving me down into the dark vaults. There were low lights hanging from black arches; gas lamps swung midway between each.

Shocked, I gazed at the colossal catacomb of precious vintages, which had been sent from vineyards across the globe: thousands of tiers of casks, pipes, barrels of French or Cap wine, brandy or rum. The powerful fumes mingled with the peculiar one of dry rot. As I limped onwards with Ruby, it was like strolling through a city of the dead, but instead of bones and skulls, there were barrels and casks. 'Are you trying to get me ran-tan?'

'No, not that.'

That's when I saw what the smell was. The blood and fear, which made me thirst to consume the world. *Who* it was.

Grace - my first love and sweet torturer for the last three years. My tempter and betrayer. Destroyer of my heart.

Grace was strung in chains, her feet dangling helplessly above the ground, like a frog stretched out for dissection. Her back was arched against the barrels. She was gagged and when she saw us, she started up with these odd little squawking noises. She'd been stripped down to her corset; the stiff whalebone bulged her dugs out, like apples.

I suddenly remembered the many nights I'd wasted alone, tossing off over the glimpse of ankle, which Grace had flashed me with a coy smile, as she'd climb into her carriage. Now her pale body - this weak flesh - which was laid out like it was in a butcher's window, repulsed me.

Ruby was watching me intently, as she nudged me closer. 'My gift, darling Light, do you wish to unlace it?'

I wasn't shaking now. There were no more doubts or qualms. Nothing holding back the predator inside. There was just this tiny sliver, which watched with horror, at how *right* this felt.

So this is how it went down: I derigged the drab down to bare skin and then I grinned because you know what? Grace was chicken-breasted under that corset - another First Lifer lie.

Strange, all Grace's thin body did was remind me how much I'd relished Ruby's curves, tipping the velvet, until I saw nothing but red. I still smelled of Ruby; she was on my lips. This blonde beauty had made me weak. But now I was strong.

When Ruby propelled me closer, there was safety in her touch because she was united with me in the kill.

'Blood is our birthright,' Ruby's voice was low; it swallowed the darkness, until the vaults echoed with it. 'It's the natural order. We would never have existed on this fair earth, if it was not. We would not have these,' as Ruby's two thin canines extended, Grace squirmed frantically, 'or our venom, which paralyzes and stops their weak hearts, as if they were clocks. We are so perfectly designed for their blood, as they are so perfectly designed for us. Blood Life is not hunger. It's fulfilment. Freedom.' Ruby's hands caressed around me, naughty as before, to those places that had never been touched before my death and election. 'Dearest prince,' she breathed, 'free yourself.'

I edged the gag out of Grace's mouth.

Grace gasped, panting and then stared between me and Ruby, whose hands were still wandering wherever they fancied.

I knew what Grace was thinking: how could some nobody, like me, have done this to her? Her little plaything turned round to bite her?

When I saw the tears glistening in Grace's peepers, it was like being booted in the gut. The death throes of my First Life. Then it was over.

'Thomas, please--'

'My name is Light.' The fangs shot from my teeth; I sank them into the milky white of Grace's neck. It was pure bloody instinct.

Grace screamed, but I was lost by then, engulfed in the blood.

Grace shuddered to paralysis, as I drained her. I was bursting with it – Ruby's gift of new life. It was like nothing I'd ever experienced or imagined. I wanted everything the world could bleeding well throw at me.

When at last I fell back from Grace's still body, I was laughing with excitement, shock, mania... I draped my arms around Ruby's neck. 'My thanks for your most perfect gift. It was...' I laughed again.

My nut was ready to explode – *boom* – with the rush and roar of the blood and the beat of my own heart, powerful in my chest.

Ruby glanced at Grace, whose eyelids were twitching feebly. 'It's the river for this Athanasian wretch; let it carry her away with the rest of the filth. Then you'll be free of her most completely. Free of all First Lifer ladies. Do you not feel it? That roaring call? It's the world unfolding before you. The next step into the light, even though we dwell in the dark. Are you ready now, dearest prince?'

I gripped Ruby hard by the shoulders, as she traced the blood from my lips, slowly sucking it from her fingers. Then we were kissing.

All the nasties and wankery? Yeah, that first kill was the most complete moment I've ever experienced in First Life or in Blood.

I'm not going to lie to you, not one word when this is the last time...

Well, you know, right? And git that I am, less or more than human that I am, *it was bloody perfect*.

When Ruby held up her neb to be kissed - it's true - I loved her. And I was turned on because I wanted her, the same as I wanted the blood.

I'd have done anything for her. The two of us could do whatever we pleased.

It was intoxicating.

When I pushed my hand down towards Ruby's quim, however, she caught my wrist, with a laugh. 'Just the blood heat. It will pass.'

'What if I don't want it to?'

'You are young, and this is new. When it fades-'

'I won't let it.'

I saw Ruby's expression change then. For the first time, there was a mixture of confusion and doubt, rather than contented control. Ruby stepped back. 'I know a place we could... Where our own kind...'

'Others?'

Ruby frowned. On her brow it was terrible. 'You do not want that?'

I slipped away from Grace's naked body, noticing with surprise that no blood had leaked from the tiny puncture wounds at her neck, as if something in my venom had sealed the holes, after my teeth had withdrawn. It was a marvel of evolution.

Grace was still alive – just - her gaze seeming to follow me around the dark vault.

I leant against the caskets; the wine fumes were making me heady. 'I don't play nicely with others, or at least they don't with me. I never was much part of the world, even when I walked in it.'

'But *we* play very well, do we not?' Ruby was at my side, even before I'd seen her move. Her fingers teased my tackle with long strokes.

'You're different,' as the rhythm of Ruby's hand increased, I struggled to stay still, 'you're my Author, muse, liberator...'

'Love?'

I caught Ruby's fingers before I climaxed, raising them to my lips. 'Is that not why you chose me? So I would love?'

Ruby slunk closer, entwining her fingers around my throat. 'So, lover, if you do not wish to walk in the world, will you let me be your guide to it?'

'A Grand Tour?'

'Of sorts. The two of us.'

'And the earth to eat whole.'

Ruby's nails bit crescents into my neck. 'Patience. Learn its secrets first, before we dance. You have a mind, as well as a heart. I elected you for both.'

When Ruby wrenched her fist back, I waited for the clout – this one liked to play rough. But the *smash* came beside my head with a loud splintering of wood. Then an explosion of red, a blast of wine fumes, and I was flooded with it, as a crimson gush poured from the gaping hole.

Christ in heaven Ruby had some power in her; I wanted some of that.

No, *all* of it. Ruby and her secrets wrapped up in a bow.

Ruby thrust me back, until we were caught in a fountain of French wine. We were giggling like kids, opening our mouths wide, drinking deep, as it coated us in a second skin.

'Thought you weren't going to get me ran-tan?'

Ruby licked the red tears streaming down my cheeks. 'This is a celebration. There must be wine at a man's...' She caught my hand between her sticky fingers, twisting it back towards the contorted corpse of the First Lifer, who I'd once wept for. 'To Grace.'

I blinked the wine from my peepers. The blood was still hot, pulsing through me in a howling haze of ecstasy. I smiled. 'To the world.'

Ruby. My red-haired devil, Author, muse, liberator, guide: my gorgeous nightmare.

Ruby did it, you know. She showed me the world's secrets.

Yet here's the thing, to do that she took me to darker depths than I'd ever dreamt of, let alone knew had beat in my own Soul.

But that's bollocks, right?

Because I'd only thought they didn't, until Ruby showed me those places, which we all hide locked away, reckoning we're dead civilised, rather than bloody cavemen. As I said, *bollocks*.

We're animals when it comes down to it. Predators of one type or another. You First Lifers war over territory, your gods or your women, as if you've only just discovered bleeding fire. If you ever try and get between a woman and her cub, you'll soon discover you've got a tigress on your hands.

See the truth of it is, everyone enjoys a good barney - win or lose - they hunger for the fist and the boot. Who doesn't want to get a bit dirty, once in a while?

Modern life tries to smother it, but it's under there, if you lift up the corner and peer beneath, then you'll see it's bubbling to get out. And Ruby, sod it, did she let it out.

Ruby brought me to life by killing me.

Every emotion amplified? Mine – love, curiosity, an aversion to authority – they survived but twisted, like a blasted tree after lightning. Where once they were pale and sickly, now they were intense, powerful and dark.

It's not as straightforward as good and bad. You don't get to sticky label me. No one does. It was simply *different*.

It made me feel like loving Ruby would be the death of me, even as I lived for being close to her. We relished breathing the same air. Draining the same First Lifers. Shagging and hurting, until we knew each other's bodies the same as our own. All was nothing outside our love. It smashed on us. Broke on us. We savaged it. Together we screamed at the world and when we had the world by the throat, the world screamed back. There was nothing we couldn't do, or take, together. Nobody else we needed.

I thought Ruby was mine, stupid bastard that I was. But I was young, so yeah, I didn't reckon I'd be the one who got burnt.

It should've been impossible for us to understand each other, what with Ruby being an Elizabethan bird, and me not being born until the age of steam power. In First Life, if there's a single generational divide, the parents can't understand a word their kids are spitting, whilst the kids reckon their parents are dinosaurs, who should be euthanized for not keeping up with the latest slang.

So how can Blood Lifers bridge the centuries: Tudor to Generation X? Punk Rocker to Georgian dandy?

Because we don't stand still: mosquitoes teared in amber or museum exhibits in wax.

Each moment we travel through - in our parallel lives to yours - it sticks, clinging like caught gossamer spider webs to our skin. The worlds of First Lifers never die. They live on in the blood of those who witness their crawl from the cradle to the grave, which just sometimes is a brilliant burning dance across the stage.

Me? I'm the bleeding audience.

True, some Blood Lifers despise this adaptation and mingling of species; they want to keep themselves pure and uncontaminated. The wankers. But me?

First Life fascinated and consumed me; it haunts me still. The ease of it, which I'd never learnt. Its warmth, joy and *life* drew me, like the sodding moth to proverbial flame; I hungered for the burn. In turn, your world clung to me more than most. We suckled each other as the years seeped by, one year crimson into the next.

But I was only ever on the outside, looking in.

It all started with stuffed hedgehogs. The Great Exhibition of 1851. Of course I was too young then. But papa's lot? They went bloody barmy for them, starting a craze (and you know what us Victorians were like with our crazes). We never knew where the bleeding line was.

Ruby decided the first thing on our list, after we'd sampled the delights of London, was to have a gander at Potter's Museum in Bramber. We broke in one night, when the well-to-do tourists had already gone home.

We strolled in the silence, between tableaux of dead kitties with ribbons tied around their fluffy necks, as they posed on hind legs, like miniature First Lifers at the altar: bride, bridegroom and vicar. Others modelled frilly costumes, as they sedately supped at a tea party: a polite society of corpses.

That was Ruby's number one lesson, and it didn't take me long to get it: it's not us Blood Lifers, who dream of death - it's you First Lifers.

It fascinates, possesses and *excites* you. So you hold it close, precious for those quiet moments. You fear it. Yet you still seek it out vicarious. Even though you always know it's coming, you still love the shadows.

Blood Lifer's aren't death; they're merely part of something bigger.

'See how they play games too?' Ruby whispered.

After, we travelled by night to Dover, crossing the English Channel to Le Havre, by coach again and then a trip by boat up the Seine to Paris.

When Ruby spoke French it was beautiful, mesmerising – and perfect. I foolishly reckoned she'd be impressed with my mimicked attempts.

Ruby, however, only laughed, dragging me away. 'Do not frown so. We will find you a tutor. A good tutor. A *proper* tutor.'

'But I...Wasn't it right?'

'There's a difference between right and the feel of it coursing through your blood. You must learn to listen and feel. Not parrot.' *Tutors*? It was like being a kid again. Every evening I awoke to Ruby's naked outline pressed to mine, in the crisp Parisian air, with her long, red hair spread like curtains, over the white of the sheets. Yet when I'd roll over in the four-poster (a new luxury indeed), and slip my hand to Ruby's knockers, her emerald peepers would snap open, cold and hard as hell. 'If you wish your trinkets not to be rent or be-torn, I would remove your hand and concentrate on your lessons instead.'

Fencing, riding, dancing... Ruby said all men must have these accomplishments. Even Blood Lifers.

When at last Ruby was satisfied (and she was bloody hard to satisfy), we hired a carriage and flew on to Italy.

It wasn't until we arrived in Turin that Ruby finally rewarded me for *my patience* in my lessons, teaching me new ones as she did so, which I never wanted to end.

We didn't surface for several months from the ecstasy of each other, except to hunt in the ancient streets.

From there we rode to Florence, where Ruby became my Cicerone, guide and tutor; it was a revelation. I was walking in this vast world, which I'd once enviously watched gliding by on the Thames. Now the earth was revealed, spread before us like a sodding banquet; the greatest works of First Lifers, were as if ours alone.

In the blackest night, we'd wander the deserted piazzas, staring up at the Duomo's terracotta and white dome; *Brunelleschi, fifteenth century*, Ruby would murmur and then point across the piazza at a Gothic bell tower, which soared into the star-lit, Tuscan sky: *Giotto's Campanile*, she'd add.

Or we'd perch on a crumbling wall high over the city. Ruby would rest her nut on my shoulder, as we were serenaded by the haunting Gregorian chants of San Miniato's Benedictine monks, during vespers.

We ate two of the monks after; they tasted sweet, like nectar.

You'd expect monks to be peaceful, but one duffed me right up, before I bit. I guess it was the outfit, which caused me to hesitate - all that black - or maybe the chanting had made me sleepy. Yet after the first taste, I fumbled, and he legged it, his skinny shins kicking, like a long-legged hare.

Ruby laughed at me; I hated it when she did that. 'After him then, my brave hero.'

'In this heat?' I leant against the cool stone, probing the swelling around my purpling peeper. 'Lost my appetite.'

I watched Ruby guzzle at the neck of her fat prize; it hadn't been a fair contest between our two - hers wobbled with too much lard to fight back.

She gazed at me over his sweaty neck. 'Eat. We can share.'

'I don't need charity.' Churlishly, I turned to watch my monk's stumbling collapse. He'd only fled halfway down the hill, before he'd staggered, clutching at his chest, with a comical strained look.

All right then, here's where I come clean: how it really works. The truth is we don't drain dry, that's the bollocks. Blood is pure and powerful, even the smallest drop. One pint is more than enough to satisfy us. It's our secret, which is deadly.

It's not the loss of blood that does you in, not when we're taking so much less than the half, which causes a First Lifer to cop it. It's what's invisible on the tips of our fangs.

You can beat us off, or escape entirely. It won't matter. If you've been bit, you're dead.

The heart – *bam* – explodes. The blood flow is blocked. The heart's starved of oxygen. And then it's all over. I believe the quacks, who reckon they're dead clever men in this modern age, call it *myocardial infarction*.

In autopsy reports across the world, low blood levels are only minor footnotes, where the primary cause of death is... You guessed it. *Not us*.

We're the perfect camouflaged predator.

It'd be a bleeding crime, except in case you're not getting the through line here, this is about survival, and I'm all for that. In the past, the only thing we left was a pale but peaceful corpse, before the wailing began.

Now *that's* evolution.

A First Lifer's heart, who lives an average life, beats 100,000 times a day, 35 million in a year, two and a half billion in a lifetime. All that thudding and squeezing simply to pump the blood round because it always comes back to... Yeah, you know what.

You reckon every single weak heart gave out on its own? There must be part of you, which finds it reassuring that some were helped along?

You used to hate it when I talked like that; you'd get so shirty with me.

Yet the memory of blood is the only thing I have left now I'm on the pig gruel.

One night we slipped into La Specola, a museum next to the Pitti Palace, which stank of something sweet but rotten. When Ruby gripped my hand tight, I realised I'd never felt this radiating from her before: it was something alike to fear but not. It was revulsion.

'The First Lifers are proud of this...museum of death,' Ruby breathed. 'They call it science.'

'We can go. Let's find some piazza with music, drinking and dancing. The land of the living for once? Then we can...'

Ruby held her finger to my lips. 'You need to see.'

Ruby's hand curled tighter around mine. I glanced up. The walls of the museum were pinned with dead butterflies: every type, colour and size. They were neatly ordered, categorized and labelled. As my pulse quickened, Ruby caught my eye. She nodded.

Room after room was the same: display cases lining the walls, standing from floor to ceiling, or lying open, like glass coffins. Snow White in some twisted rendition of the tale. Rooms of stuffed birds, stilled forever on their perches, with predator next to natural prey: herbivores, carnivores, a huge hippo and a gallery of primates staring back blankly from their boxes.

We paced in silence, until we reached the primates. Then I rested my forehead on the glass, holding my palm up to touch the grasp of the chimpanzee on the other side.

Poor bugger.

Death was so close it throttled me. I'd lived close with it, intimate-like, as a Blood Lifer.

But this?

I'd known science in my First Life or reckoned I had. Yet somehow I'd failed to see the darkness underneath.

'All that's missing is one of us,' Ruby's fingers were stroking the back of my nut. 'Then they'd have the full collection. We're the Lost species. Why do you think we hide?' I twisted to Ruby, shocked. She raised her eyebrow. 'Are we not superior? Evolution's advancement? Yet we're adapted for masking our true face, whilst relying on humans for sustenance. Just as we do the night for protection from the sun. Prithee tell me how beggarly is a divided world, in which half does not fathom the truth? And for it to be danger akin to heresy to reveal it? Consider what these First Lifers pay to see.'

With disgust Ruby led me around the exhibits. For a moment, I thought there were mutilated cadavers laid out in the glass cases (which gave me the willies I can tell you), but then I saw they were anatomical wax models, copied from real corpses.

All right then, so that wasn't much better because on every side were these torture victims, with their guts out, their chests ripped back and lungs offered up, as if we were about to dig in, whilst twins curled around each other bonded in uterus. The skinned man was laid on his side, arching in agony.

When I paused at a man reduced to one large circulatory system, I felt Ruby's arms snake around my waist. She rested her chin on my shoulder. Blue and red coils circled the corpse: First Lifer reduced to food and all it'd needed was a little flaying.

Here, laid bare, was the proof that man was created for our needs.

'They want to be feasted upon, even if they do not know it. A First Lifer is our prey. We grant the death he seeks, so he no longer needs to fear it.'

I reckon Ruby experienced unexpected guilt for taking me to that place and giving me the collywobbles.

No, all right then, not guilt - whatever was closest to that emotion, which she was still capable of feeling. She was tenderer than usual for the next few days.

At least, she tied me up less often.

I'd wake to Ruby just lying there, watching me. She'd kiss my neb lightly over and over, as if dispelling something.

Then Ruby bought me a whole new set of close-fitting clobber: a double-breasted reefer with military stand-up collar in indigo check and a velvet trimmed overcoat. She twirled me round and round, clapping her hands in delight. Then she promenaded with me - all dolled up - in front of the fancy ladies and gentlemen in the piazza d'Azeglio, who were spilling out of the light and buzz of theatre performances, into the quiet of the night.

They'd always felt off, however, those threads. Maybe because Ruby had chosen them for me, as if I was her sodding Mary-Ann.

So later, when we were caught up in France during the First of the two bloody wars, I took the opportunity to filch a British Officer's Great Coat. He didn't need it, since he'd been shot through the head (poor sod). The coat, however, was fine.

We weren't meant to even be there, shouldn't have been within a thousand miles of those bleeding killing fields and that madness, where I truly learnt where the science I'd once worshipped could lead.

All the beauty and terrible splendour of this earth, yet First Lifers were racing to develop new ways to annihilate it?

Death, you see, that's all right – natural - carnage raw in tooth and nail. But apocalyptic machines, which dealt it out with a twitch of a finger, chattering *ack-ack-ack*, whilst dying soldiers were entangled in aprons of barbed wire, like puppets shuddering on strings..? The *whomp* above your nut, before the whole world dove for cover, and the earth shook to dust; metal beasts lumbering through the heat and churning the world to nothing but mud and sleet, nothing but sodding mud and sleet, whilst the neat white crosses were erected between blood-red poppies..?

And the *boom* of those guns...

If you haven't heard those guns, you're not haunted by them. But me..?

We got trapped once for a full month between those lines of First Lifers. The blood of either side smelled exactly the same; the mound of rotting corpses, which we were forced to hide under, stunk just as badly. Yet they were still trying to mechanize slaughter each other, as if they weren't the same species.

And *we're* the monsters?

Boom, boom, boom...

Those bloody guns bore into me, day and night. They drove Ruby half-crazed, buried as we were under the mud and the soft ooze of decaying soldiers, until she tore at herself with her nails. I had to hold onto her to stop her.

Then Ruby lashed out at me instead. Still, that was better because I could take a hiding but what I couldn't bear was to see Ruby hurt herself.

Our extraordinary senses can be our weakness or our strength. Like all creatures, we have to adapt.

The light shows in that war? They burnt my peepers. I can still see them.

Hell came to earth in those days and not in the form of us Blood Lifers. Humanity invented it for themselves.

All that said, I did get a blinding coat out of it.

After that, we wandered the world seeking nothing but each other and solitude. Not that easy with my kind because if you don't play by the rules, they'll find some reason not to like your mush. Then they'll bottle it, faster than First Lifers, after a curry and lager on a Saturday night.

I'd witnessed thousands of bodies heaped on the fiery furnaces of Flanders. It was a sense of connectedness to the earth itself, fresh and unsullied, for which I hungered.

It did fade, the shock or whatever, of it. Yet for years the sight of First Lifers triggered something sickening, jolting me back with flash shot clarity, to the *boom* and the lights.

At those times, Ruby would sit with me as I shook, holding a woman's neck pressed to my lips, so the blood would run in because I couldn't hunt, more quietly patient than I'd ever have guessed my lover could be.

Sometimes Ruby would disappear for days, weeks, even months...

But she always came back. I reckoned Ruby simply needed to be alone: I sodding knew how that felt.

We settled in Deadvlei - death valley - in Namibia, which in the twilight, looks like a surrealist painting and in the dawn is otherworldly; withered trees are silhouetted, against the highest sand dunes in the world. Where once there was a whole bloody forest, now the encroaching desert had smothered all life.

Ruby and I felt at home there, like the sands and we were kin. We kept only the company of the black mambas, which coiled round us as we slept, as if we were no more alive, than the branches of the murdered trees.

Years later when I was much more myself again (don't roll your eyes, I get there's no such thing as *myself*, all right?), when my mind was in fewer fractured pieces and spent less time screaming, stuck in that hole in the Great War, we were in Waitomo, New Zealand, as I prepared a special do to celebrate the day of my election into Blood Life.

Ruby and I hunted together through the undulating green fields. Then fed on the same farm girl, whose lips smelled of the lad she'd been snogging, only moments before we'd snatched her in the dark.

We whooped through the ice waters of a waterfall, in a rite of shared blood and bond of love.

I wanted to surprise Ruby, so I led her down into the limestone Glowworm caves. Thousands of tiny, luminescent glowworms lit the ceiling of the grotto an eerie blue.

'My dearest prince has indeed been busy.'

'For you. Anything for you.'

We were on the deepest level. I'd strewn furs over the damp cavern floor, along with a bottle of local gin, which I'd nicked (and might just blind us), and Ruby's favourite toys: ropes, blindfolds, leather braided and knotted floggers...

That's when Ruby turned to me, serious all of a sudden and commanding as any aristocrat ever was. 'I wish to go back to England,' she said, her brow furrowed, 'we should go back.'

Bollocks.

I knew, don't reckon I didn't? We'd go, there was no doubting that. But it also meant something was wrong - dead wrong - and for the first time Ruby wasn't letting me in on it.

Where was my Author, muse and liberator now? Where was my love, if secrets abided in Blood Life, just as much as First?

Lost to me, that was where.

I could feel Ruby slipping.

4

'Looks worse today, doesn't she?' Wednesday was peering into your still face, her sour mouth pulled down at one side. 'Another *accident* earlier. They get like that at this stage, although I know it's part of the job. Oh yes, I've seen a lot of clients go downhill fast when they're close to--'

'Shut your bleeding mush, all right?' I threw myself away from the wall and down onto my knees next to you, as you lay entombed under the white sheets, as if I could protect you from the likes of Wednesday and every poisonous word, which dripped from her venomous lips. I grasped your limp fingers between mine, stroking the backs of your hands, in the way you always loved. They were cold. But I knew you could feel me. I just sodding knew it, all right? Affronted, Wednesday had raised her sharp eyebrow. 'Just...don't yammer on like... Not in front of her.'

'I see. You really think your...*grandma*, is it?' Wednesday inflected the word with cruel mockery.

'That she can still hear us? She's lost to the world. I'm putting a brew on.'

Wednesday bustled down the stairs, sniffing loudly. I flinched, when I heard her banging the mugs about.

What the bloody hell did any of it matter?

As soon as the lazy bitch had slurped her tea, her time would be up, and I could sign her timesheet. Then she'd bugger off for another night, leaving us alone together, like it's always been - well, for you.

For me? There was my First Life, followed by a century of Blood Life with Ruby.

Yet when I think about it, it's odd how alone I still was, until we...

I never knew it though. Or admitted it. We're all practised liars to ourselves.

Funny thing, the lives we paint in pretty pictures, drawing ourselves a world to trick our minds, hearts and Souls that we're part of something dead important. Even a great love.

Love - yeah, I was always one for that.

MAY 1964   BRIGHTON, ENGLAND

'By heaven, look at these ruffianly roaring boys. This is it - your tonic - to get back into the fray. The blood and heat of it.'

I'd nicked a bright red Jaguar E-Type (beautiful little number), and we'd tonned it up to the coast for Whitsun Bank Holiday. Yet now we'd found ourselves caught in a war between two gangs.

A Mod in smart Italian suit and fish-tailed Parka sped past us on his Lambretta Li150, only to be blocked by a wall of hard men Rockers, in dirty motorcycle jackets, who were swinging heavy bike chains. The poor git was dragged away by his lapels, like a fancy sacrificial offering to the gods of leather.

'What do they want?'

Ruby shrugged. 'What do First Lifers ever want? Question is, what do *we* want?'

I hesitated, before grinning. 'The Bedlam. To revel in the madness, like we used to. I want--'

That's when Ruby kissed me. She hauled me close, as her tongue thrust deep, like she'd only just discovered me again after a long absence: I realised she only just had. When she drew back, we were both smiling. 'To live in the world again?'

I nodded.

Screams? The shattering of glass? Curling smoke on the night air?

I was bloody alive once more.

Ruby and I swaggered through the shadowed streets, towards the promenade and Palace Pier - her in crimson silk, me in military Great Coat - two creatures from another world and time, unnoticed by these petty First Lifers because we weren't painted in the colours of their tribe. We twirled each other round, dancing in the carnage and the flames.

Mods fleeing, with gashes on their foreheads, their coats flapping behind them. Couples sprawled under the stars, on a beach where the pebbles met the sea, as turned on by the violence and danger as any Blood Lifer, pretending to be oblivious to a ring of Mods, who were kicking a curled foetus of a Rocker bloody with their sharp winklepickers. Deckchairs smouldering in orange bonfires, which lit a town prowled by leather clad kids on Triton motorbikes.

Flick-knives, coshes, knuckle-dusters...

Here's the thing, the deadliest weapon of all? It was this type of wild confusion, which was like a force of nature. The quick change from predator to prey and back again, in the turn of a corner.

It was glorious to watch: it fizzed. We laughed at the brutality. It was a cosmic bloody joke. But I know you won't get the irony. First Lifers never sodding do.

It was powerful - the smell of all that free flowing blood, which surged with adrenaline.

Remember what I told you about Grace's blood? Well take that and amplify it tenfold, hundred fold, sod it, *a thousand fold*. Bugger me, was it mind blowing.

It had this added masculine, tooled up excitement; don't tell me those blokes weren't getting off on it because they were and without the excuse of blood drugging their veins. They were high on the fear and the fight and it was delicious – to them and to me.

That's what awakened me to the world again. Ruby had been right: all I'd needed had been a right good barney.

As we flitted towards the onion-domed Palace Pier, however, the night was quietening, as the pigs rounded up the oiks and battered them. Those who were left, had broken down into aimless wandering. All right then, so there was a hard-core, still battling it out in the blackest corners, slashing and carving or giving some bleeder a hiding. But do you know what I saw? Amidst a night of folk devils?

Some hulking Rocker, with skull and crossbones on the back of his grungy leathers, jumped off his motorbike to help an old biddy safely up the steps of her Regency terrace.

Ruby and me exchanged a disgusted glance.

Bored, Ruby slipped her hand down towards my todger, but I caught it.

Swearing. Loud scuffles coming from the Palace Pier. Ruby and I both turned to listen.

The pier was spooky in the evening light (and yeah, I can still find things spooky because we're not the only things that go bump in the night). The lights were blazing down the pier's ornate length, even though it was closed up. The funfair was shut too, which was a shame because I could've done with a game or two.

Ruby nodded. Then we swooped towards the pier, hands entwined.

A Mod - not a scratch on him and dead smart in a reversible jacket and polo shirt buttoned up to his pale neck - was scrapping with a Rocker, who was twice his size (and twice his age as well). Strange thing was, there were bands of Mods and Rockers slouched around watching, smoking and bantering, as if they were at a bloody football match.

This wasn't the white hot rush of Bedlam: it was the cool truce of Christmas day in wartime.

Then I saw him - this wanker of a photographer - snapping away at his staged fight, like a god.

And I knew I was going to taste him, just to hear him pose for me, whilst he screamed.

'They came for a real fight, did they not?' Ruby's mouth curved into a smile.

I hunched my shoulders, as I pulled Ruby closer to me by her waist; I wanted to feel every inch of her. 'Then how about we give them one?'

We threw ourselves down the pier as one, towards the make-believe. We, however, were real - we were *too* bloody real and with fist and boot, like the Blue Fairy, we made them into real little boys too, Mod and Rocker alike: bleeding little boys.

I launched myself at the photographer first. Just like I'd reckoned, he had no bottle for reality. He turned, scarpering before I'd even duffed him up.

That's the best part, when the hunt begins: in and out of the closed stands, dodging the railings and kiosks.

I got to play after all.

The photographer's panted terror was the beat I danced to; I extended the cat and mouse because we all deserve our fun, right?

He blubbered when I let myself catch him.

Don't get shirty, not over him. What type of geezer prefers to watch, than do? Dodgy, that's what that is. Psycho written all over it.

I did the world a favour.

At least, that's what I tell myself.

I know what your view would be; you've lectured me about it often enough. But all the *nasties and wankery*, right?

Tell you what though, I nicked his camera: blinding little model.

Those daft berks laughed, when Ruby first leapt into the rumble. They weren't laughing, however, when she broke their arms, noses, legs and less said about what she did to their goolies the better because that one's a queen of hurt (and I'd know).

We did our bit for First Lifer peace, as Mod and Rocker united against us. The blood in me soared, when I picked them both off equally in the roar of battle.

Mine was no pretence, you see, no peacock preening or nomadic romanticism of anti-authoritarian anarchy. It wasn't a sham loner status, culled from the flicks or the clobber on my back. I was the true outsider, and these First Lifers were too busy playing at it, to even notice.

In fact, you know what? You First Lifers still are.

I booted the last twitching body, trapping Ruby in my arms, before dragging her away, back to the seafront.

I buzzed, shaking, nauseous now with the hunger for blood. Tonight hadn't been about feeding. Somehow Ruby seemed to always know just what I needed.

Yeah, you're right: I was her good doggy on a leash.

The fat stars were bright, pulsating shards in the sky; the salty air was sharp. We strolled arm in arm between the puddles of light from the lampposts, staring up together in silence.

It was beautiful.

'Wanna go to the chippy tomorrow?'

Ruby shrugged. Then she nodded towards a pale stuccoed hotel, through the green railings of the promenade. A young Rocker, with a dark pompadour, was wearily knocking up its owner.

'Would you rather not feast tonight?'

What do you want to hear? Every crunch and bite? I bloody promised, didn't I? It'd be a piss poor attempt at honesty, if I got poufy now and... Oh, sod it.

Ruby took the old bird splayed over a counter in the kitchen, amidst the remains of her shattered Portmeirion coffee pot. Then we worked room by room, dividing up what we found on gut basis because blood calls to you, sometimes to one more strongly than another.

Here's the thing, we can smell, long before we open a door, the First Lifer inside. Look, that's important, because I don't have a go at kids. That's a line for me, especially as they smell...*unripe*. There's no urge to touch or taste. *All the wankery, yeah*?

Some Blood Lifers specialise in the young, like a niche market. The same as veal. Every emotion amplified? You don't need to think too hard to guess what dark corner Blood Life shone a light on there.

Most Blood Lifers are repulsed, but it's the choice of the few, who justify it on taste grounds. They insist the blood's sweeter on account of the innocence.

Bollocks to that.

Kids aren't innocent: being closer to birth, simply means being closer to animal instinct. Society artificially imposes civilization, as age teaches self-control. Kids are humanity at its rawest.

I imagine they taste nasty.

So we got to the last room and discovered the young Rocker.

Ruby and I were already throbbing, pulsing with the fresh blood ripping through us. We were tripping like we hadn't in years. The world was detonating in colour and light; we were licking the walls and each other - tasting the universe.

We were laughing - I know that - giggling at sodding nothing.

The Rocker actually opened the door to us with this look of surprise, like we were interrupting his kip and he intended to tell us to keep it down. Then his expression changed to a sort of stupid incomprehension, when he saw the blood dribbled down our chins, since we were too bleeding gone to even wipe it off.

Before he could slam the door, we were in and like all the rest, we didn't give him the chance to scream.

Ruby snapped the bloke's neck before we drank. Our fangs sank in deep, as Ruby held the Rocker between us, like a fallen antelope. Then we let him drop to the orange shagpile.

I sighed as his blood mingled with the others': the magical mix popping in my bloodstream. A blood rush overload.

When I swayed, Ruby steadied me. Her nut was on my chest, listening to the thundering beat of my heart.

I glanced around the Rocker's room: at the combs, keys and Brylcreem on the dressing table and his clobber stuffed in a scruffy suitcase. I bagged his still smouldering fag from the glass ash tray, taking a deep drag. As I flicked the ash off the tip, I noticed a ten inch record sticking out underneath the Rocker's twisted body.

When I disentangled myself from Ruby, I slipped the LP out. I wiped off the smears of blood with my fingertips; music should be treated with respect.

"The Sound of Fury" by Billy Fury and THE FOUR JAYS.

The bloke on the front was a dead cool Rocker with pompadour hair. I liked the look of him, so edging the LP out of its jacket, I dropped it onto a record player, which balanced next to the messy bed.

As soon as the needle touched the vinyl, Ruby and me were hit by a raw vocal and guitar, which only made the blood in us move the more, until we were ripping at each other's threads. We tripped over the corpse, as we stumbled to the bed. Then we were rolling naked in its filth, lost in each other and the moment because that's what it's like: blood.

Real blood. First Lifer.

It's everything, and you're everything but in that second only. So you've got to take it. Ride it. Live it...

The music built its rhythm - our bodies' rhythms against and inside each other - spun a web for our world, where nothing else existed. Ruby threw me on my back, holding me down as she snogged me.

Bugger she was strong.

I rolled onto her. Our thighs were hot, entangled. Then we were feasting on each other. First the sweet agony of Ruby's bite on my chest, and then I suckled from her pure white throat.

Our venom, perfect design in all things, heightens the pleasure; when taken natural in small doses it isn't toxic to our own.

Isn't evolution a hell of a thing?

And our blood? It makes yours seem as water is to wine. It's like the world's singing: a choir of dirty angels. To Ruby, it's close to Sacrament. That's why I didn't get to taste often but when I did? I achieved the only true moments in a whole century of Blood Life, of total peace.

Why? Because it makes you complete.

Is that happiness?

I'll tell you something, it's not hell.

At last, Ruby pushed me away, lapping the last blood from my wounds, up my chest, to my neck and then my mouth.

Then it all started over again...

In the morning, as we lay sprawled starkers in the silent hotel, the curtains firmly closed, we heard the brawling start up again outside.

Bollocks vampire myth... What am I even up to now? Look, we can be awake in the daytime, we're just knackered because we've been up the entire night. *You* can pull an all-nighter if you have to, can't you? That's classic vampire prejudice, seeped into public consciousness or culture, that's what that is. I'd say Blood Lifer but then First Lifers don't even know we exist because we're camouflaged.

So between kips, we'd spent the day wandering the corridors of the now deserted hotel (*no vacancies* sign up, of course), whilst I messed around with my new camera, which really was a blinding little piece of equipment.

We'd been listening out for broadcasts on a transistor radio, which we'd discovered in the kitchen, once we'd stepped over the stiff corpse of the proprietor, about how the Mods and Rockers were still going at it, like a bad repeat. It was as if they hadn't learnt a thing from yesterday.

Or maybe like it'd been as much of a game to them, as it'd been to us.

'Naughty boys are foolish indeed to behave so,' Ruby had held the radio close to her cheek, her nails clawing so tight around it, I thought she'd snap it. 'See how lessons do not seed with First Lifers?'

Ruby would narrate stories to me, in those difficult years after the Great War, when I'd lie shuddering in the grip of night terrors (reliving the *boom* of the guns, flash of the lights and the stink of rot).

She'd tell me of how she remembered a time when armies would agree to fight well after breakfast, with the steady march of two battlelines towards each other. How both sides followed chivalrous and honourable rules. But the whole rulebook's blown to pieces now, isn't it?

After World War Two, it was nuked.

Look, First Lifers fight, get it? It's what you do. Kill. Rape. Destroy. It's worming in your nature. Every day you sit calmly at a desk and don't rip out the heart of your piss annoying, bully of a boss, you're simply supressing it. You know it, even if you won't admit it.

First Lifers wail about butchering wars, rebellions or massacres half way around the globe. Yet you never stop to ask why they're still happening. You just want them to stop.

Bloody genius.

Want to know something?

They're never going to stop.

Not whilst you reckon you're the apex predators, stomping around this planet, like the King of the Animals.

If your boys don't have a war to be sent to die in, they'll make one at home. If your Government acts like a pack of tossers (and that's not much of a stretch of the imagination), then they'll riot, burning their own streets to ashes, like bloody heroes. It's skin deep, this twenty-first century lark.

Us Blood Lifers? We're merely more honest about it.

In the afternoon we got some shut eye, curled hot in each other's arms until sundown.

Whilst Ruby was dressing, I strolled naked to the mirror, grabbing the Brylcreem and comb as I passed; I shaped my hair up with them into a pompadour. I grinned, modelling my latest look for Ruby, like a mannequin.

'My own Billy Fury,' Ruby smiled, catching me close and hard against her, for one long moment.

I loved this new age, freedom, music, clobber...

Our weekend had resurrected me once more into Blood Life. I needed a fragment of it to wear as a second skin, in case I forgot who I was again.

I dragged out jeans and a black t-shirt from the dead bloke's suitcase - just my size.

Ruby was watching me with narrowed peepers.

I wrenched the tall motorcycle boots off the Rocker, who'd started to soften down the path of decay; he'd already passed the rigor mortis, which had comically stiffened him all day – they'd do.

An arm at a time, I heaved off his motorcycle jacket, which was studded and decorated with a gold *Ace of Spades* on the back.

'You're a rebel now?' Ruby assessed me, transformed into head-to-toe Rocker.

'I was always a rebel,' I lit up, striking the match against the wall with a smile, 'just got me some new threads.'

Then I glanced down, noticing the motorbike keys on the dressing table: *a bloody Triton.* I caught Ruby's eye. She shook her nut, but I grabbed the keys anyway, before sauntering to the door.

I looked back at Ruby over my shoulder. 'Wanna take a ride with me?'

'Do you wish to take a ride with *me*?' Ruby snatched the keys from my fingers. Then suddenly serious, she traced down my cheek. 'I'm glad we came back. I'm glad *you* are back. Yet I sense something's happening in the First Lifer world: a change I've seen before. But this time, we need to be ready to play our part.'

5

'Change is always difficult for everyone involved. Sometimes, however, we need to have a long, hard think about what's best and accept--'

'I'm not sodding accepting nothing.'

Wednesday sighed, straightening out her uniform in quick, frustrated motions. 'Try to be more open, yes? You need to seriously consider, well, what we talked about earlier.'

'*You* talked. Did you hear me yammering on?'

I edged further away from the bedroom window, wincing as my back began to smoulder.

Wednesday had been late this morning - of course she had - because reducing stress for carers is so buggering important in our care plan. I know that because they've kindly written it down in black and white. If it's on a piece of sodding paper, it's got to be true, doesn't it?

Black ice on the road, Wednesday had moaned, *you're so isolated here on the moors.*

Another complaint and mark against my name.

So now my best mate the sun was smoking over the horizon; slivers of light scorched around the corners of the blind.

One toasted Blood Lifer: not the best bloody start to my day. If I melted much more, I'd look bleeding dodgy. Still, Wednesday was ripe for a heart attack...

All right, I'm just pissing about here. I'm not that tosser anymore. Especially not when you were lying there off colour, your thin fingers clutching the bedclothes and then *tap, tap, tap,* like you were trying to pass on a message because you can't talk to me. You can't tell me what you really want to say. I scanned your mush desperate to understand but - *tap, tap, tap* - I couldn't. Not anymore.

Your mouth twisted in frustration.

'They did leave the leaflets with you yesterday?'

'Binned 'em.'

'No you didn't,' Wednesday smirked. 'Read them.'

Tap, tap, tap. That desperate wringing of the covers. *Tap, tap, tap.*

'I don't need to.' I stormed towards the door, flinging it open. The band of light from the window scorched my cheek. But only for a moment.

When Wednesday grabbed my arm, I stared down at her wrinkled hand in surprise. 'Whether you want to admit it or not, it *is* going to get to a stage when your...grandma needs a higher level of care than you can provide. Or than we can. The local care home's excellent. They're specialists with her type of--'

I shook Wednesday off my arm. 'No one's bloody taking her, got it?'

Wednesday's gaze gave me the once over. Then she shrugged, as if having done her duty, she could now wash her hands of us.

'Advance,' you muttered between clenched teeth, as your back arched. 'Advance.' Your eyelids flickered.

I dropped to my knees beside you, stroking your candy floss white hair. But I knew I wasn't there because you couldn't see me. Worse, there was sod all I could do about it.

'Always wanting to advance this one,' Wednesday stared down at you perplexed, 'but never says where to.'

Here's the thing, I could explain it to her. What your splintered mind's drawn to at the end: what it can't forget, when it's obliterated all else.

Why it's not at peace.

Yet even I didn't know what *Advance* meant before the summer of 1968.

Everything comes back to then.

And before?

Before came the decades of lies and my beautifully gilded cage.

It wasn't until that glorious summer that my world expanded to more than an orgy of blood, thrills and discovery. They were my buttons, which Ruby knew how to push and in what order. I was caught up in her tempest.

It wasn't until then, that my peepers were opened to the consuming darkness: how each kill inexorably pushes you into the shadows. Until you don't even know where you end and the gaping dirt mouth of the earth begins. Until you don't know what tiny shard of what you once were is left.

All right, so here's the truth of it: I thought in death I'd shed fear and sin. That's the refrain we Blood Lifers hold aloft, like a bloody standard.

What I didn't understand was that my Soul would claw at me to be saved. Not by a god but through my own graft, bottle and the ball of squirming terrors tight in my gut.

I only started to taste the truth of that, when Ruby finally brought me to Advance.

JULY 1968   LONDON

The Who's "My Generation" – a tribal bloody howl of Mod rebellion and youth's hymn of raging, stuttering disgust at humanity's inevitable, ageing decay - blazed up the wide staircase of Advance Record Company, as I descended. I was already sweating patches through my t-shirt in the muggy heat. I jumped the last two steps.

Then I pressed my ear to the closed double doors. All I could hear, however, was the twang of guitars and the same pounding two chords, overlaying the clash of drums.

'Don't sulk in here all night, dearest prince,' Ruby had insisted, curling her hand down my chest, in the way she knew made my blood roar. 'Come join us, the twins and me.'

Yeah, see there's the lie. The darkness wormed in our crimson bed for so many decades, ones in which I'd done nothing but follow Ruby: my Author, muse, liberator and love. The reason I'd known there was something Ruby was hiding about our coming back to England. Something more than the need to resurrect me into Blood Life. And what was behind those doors was it: the sodding twins... Ruby's *brothers*.

We'd set up our crib in Liverpool, behind the Mersey docks in the shadow of the cranes, hulking

times you just left. Days? Weeks? Months? And that one time..? And *me*..?' I'd raged towards Ruby (although damned if I'd known what I was going to do) but then had found myself slamming my fist clean through a shipping crate instead – *crash* – tiny splinters embedding in my gashed knuckles. 'Not once even a message or... You know what? *I'm* the one buggering off now, all right? Maybe you'll understand what...'

Ruby's move towards me had been so fast, I'd felt her hand crushing my throat before I'd seen her, as she'd slammed me against the damp wall. Ruby's sharp nails had torn through my skin.

'Darling Light,' Ruby had whispered, tightening her hold on my neck. I'd struggled to breathe. 'You do not possess me. No man does. I am not yours; I'll never be anyone's again. What I tell you, I tell you but what I hold to my heart is private to me alone. Do *you* understand this now, my naughty lover?'

My eyelids had fluttered. A stabbing pain had pierced my lungs. A dark mist had descended.

Being throttled's really not my cup of tea.

I'd struggled to nod just a fraction.

Ruby had held my gaze, as she'd smiled. 'I allowed you to follow me. But I will not be led. Never again.'

Then I'd been lost in the cruel green of her peepers, whilst I'd slowly blacked out.

I pressed my ear to the rosewood doors, taking a single breath. This was it then.

When I flung open the doors, before I could bottle it, I was hit by a tidal wave of light and sound. 'Blimey...'

Everything was chrome and white, like stepping into one of those rockets, which they'd been promising to land on the moon, ever since Kennedy and the space race alpha male jostling *my Johnny's bigger than yours.*

Territory, that's what it's about. Planting the flag and making sure the rest of the world's enviously watching because they didn't get there first. Ruby witnessed centuries of such imperial expansionism before it shrivelled. Everything withers eventually. And yeah, that's morbid, but I'm dead, right?

You First lifers don't see the beauty in this transcendent world around you but you're still greedy for another to bugger up. Or maybe you were just desperate to prove you had the balls to do it.

Science marches on and it drags us all in its wake.

White and silver Moon lights hung in clusters of iridescent mother of pearl discs, like satellites to the humongous chandelier, which illuminated the room brighter than day. The black and white paintings made me dizzy, fragmenting and distorting the world, as if I was on something.

I hadn't fed, however, since I'd tonned it down here on the Triton, with Ruby clutching tight around my waist and my neck still purple with bruises. Not feeding was a form of silent protest.

Ruby, however, hadn't even noticed.

And then there was *him*: brown velvet jacket despite the heat, blush of eye shadow and smudge of eyeliner and a dark mop top – head-to-toe the uber-Mod.

This Beau Brummell dandy, dancing in the eye of the whirlwind, jumping and twisting – he *was* the whirlwind - belting out the lyrics at the top of his tone deaf voice.

He was my new family?

Christ help me.

Whichever bloody twin he was - Donovan or Aralt - lost in the throb of the music and the blood high, he didn't see me.

I'd been invisible to Ruby the moment we'd roared into London, or at least that's how it'd felt. I could still touch her body. But underneath? Ruby wasn't with me anymore.

When the Mod swung over to a lounge chair, which was translucent white plastic, I noticed the First Lifer cowering in its angular frame; she was nothing but legs in her pop-art micro-mini. The Mod dragged her up into the dance and then jived around the chair with her, like she was a doll. Her petrified peepers were focused on him, with a shuddering intensity.

He liked to play with his food, this one.

I could see now where the Mod had necked her, just under her daisy clip-ons and the stiffness of her limbs, as the paralysis set in. His fingers played up and down her bob, through her thick fringe, like she was a bloody guitar. Then he hurled her back into the lounge chair, before straddling her. Her little feet twitched, when he tore at her in overexcited mouthfuls.

All right then, so remember I said sometimes we come back wrong? But there's no wrong, only different?

This berk? *He was off his bloody nut.*

Just take it from me that you learn quickly the ones whose Souls got butchered in the cross-over.

Or who choose to slash and burn them after.

I have lines right, ones I don't cross?

I didn't reckon this one's lines were blurred: he wouldn't have had them to start with.

Then over his nut, I saw Ruby.

And when I did, I wished I'd stayed upstairs sulking.

Ruby swivelled round, enwombed in the scarlet folds of a chair, which was like a space vehicle opening. She was half-submerged under the naked body of a First Lifer.

Why did he have to be such a bleeding hunk?

Were First Lifers bred differently now, or after the end of rations and this sudden rash of peacock preening, had the muscles evolved like that?

Ruby was writhing. Touching. Snogging... Like she did with me. *Only* me, I'd thought. She was feasting too; the poor sod was nothing but a paralysed puppet to her desire. He couldn't have got a stiffy if he'd tried. It didn't matter; I was still alight with jealousy.

A century of love and loyalty and it'd only taken one night in this place for Ruby to cuckold me?

That's the thing with passion - it curdles when you lose control. Yet I was beginning to realise I'd never had any control to start with.

The twin threw himself off the skirt. Blood stained his mouth like lipstick - just one more touch to his costume - as he boogied to the far corner.

I slouched back against the door frame. Into the shadows. I'd lost my appetite. I still watched, however, when the Mod dragged up this young bloke, who was all polo shirt and tight jeans and had been trying to make himself as small as possible in a quaking ball, as if somehow he'd be forgotten about that way: you're never forgotten in the heat of a hunt. Once we've got your scent – *bam* – you're in our blood, gut and Soul: we couldn't forget you if we tried. It's an obsession. A bloody addiction.

Ruby once told me not to feel guilt about feeding because we're designed like this. In the same way every animal has its adaptations.

It took you to help me see we have something animals don't – a conscience.

Remember that? I'm still not sure I get what it means; I try and grasp it, but it slides through my fingers.

How long will you be with me to make sure I remember?

The Mod caught the bloke around the neck, pulling him into the dance. He wasn't bitten yet; he was still alive and squirming. He was swung out onto the virulent orange rug - back and forth. The twin's fangs pressed the skin at his neck. But didn't quite break it.

So the prat was a prick tease too.

I wasn't into those types of games: that was Ruby's thing.

The Mod was laughing; the boy was crying. The twin's fingers caressed the tears...

Then the twin plunged in his teeth, drinking hard. He was tripping on the music. Blood. Freedom. The drums were beating out a frantic rhythm. A clash of nothing but raucous noise.

When Ruby coiled round the now motionless body of the First Lifer, with an ecstatic, *satiated* expression (which I hadn't seen for decades), agonising hurt and resentment ripped through me.

Why wasn't Ruby like that with me anymore? What had changed? *Me*? Yeah, bloody well blame the man.

What was so special about this *Advance..*?

The Mod twisted back to the totty, who was limp now in the chair, yanking her up in his arms.

Her nut lolled back, like the bones in her neck had melted. He wrapped himself around her, holding her tight on his left side, at the same time as tugging the struggling bloke closer on his right. He laughed. First, he snogged the bird's drooping mouth and then turning to the guy, he tasted him more lingeringly.

Bang. The door on the far wall slammed open.

Bloody hell, who was this now?

An identical copy of the Mod. But this smarmy geezer was in a vintage 1950s Savile Row suit and his Ivy League hair oozed oil – *bastard twin number two...*

'Turn off this fecking racket.'

There was a *thud*, as Ruby nodded and shoved the First Lifer's corpse rolling off her. She scrambled out of the chair, in a flurry of scarlet hair and silk.

Bugger me, it was like angels had trooped from Heaven in blinding rays of light because I'd never seen Ruby scramble to do anything before. Certainly not for me. Yet now she flew to the hi-fi, cutting the music dead.

His Nibbs in the charcoal suit scanned across to me with dark peepers; I didn't reckon he was the sort to miss much, or maybe he was simply the only one here, who wasn't spaced out of his head. 'This your babby then?'

I raised my eyebrow. 'Don't see no bloody rattle, mate.'

For the first time Ruby seemed to notice me. She made a strange type of hushing motion. 'Aralt, he is--'

'A wee gobshite?'

'Name's Light,' I pushed in from the doorway.

I tried to read Ruby's expression but found I couldn't. It was different from the one I knew. It nearly sodding killed me to see that in the years we'd swum in each other's Souls - together in Blood Life – she'd held back this fragment from me.

'Someone's big on irony,' Aralt deadpanned.

'Hey man, so you're a Rocker?' The Mod briskly snapped the necks of his two First Lifers – *crack, crack* – dropping them in stricken, blue-lipped piles. He eyed my studded leather jacket, before sauntering towards me, wiping blood from the corner of his mouth. 'Guess we're gonna have to fight then? What a drag.'

Bollocks – Aralt and Donovan, Ruby's twin brothers, the most powerful Blood Lifers in London - and already one thought I was a wanker and the other wanted to give me a hiding.

Yeah, everything was tickety-boo.

'Depends how you figure it. Ate some bloke, nicked his coat. But you? Bought those threads, right?'

A black threat swept behind Donovan's peepers: murderous, powerful and sadistic.

Adrenaline surged in response through me. All right, it was back against the wall time. That suited me just fine. I could do with a right royal scrap.

The only thing I could hear was the blood: the world aflame. Soaring and crescendoing.

Then the danger passed. It was like Donovan had closed the box, trapping all those shadows inside.

Donovan laughed, clapping me hard on the shoulder. 'You're crazy dark; that's cool, man. We're gonna have a blast, our little family. I can taste it.'

Aralt's smooth features soured. 'Now the hugs and blather are over, some of us have work.' Testily, he marched to a long, rosewood desk, where he dropped behind its shining surface, whipping out a silver fountain pen from his pocket. Donovan draped his arm through mine, drawing me further into the lounge. When we stepped over the corpses, my boot sank into the boy's outstretched hand; the bones crunched. At last, I had the bottle to glance up at Ruby. She was bent over Aralt, studying a file, as he scribbled notes like a businessman. Ruby's hair mingled with Aralt's, in a way it only ever had with mine for a hundred years. Yet Ruby was staring across at me: in that moment, she was mine again. How hadn't I recognised her: my red-haired devil, Author, muse, guide and liberator? My gorgeous nightmare? All I wanted was to devour her, there on the desk. But then Ruby had turned back to Aralt again and was listening to him keenly. 'I've booked the musicians for the gig at Heartbeat. But with the release of--'

'Why don't we just bite them? I'm up for it, man,' Donovan interjected, pressing me down into the lounge chair, his fingers massaging my shoulders. I tensed.

'Shut your cake hole, adults concentrating.' Aralt glanced from his brother to me; somehow I seemed to have got swept up in his rage. 'And what job exactly were you planning for your boyo?'

'Job?' I straightened. 'Who says I was applying?'

Donovan sniggered. 'You are so gonna bug my bro. Right on.'

Ruby ignored me. 'He could work at the club at the weekends? He understands this...modern music--'

'Does he now?' Aralt rapped his long fingers – *tap, tap, tap* - on the top of the desk. 'Until I know he's not a chancer, he can pair with Alessandro: two babbies together.'

Alessandro was hunched on the floor over a glass chessboard, his hand hovering over a pawn with rapt deliberation, as he battled an invisible opponent.

Christ in heaven, he was a *kid*.

A blonde teen in indigo sweater pullover vest and dot bowtie. His feet, however, were bare, poking out from under his crossed legs.

Alessandro pushed the pawn one move and then swerved the board 180 degrees.

I slid down next to him, as I lit up. 'Winning?'

Alessandro glanced, not directly at me but somewhere to the side. 'There's no winning, only learning.'

'All right then.'

Touched. The kids always are.

I leant back against Alessandro's hard bed: his sheets were tucked in tight hospital corners. When I glanced around, I noticed there was nothing else in his room, except for a Modernist desk and chair, which was made of cold aluminium strips. It could be a bleeding dormitory.

Alessandro was watching me expectantly. When I flicked the ash off my fag, he flinched.

I shrugged. 'Sorry, mate. I know sod all about this chess lark.'

'Alessandro Salvio was a chess genius - one of the first - back in 1600 he was unofficial world champion,' Alessandro jumped to his knees, fiddling at his bowtie excitedly. 'He wrote *Trattato dell'Inventione et Arte Liberale del Gioco Degli Scacchi*, in which--'

'You read Italian?'

'Don't you?'

I laughed. *This was my new playmate*?

'When Aralt elected me, he insisted I choose a new name, so I chose Alessandro - impertinent I know - but in that moment I couldn't think of... No other words would form. As I was working through this game in my head, which was based on one of his theories, his name popped out. You know, like words so often do. It's better than my old one. Everything now is better than my old.'

See here's the thing about us Blood Lifers: we have the name they wetted us with when we wailed all bloody from the womb but we also get the one *we* select, when the blood elects us from the ranks into something else. It used to be like a holy anointing, with ceremonies, night long orgies and feasts of the slain. I've had a gander at the pictures: they wouldn't make a good bedtime story for the kiddies.

Me? I chose Light because... Let's just say it wove me to the best of my First Life and everything I never wanted to lose. Wanker that I am, I'm something else even amongst a breed of something else's.

'Aralt's your Author?' Yeah, he seemed the type to go for kids; I'd known there was something dodgy about the smarmy git.

'And you're Ruby's?'

'Used to think so.'

Ruby once told me that she'd elected me because she'd fallen in love with the taste of my Soul. Every emotion amplified: hatred, jealousy or passion, like flavours of an ice-cream. Each one unmistakable.

It's not random, our election: we only choose the best of each generation to exalt from their humanity and twin eternally blood to blood.

Or that's the bollocks.

You're rolling your eyes, right? I know the look, like you reckon that's all grandiose, poncey codswallop? You never let me get away with the superior species spiel.

Yet that's how being chosen into the Blood Life works - the *something more* - which everyone craves. *Feels*. The black core gnawing through their First Lifer hearts.

I know because I felt it too.

It's not the most successful, who are elected, not by First Life criteria: the rich, parliamentarians, aristocrats, heterosexual males in their suits or bimbo celebrities.

No, we smell the true scent of you First Lifers. The bubbling emotions, which are veined underneath, like gold in rock: the ambition of true leaders, unrecognised genius of thinkers and courage of warriors. Beauty is skin-deep, I'll give you that, but we see it in the faces of the poor, unmasked by makeup or fancy dos. In the capacity for love, rather than its cold cruelty.

See our society (if anything so bleeding dysfunctional can be called that), has strata, like the layers of the earth, down to its burning magma heat. We're chosen but with different roles.

Some are thinkers, prodigies like Alessandro. Others warriors, so steeped in blood you won't find their names in any First Lifer chronicles because no one lived to write them. Then there are beauties, like my Ruby, who mesmerise with a look. And of course there are leaders: the twins had taken the egg on that one.

But the very bravest Authors? The ones with the real balls? They uncover First Lifers with a little of all four bleeding through them: thinker, warrior, beauty and leader.

Yet that's the risk right there because if you mix it up, you create one hell of an individual: a loner who doesn't play nice or by your rules. We bite the hand that feeds us.

As Ruby would soon discover.

Alessandro was absorbed in his lonely chess match again, shuffling his King out of check.

I shoved myself up, wandering around to have a shufti at these posters of ugly great lizards, with long yellow tongues that forked out of blood-stained mouths. They were plastered over every inch of wall. 'You got a thing about Komodo?'

'Komodo dragon, monitor or Island monitor. Known to natives of the Komodo Island as ora, buaya darat, the land crocodile or biawak raksasa, the giant monitor.' *Bloody hell, Alessandro was a Blood Lifer encyclopaedia.* He caught my expression and shrugged. 'It's one of my...obsessions. Aralt's too.'

'If Aralt's into reptiles, I'm a Dutchman.'

'He is,' Alessandro neatly hopped up, peering over my shoulder at the Komodo. 'He insists I research them and keep files on the data to present to him. He says he's going to elect other scientists, so they can...' Alessandro broke off, as if he'd let something slip.

'What type of research would that be then?'

'Oh you know, how they're closer to us than any other species.'

'Is that right?'

'First Lifers believe Komodo kill because of virulent bacteria in their mouths but it's my suspicion they have...' Alessandro paused, as if imparting some massive secret or insight, 'venom glands.'

I tried to look suitably impressed. What kind of squares were getting elected nowadays? 'You been there then? Seen them?'

Alessandro goggled at me. 'Why of course not. Who would take me?'

I choked on my ciggie. 'How old are you in this Blood Life? Still have to ask permission from papa?'

Alessandro paced to his bed, curling up on its hospital style sheets. 'Aralt wouldn't like it if... I have a job...an important job here...'

'We're Blood Lifers, mate. Not bank clerks.'

Alessandro wrapped his arms tighter around his knees. This kid had been elected but not into Blood Life; he was still in a twilight caught between child and Blood Lifer. His eyes hadn't been opened to the glories of the world, as Ruby had opened mine. He huddled in a perpetual half-life.

'The twins went to the Komodo Islands but they wouldn't, you know... Aralt said it was private...'

'Bastards.'

Alessandro's arms burst into a frantic flapping. 'Don't. Be quiet. They'll--'

'Reckon I'm scared of those tossers?'

Alessandro studied me with serious peepers. 'I don't know. I am.' Glancing down, he tore at the grey sheets. 'Aralt freed me. Before him... I was put away. Forgotten. The doctor told my parents to leave me in an institution and get on with their lives. I believe he put it that they were still *young enough to have another baby*, who would be *normal this time*. I was in the room when he said it because no one considered I could hear or understand, since I couldn't yet speak. It's impossible to put into words what it was like to be taken there and left behind forever. You cannot understand what it's like to lose your family in such a way.' Alessandro stopped, his tiny fingers twisting at his bowtie. *But I could, I bloody well could.* 'Then at last, someone came for me, just as I'd prayed every day they would. Aralt came for me. He was my saviour.' Alessandro shifted on the bed and then his voice was strangely monotone, as he added, 'My first kill was that doctor, who'd been too small minded to see my true hidden mind. With that kill, I slaughtered the label of *idiot*.'

'And your parents?' *They always went after them, the kids did.*

Alessandro blinked. 'I broke in one night and crept upstairs. But then in the dark I heard this babbling sound from my old nursery. They'd done it: what the doctor had suggested. There was my baby brother tucked up tight in my cot. The new heir. They'd moved on and I simply couldn't...' Alessandro wiped at the corners of his peepers. 'I never saw them again. I've often wondered if anyone ever told them I went missing, or if they still think I'm shut away from the world.' He gave a high laugh; Christ in heaven, it was unsettling. 'Still am I guess, aren't I? At least, from their world. But Aralt freed me, which means I owe him everything. To be alone and trapped, that's worse than death.'

Abnormal, normal. See what I mean about sticky labels?

All right, so Alessandro had always been barmy in his own way. But so what? Who'd got the right to chuck him out with the rubbish and breed another kid in his place?

There's nothing but snowflake patterns.

We're all individuals, that's the long and short of it: born alone, dying alone and grasping at each other as we fall.

And I should know.

6

JULY 1968   LONDON

Remember when there was only one correct way to act, decorate or dress? Paris and Milan, the trend setters?

Us Blood Lifers? Do me a favour. We take what we fancy and drop the rest. We're not slaves to etiquette, dictates or form. We're not tied to someone else's apron strings.

But then something happened in those hot, spacey 1960s summers, as if a switch had clicked collectively in your brains. At last you could see through your brutish First Life enslavement, out to the untold combinations, possibilities and wildness beyond. Or a glimpse of it anyway. To the life around you, which sears with spark and Soul.

You grasped it all in a moment - at least in London. The rest of you? Well, you got there.

Sauntering down Carnaby Street in the early evening, the sun just set, was like bursting out onto a madman's canvas.

There were myriad creations and not one the same: colours, prints, styles and no decorum because no one was waiting for some stuck up bint across the channel to tell them what fashion meant. Yeah, here's the cool bit, they were going to invent it fresh, nicking whatever they liked from their ancestors: Art Nouveaux or my beloved Victoriana.

It was the age of freedom.

Even if you First Lifers will never taste *real* freedom, not like the burn of death and then election.

I'd slipped out, whilst Ruby was in another one of her sodding meetings in Aralt's study, which I'd discovered I was shut out of. I was relegated instead to glorified bouncer at their club and babysitter for the child prodigy.

I'd pressed my cheek to the rosewood door before I'd left, deeply breathing in Ruby's scent.

It was maddening.

I could almost taste her; my blood sang for her.

Yet she was with *him* now.

My jealousy bubbled; the pain was hot. My imagination went awandering about what was happening on the other side of that door...

So now I was exploring this brave new world of Carnaby Street - by myself - to keep from thinking of the study and my rage.

I wove beneath Union Jacks, which were strung across the narrow road between the taxis and parked vans, passing under a pale blue awning and then spying a boutique, where starkers mannequins with humongous knockers lounged in the windows. That made me stop and back up for a second look, I'll admit.

There was this buzz: a heat of chatter, music and laughter. Donovan would've called it a *scene* but you know, that's what it was.

The First Lifers' threads were an eclectic vintage mix, which transformed the whole bleeding lot of them into Blood Lifers.

Apart from the scent and the blood, there was no way of figuring the difference, as one strutted towards me in the twilight with a swaying afro and an old regimental jacket and faded waistcoat.

Bloody hell, what was this?

It brought me up short: me standing there, like a right berk, in the middle of the stream of humanity. Because all I could think, was that never had the divide between our species been so slight; I could sense it sticky on my skin.

Ruby would've choked me, if I'd ever said that out loud: I'd be blacked out for a week. Yet it was true. It was like First Lifers had jumped up several rungs of the evolutionary ladder, in one drug fuelled bonk fest of love.

This mutation (or whatever it was) meant I could see more of me in you, just as you saw more through our peepers.

That's when I started freaking out.

Because this was the bastard of it: now it wasn't so easy to dismiss First Lifers as prey or hunt you down. Ruby's justifying of your deaths, using our inherent superiority, began to feel like simply more of the black and white bollocks, which I didn't go in for.

I was stiff with the shock of these new feelings. I wished I could go back to the old, safe certainty and be wrapped in its flames.

An idea once freed from its box, however, won't let its wings be clipped twice.

I forced myself to be swept along with the night. I couldn't go back to Ruby. Not whilst I was still thinking like this. Otherwise I might say something wild about these whirring ideas and I knew bloody better than that.

I found myself standing staring blankly into the window of the boutique "I was Lord Kitchener's Valet". As I slowly unthawed, I realised what I was looking at.

This was the dog's bollocks: the source of those vintage jackets, which had been blowing my mind and sending me into poofy angst, as if an undead army had suddenly been resurrected. I grinned, studying the pairs of Union Jack trousers, which crowded the windows. They were sheer Donovan; I'd wager he already had a pair.

I edged round, jimmying a back door.

I had a tradition that on forays to new places, I brought something back for Ruby: some trinket, whiskey or a pretty little something to bite...

You've got to show your love somehow, right?

Just because we were back with Ruby's brothers, didn't mean everything had to change. In fact, more reason for our traditions to continue. I needed to remind Ruby of what we had too, using our secret language, which was all our own.

I took a shufti around in the darkness, before spotting a Union Jack mug. I knocked it off quickly, before scarpering back out into the alleyway. My blood was up and pounding.

The night was fine and the world new in a way it hadn't been for decades, with that added rush I always get from a lay – mug or bar of gold, it doesn't make any difference. A lay's a lay and a hell of a kick.

I was soaring in the sweating heat - not even thinking about the feeds I'd missed - when I bumped headlong into this posh suit.

He wasn't looking where he was going either, whilst he lit up his cigar with this blinding gold lighter.

Then it hit me: the memory of every bastard I'd known in my First Life (and there'd been a sodding ton of those), who'd treated me like I was vermin.

In fact, with the same contempt as that wanker registered, when he recoiled, examining my leather jacket, like I was about to rob him.

The bloodlust engulfed me; I hungered to rip out his jugular.

Something, however, held me back.

I didn't get it then - what it was. Not straightaway. Yet it was like that epiphany on Carnaby Street had infected me.

Still, the bloke reckoned dirt like me couldn't do anything but rob?

I didn't want to disappoint the man.

I snatched the lighter from him and legged it.

'Hey, stop! Did you see..? He just stole my...'

The pigs joined in the chase; I heard their hollers and the *thud* of their boots.

This was it: the run, heat and the fear.

Laughing, I threaded through those throbbing streets, pushing the lighter into the pocket of my jeans: yeah, that was nifty. I clutched onto Ruby's mug too because I had to keep that. I needed something to return us back to normal again.

I was back. Alive, fully and monumentally. Dashing through those night-time London streets, I was bloody alive.

The First Lifer's pale pink nails scratched against the stove-painted, metal arm of the lamp. Her body, which was splayed over the elliptical conference table, jerked, twisting and rotating the lamp, which was clamped to its edge. Her crochet angel dress rode higher, until I could see her muff.

Aralt's jacket was neatly hung over his desk chair, his sleeves rolled back; he was the sort of prat, who'd make sure he didn't get a drop of blood on his threads.

They're the ones you need to watch out for, who pretend they're more civilised than the rest of us savages: the ones who take off their jackets before giving you a kicking.

Aralt was suckling at the bird's throat.

Christ in heaven, Ruby was too, right on the other side of the neck. She was sharing blood, which was as intimate as communion, just like *we'd* done on the anniversaries of my election. A bond of love, which Ruby had withheld from me, apart from on the rarest of occasions because it was close to sacred.

But now Ruby was doing it with *Aralt*? Her own brother?

I could only see the curves of Ruby's body, which had tortured me for decades and the scarlet sweep of her hair. *Creak, creak, creak* – the lamp's swinging was a torment. The reek of blood like poison.

I must've backed up a step because Aralt glanced over the First Lifer then.

When Aralt saw me, his peepers sparkled. He drew back, with what I knew was a victor's smile: an Alpha male marking his bloody territory.

Or that's what *he* thought.

No man's ever owned Ruby, not since she'd been elected into Blood Life. I couldn't wait for

Aralt's slam to earth when he finally discovered that.

'No one ever taught you it's rude not to knock?' Aralt challenged.

'It's nearly dawn and Ruby wasn't--'

'Ah, you hear that? Babby was missing his ma.'

Ruby lifted her nut, shuddering from the kill. She scrubbed the heel of her hand over her mush. She was tripping. Overloaded on the blood. Her eyelashes were fluttering. Only the whites of her peepers were showing.

This bird must've been the dessert at the end of a hell of a feast.

I didn't reckon Ruby could even see me or knew I was there; she was too away with the faeries. She never let herself lose control. Not like this.

When Aralt trailed his long fingers down Ruby's neck, I started into the room. 'Is she..?'

And then I was up against the wall, my nut gashed against a framed photo of Apollo 5. Red trickled down my forehead.

Bloody hell, Aralt was faster than Ruby.

'Now listen here, you wee gobshite, the only reason you're not a puddle in the sun is because Ruby's grown sentimental in her old age. But me? I think I was right first time: you're a chancer. A thick ride, who likes throwing shapes. I have no need for one of those. When it was just the two of you dossing around, you might have been the big man. But here?' Aralt slapped me across the cheek lightly with a smile, before sauntering to Ruby, who was swaying now. Aralt hooked Ruby tight to him, before loosening his tie. 'No windows,' as Aralt glanced around the office, I realised he was right. 'I've defeated dawn. You're not the full shilling, are you?' You know those bastards, who simultaneously make you feel the idiot and burn to clock them?

Screw it, I wanted to feel Aralt's heart stop bloody in my hands. 'Run along to bed, like a good babby,' Aralt licked the blood from Ruby's lips, and she sighed, low and contented, 'and I'll take care of your Author.'

Alessandro examined the thin cut, which was rapidly healing up into a white line, with tentative fingers. 'Still not scared of Aralt?'

I shoved away from Alessandro with a shrug. 'Kids play. Saturday night in with Ruby.'

We were sprawled together on Alessandro's wooden floor, in a glorious chaos of singles and LPs, as if a tornado had hit, and we were in the eye.

I'd found them, one after the other, ranked in bright orange paper record racks, alphabetically listed. Alessandro had given this vole-like squeal, each time I'd wrenched one out, devoured its cover and tossed it aside.

I drew out the psychedelic cover of The Stone's "Their Satanic Majesties Request". I turned it over reverentially in my hands. 'You're a dark horse. Because for a square? You've got cool taste.'

Alessandro fidgeted. 'Another one of my...you know? You hear an awful lot of this modern stuff working at Advance. They even let me name the radio station.'

'We have a radio station?'

The rot had set in already – *we*? I should've cut out my bloody conforming tongue. Society creeps up on you; it catches you by the balls, taming you until you're leashed.

See here's the thing, we're all bound by our family, friends, jobs and love... But love doesn't need to be bound or to bind - it can be free.

Society's the prison we volunteer to lock ourselves in, hiding behind its bars without the need for guards because it's comfy, safe and as predictable as you First Lifers crave. Yet it's a fantasy because it's built everyday on lies: from the laws you follow gormlessly unquestioning, to the roles you mould yourselves into, so you can fit square pegs into round. That's what you're conditioned for, cradle to the grave.

Here in our Blood Life, I'd thought we were beyond that. At Advance, however, I was being exposed to a whole new society; it made me feel like I was being castrated all over again.

Alessandro nodded. 'A pirate radio station. You haven't heard it?' His arms started to flap. 'Goodness, you must.' He dived under the bed, so far I could only see his pale white feet sticking out. When he wriggled free again, he was clutching this bloody great box of transistor radios and beaming, like he was about to present his first born. 'My collection. Donovan finds them for me because he knows I... Well, see..?' Alessandro passed them over to me one at a time. Tiny pocket transistors. A real mink RL200 radio. And portable radios shaped like lipsticks, Batchelors tins or cups and saucers. He raised a red pop-art radio to his ear, twiddling with the tuning. 'Guess what I named it?'

I craned my hands behind my nut. 'Haven't the foggiest.'

Alessandro grinned, the static clearing as he found the frequency.

...And now on Radio Komodo we have another groovy record for all you hip listeners out there...

'Komodo?' I kicked at Alessandro with my boot. 'Nice one.'

All right then, so this is the moment...the one I've never told you about...I don't know why.

Sod it, yeah I do. *Honesty*, right?

I didn't tell you because I didn't want to feel like just another groupie, or any more of a sad git than I already did when we first met.

How's that for a superior species?

But now's my chance. My turning round.

So, this was our first true meeting. Only you never knew it until now.

This song started up on the radio. Then this singer and the voice... It was sultry but fragile, with a northern edge and a hint of Marianne Faithfull. Yet it was rock, rather than folk, through to its core. It belted me in the sodding gut because it was like everything I'd tasted on my trip down Carnaby Street - this new world blossoming from the earth, which made me feel old for the first time: dusty and *dead*. I craved another shot of this vibrant vitality and to suck the Soul from that voice – *you* - directly into my veins.

I'd wager it was your humanity, which we stripped away with every kill, rejoicing in each sacrificial hunt, that drew me to you.

For the first time in a century, I missed the heat of the sun.

I tried not to point too wildly at the radio. 'Who's this?'

Alessandro flushed. *Interesting*. 'One of ours. She sings at The Heartbeat Club, so I hear.'

'You've gone a little red there.'

Alessandro pressed his palms hard against his lugs, rocking backwards and forwards for a moment. Then he wrapped his arms around his middle. 'Kathy's...dishy...'

'That right? Listen,' I edged closer, 'the twins, what's up with them? All this record company bollocks? I'll be buggered if all they're building is a music empire. Are they like the Kray twins or something?'

Alessandro sharply twisted off the radio. Your voice and world was lost to me again, leaving me with only the aluminium starkness of neat corners and the festering mouths of Komodo.

'Or something.'

'They're Irish,' I began thoughtfully, 'elected after me. They're brutal, ruthless but dedicated leaders. Taking a wild guess, they're IRA?'

Alessandro clutched my arm, his small fingers digging in hard enough to hurt, as he dragged my forehead close, until it was touching his. 'Members of the original Irish Volunteers; they were involved in the Easter Rising and the later fight for freedom against England. Aralt told me it was all right though - what they did - because Ireland was in a state of guerrilla war. They're not terrorists or... The struggles made them officers in Ireland's army. I don't know if I...but that's what he said. They were special too. Members of the Twelve Apostles. Assassins.'

'Yeah, blokes who murdered their Old Bill, right?'

'British troops too. It was *war* Aralt said. And in war people do things, which are... But please, you can't... He only told me because he's my Author. He's private like that. About his past--'

'You could knock me down with a feather. And? How were the twins elected?'

'Black and Tans hated men like Aralt and Donovan. They burnt down their home one night. With the twins in it. Lucky for the twins, however, *he'd* already been watching and following their impressive exploits.'

'Who?'

Alessandro rocked back on his heels. 'Ruby's Author, of course. Plantagenet.' Alessandro looked confused at my blank expression; even he couldn't misread that obvious a reaction. 'She didn't tell you? How she was elected? About Plantagenet?'

'Doesn't look like she told me sod all, does it?'

You know when you die and are elected into Blood Life, the one thing you reckon you won't bleeding have to do any more is go to lame parties with limp, wilting grub and warm beer and make nice with the natives.

Do you reckon it's a pass to some glamourous VIP lounge?

Yeah, that'll be right, well, maybe when it was just me and Ruby and I let myself dream, like some doe-eyed berk, that we were set apart, alone and united in blood and love and bollocks to the rest.

But that was the lie.

Now I was finally waking up to the fact that this Blood Life was no dark fairy-tale: it was hard science. Ruby had warned me, hadn't she?

Pissing evolution.

There are some amongst us, who claim there's no difference between magic and science.

But I've seen the numbers streaming in my head. I've witnessed words whispering from across the globe and tiny bastards trapped in TVs for our entertainment.

And in the 1960s? I even heard First Lifers boast, like a declaration of war, that they'd walk on the moon and at its tail end, I saw them take the very first step. You can't experience wonders like that and not reckon them beyond magic.

We're all creatures of the earth; it's simply nature. And we all want to survive - even you.

That's why you should fear us.

Gammon, pork pies, cheese straws, scotch eggs, sausage rolls and crisps: ready salted, cheese and onion, smoky bacon and roast chicken. Like an alien hedgehog, a halved grapefruit in foil, stuck with pineapple on cocktail sticks, acted as a centrepiece on the plastic table. To the side were stacked crates of brown ale and tall bottles of wine.

See here's how it stacks up: one pint of your blood (which is what we generally speaking drain), that's only 500 calories. You reckon we could subsist on that, even if we killed once every twenty-four hours?

Man would die of bloody hunger.

We'd need to guzzle four First Lifers a night, if we didn't eat up our meat and five a day.

Still, there are some Blood Lifers who rise to the challenge. It burns them out quickly, however, so they don't tend to last long.

Since our senses are enhanced, I think about food almost as much as I obsess about blood and sex because we still dig the flavours, the same way as you crave chocolate or that third cocktail. It's about indulgence, revelling in the moment because who knows, tomorrow you may die, right?

They'd pulled out all the stops for Ruby's *welcome home* party in the cavernous dining hall, which I reckoned, with the sticky party food, banners and glitter was Donovan's, rather than Aralt's, do. Of course, like a piece of battered luggage, I didn't figure.

Yet when I'd tried to skulk up to our room rather than play nice, Ruby had grabbed my wrist and dragged me down after her with a smile that melted, as much as her nails sliced.

Ruby was stronger now than she'd ever been. It was because she was flooded with so much blood.

She was also lost in it too, or from me anyway. Whatever she did at night knackered her. Yet after the last time I'd gone searching for her - finding her tripping and blood sharing with Aralt - I wasn't going investigating again.

Instead, I got used to being on my own.

Ruby was worn out, when I woke in the day and lay next to her, stroking the soft hair from her cheek. They were the only moments of quiet we had together, but she always slept through them now; her peepers didn't flicker open for a moment.

I wondered whether Ruby saw me, even when she looked at me.

"All or Nothing" by The Small Faces - the Mod band to end all Mod bands - buzzed from the hi-fi, as Donovan strutted his stuff by himself, where the chairs had been pushed back to create a dance floor. He used a weird combination of those dances with animal names, swinging his arms round in joyful communion with his Mod god.

A bird, who I hadn't yet met, was watching Donovan, like she was his bodyguard. Her brunette hair was scraped back dead tight and she was wearing - over a pair of pressed jeans - this blinding pilot's jacket; I reckoned it was Second World War. But it wasn't British... Nazi maybe? She didn't look German, but then I've come to know there's no *look* about it. Not for any of us.

Aralt and Ruby were pressed close together by the drinks, yakking away. I couldn't hear a single word over the music, although I was straining to. Of course the fact I knew I wasn't meant to hear, was even more infuriating.

I could see it played out, however, like a silent movie: Aralt's fingers massaging the small of Ruby's back. I could've broken every bone in his hand – *crunch, crunch, crunch.*

Alessandro was crouched in a shadowed corner, his knees drawn up to his chest. His hands would flutter in front of his peepers and then clutch to his lugs. I dived to the crate, pouring out a beer. 'Here, wet your whistle.'

Alessandro took the drink from me with shaking hands and a look of surprise. 'Thanks.'

'Not your scene?'

'Too many...you know.'

'Yeah mate, for me 'an all.'

I glanced over at Ruby, bloody moth to flame. Aralt's hand was on her neck now, playing with that delicate place where it meets collarbone and then tracing down to her blood-red pendant. Just like she'd beg *me* to when we'd lie naked, wrapped in each other's arms. And that was it - right there: *that was the line.*

A bloke can only take so much.

I hunched my shoulders, as I swaggered towards them.

Bollocks to it: Advance, the twins, whatever screwed up game they were playing and this whole crazy set up – I was out.

I grabbed Ruby by the shoulder, swinging her round. I loved the shock in her peepers. I used to delight in that; we'd cross continents to do no more than jolt each other with some new wonder or horror.

'You're interrupting,' Aralt's voice was low and dangerous.

'Sorry,' I ran my hand down the crease of Ruby's neck, which Aralt's fingers had desecrated a moment before, caressing the pale, sensitive skin beneath her ruby pendant. I grinned when she groaned. 'But I was here first.'

I saw Aralt's gaze dart around the dining room; we were now the live act. 'Throwing shapes? Ma not giving you enough attention?'

'She's my Author, muse, liberator and my *lover*. She's not my ma.'

Ruby laughed, clapping her hands. 'Foolish men to brabble and lock horns to put on a play.'

'His death will not be a play--'

'Dance with me,' Donovan darted off the dance floor faster than his brother's slam towards me, spinning me away against the far wall.

I was het up; my pulse racing in fight or flight.

Donovan twisted towards me, blocking his brother's view.

I dragged back from him. 'I don't dance.'

Donovan smirked. 'You know what they say: doesn't know how to dance, doesn't know how to shag.'

'I didn't say I don't know how to. Just that I don't.'

Donovan's thin tie was bobbing up and down like a snake, as he cornered me. 'See my bro, he freaks out easy. And Ruby? You two are tight, but she's not your chick; she'll never be anyone's chick, you cool? If not, you're gonna get yourself dead real quick. So whilst she's otherwise engaged, I've got some fab ideas how we can--' Donovan's hand was on my thigh, tarantula crawling higher... *Bloody hell...* I tried to concentrate on seeing round Donovan to Ruby and whether Aralt was back nuzzling her. I couldn't see anything, however, as Donovan pressed closer still. 'I've got this stuff that'll blow your mind. You and me should...'

Thank Christ in heaven, the bird in the boss World War Two jacket flung herself against the wall next to me, just as Donovan's hand reached my tackle. He sighed and flexed his fingers, reluctantly pulling them away.

I was starting to get shirty about being treated like a pretty toy, passed between this family, for a bit of slap and tickle. But I didn't want to explain to Ruby the reason I'd decked her brother. Or more likely had been duffed up by him.

All the same, I couldn't help noticing this edge to Donovan. It wasn't exactly sadness, more akin to an aching emptiness, in the way he studied me. It was strange next to the waves of vibrant energy, which he radiated, like a bloody bunny, in every other bouncing moment.

'She says time for a toast.' *Soviet* - that was the accent - not German. Miss Pilot's Jacket ignored me, like the disposable trinket I was beginning to feel. She tossed her nut towards where I realised Ruby had been watching us all along.

No explanation needed then.

'Right on, Kira,' Donovan was unperturbed, waving me towards the plastic table with a grin.

Ruby gripped my arm, her peepers glittering mischievously. 'Out of the frying pan, into the fire?'

I forced myself to shrug nonchalantly. 'When was I frightened of the flames?'

Aralt passed out the glasses. 'Let's welcome Ruby into the family again.'

Again?

And what was I? The bastard son?

Aralt poured wine bubbling into our glasses, even into Alessandro's, who was quivering on the edge of the circle, his peepers averted.

When Aralt reached Kira, she whispered what sounded like a question in Russian.

Aralt replied something to her (in a surprisingly placating tone), before Kira's neck flushed and she looked like she was about to go nuclear. Her lips snarled and she hurled her glass at the wall; the wine stained, dripping down to puddle amongst the shards.

No one said anything, as if nothing had even happened.

I glanced between them. 'Right, so that's like a Greek thing?'

Kira glared at me. 'Nyet. It's a die all Nazis thing.'

'German wine,' Alessandro muttered, behind his cupped hand.

I shrugged, draining my glass. 'Don't think they pressed those grapes personally, luv.'

Kira was like bloody lightning searing right at me - *bam* – but just as fast, Ruby's body was crushed in front of me, one naughty hand having a wank wander, like it'd forgotten the feel of me, the other hard on Kira's chest. 'Don't damage another's goods.'

'I was known as a Night Witch,' Kira hissed, 'but at least those bastards knew to fear me.'

'But dear woman,' Ruby smiled, 'do you not know to fear *me*?'

'Chill,' Donovan hurriedly wrapped his arm around Kira's shoulder, landing a smacker on her cheek, which left the faint impression of lipstick. 'Light treasure, this here is my shadow. More kills than any other fighter ace - male or female. So when she was downed...' He mimicked the plane's crash with his glass. 'I offered her revenge. And together, side by side, we became known as--'

'The Night Terror.' Ruby smiled.

'You 'an all?' I grabbed Ruby's naughty hand, pulling it away from me. So that was where Ruby had been in those vanishing times of loneliness? Battling the Jerry in some dodgy blood pact with the Night Terror? 'You the unholy trio?'

Ruby's fingers batted mine aside, crawling back to their teasing. 'I didn't fancy you would welcome another dance with war, dearest prince. Not after the Great one.'

Donovan sniggered.

Aralt leant against the table, his dark gaze level and unflinching. '*Boom, boom, boom?*' Then he raised his wine glass to his lips, which were curling into a smile.

She'd told them - the bloody bitch had told them.

Instantly I was back there, trapped in that hole, with the stink of the putrid corpses, the lights flaring, until my retinas burned and with those *booming* guns bellowing.

Trying to hide the tremors, which were shuddering through me, I knocked Ruby's hand forcefully this time away from my goolies.

Ruby tutted. 'Don't take so, lover. We are not all fashioned to be warriors.'

You reckon that's what did it? The death knell to my male pride and yeah, as you know, I'm not exactly an innocent on that front. But you know what really did it? Broke something, which I couldn't yet articulate, but I felt the snap of it, sickening and sharp?

Boom, boom, boom...

That's when I'd known Ruby and me would never be truly alone. Just the two of us screaming at the world again.

Because she'd bloody told them.

I stormed down the dark corridor towards Aralt's bedroom, nothing in my head but the image of Aralt and Ruby necking from the same bird, who was bent over the desk in his study, and then how

Aralt had licked the blood from Ruby's lips. No more thought than Aralt's hand tight around Ruby's neck in that proprietorial gesture at the party.

Ma not giving you enough attention?

Jealousy flamed. Burning and consuming. My peepers were filled with it. Searing.

Love will get you like that and Blood Lifer love? Twisted obsession doesn't come close to how I felt. I was losing Ruby to that bastard but I didn't intend to go down without a fight.

I imagined Aralt bleeding at my feet. His smart white shirt soaked in red. His smooth hair messed up. His peepers puffy, but he could still look up at me - the man who'd beaten him (yet he'd called *babby*) - whilst Ruby watched.

I imagined that and it almost blotted out the rest.

Almost.

I swigged from the bottle of gin, which I was clutching and had been nursing, ever since I'd skulked away early from the party. I staggered on, wiping my wet mouth.

'Light?' Alessandro was staring at me, bemused, through the half-opened door of his bedroom. 'What are you..?'

'Not now.'

Alessandro trotted after me, glancing at the gin slopping at my side. 'Golly, how much have you had?'

I grimaced. 'Not enough.' I took another deep swig.

Alessandro thought for moment, before offering, 'Ruby's been looking for you.'

'Has she now?'

Alessandro frowned. 'Why yes, that's why I said it.'

I shook my nut. 'I wasn't... Can't a bloke get a bit of peace and quiet to seek his vengeance in this sodding place?'

'Vengeance?' Alessandro snatched at my sleeve, dragging me to a reluctant stop. His peepers had widened to startled blue puddles. 'I very much hope you're not referring to my Author?'

I shrugged.

Suddenly I found my mush shoved against the wall, my arm twisted high up my back. 'Buggering hell...' For a small lad, Alessandro was surprisingly strong. I was stronger still (and larger), however, so it shouldn't have been difficult to break Alessandro's hold. Yet I couldn't. He was dextrously pressing sharply into this one point on my back, sending sparks of pain that I hadn't expected straight to my brain.

'You see,' Alessandro's voice in my ear was light and matter-of-fact as he pressed harder, making me gasp, 'what many people don't realise is you don't need to be the most powerful to win a set to, you simply need to have a scientific knowledge of anatomy. That's another obsession of mine. The body, for example, has some bizarre quirks to it. It needs only the slightest pressure on a collarbone to break it. Do you wish me to break your collarbone?'

I could feel the thin bones straining. I moved my lips with difficulty. 'No, I sodding well don't.'

'Then please do not move and listen. Are you angry?'

'Of course I bleeding well am; you're crushing me.'

'I meant before.'

I blinked. This was one of Alessandro's paper snowflake differences; his emotions were amplified, but whatever part of the brain decoded them, functioned differently. He walked in a world of perpetual emotional mystery, where we were as odd to him as aliens. It must've been bloody terrifying. 'Yeah. And sad too.'

'That's why you're drinking?'

I gave a bark of bitter laughter. 'It's meant to numb, right? Bollocks does it.'

I yelped with pain, as Alessandro pushed harder, enough to start a tremoring crack creeping through both collarbones. 'Firstly, you will not drink anymore tonight. Secondly, you will not see Aralt or say anything to him about Ruby. And thirdly, you will not jolly well get yourself killed. Do you understand these three points?'

I struggled to answer with my gob squashed against the plaster. 'I get it.'

He twisted my arm. 'Say, Alessandro, I understand the three points.'

'Alessandro I understand the three sodding points, all right? Will you please get the hell off me now?' At last, Alessandro released the pressure, first on my back, and I sighed as my collarbones tipped back from the edge of breaking (but bugger me did they ache), and finally on my arm. I twirled round ready to belt him one, but Alessandro had crumpled to the side of the corridor. He was curled into a ball, trembling, with his chin down on his chest. He was in a worse condition than me. Shaking my nut, I hurled the bottle of gin skittering down the corridor, before ducking down to Alessandro, whilst massaging my sore wrist. He flinched away from me, expecting the volcano rained down on him, but I only gently touched his shoulder. 'Thanks, mate. I was gonna do something... Let's get you back to your room, all right?'

Alessandro glanced up at me in surprise, his quick hands fidgeting with the frayed threads of his vest. At last, he nodded. I helped him to his feet, feeling the soft quiver of him. Then we strolled together back down the corridor.

Later that night, when Ruby slipped out of her dress, I watched her derig, as I sprawled naked on our bed, in the room the twins had allocated to us.

It'd been a bland beige box, until I'd filched some dead blinding vintage Victoriana from local junkshops. It'd taken some ingenious lays: thick crimson curtains for the four-poster and a green and red Oriental rug. I'd even spent an entire night wallpapering with Gothic leaf patterns - right pretty it was.

Ruby had poked her nut in with lifted eyebrows, before disappearing for the evening, until it was finished: she never got her hands dirty. Ruby left the decorating to me, no matter where we were.

Once it would've been hard to unearth these types of pieces. Not now in this new London.

Ruby liked me to bring her presents. Elizabethan objects, however, were hard to come by, especially as museums have better security.

As I gazed at Ruby standing there, starkers apart from her fiery hair, which hung down between her breasts (every inch my Ruby of old), all I wanted – *Christ in heaven how I wanted it* – was to forget what had happened in the study and that damn dining room. But one word, three times over – *boom, boom, boom* – resounded in my brain.

How's a bloke supposed to forget that?

'Darling Light, how serious you look,' Ruby crept onto the end of the bed, her Bristols swinging alabaster white, as she crawled on all fours towards me. With a wicked grin, she licked up my leg. I closed my peepers. She wasn't making this sodding easy. With a shake of my nut, I threw myself off the covers away from her. Ruby stared at me, confused and then lay back luxuriously. 'Come, I want to play.'

There was something twisting inside me, bursting to get out. If I didn't say it now, Ruby would touch me again, and my body would betray me, sinking down into the memory of her. 'I took a shufti around the other night when you were... I went out into the streets. I discovered something: this time...these First Lifers...they're not like I remember them. They're--'

'Do you still cling to First Life?' Ruby arched her arms behind her nut. 'What is it you so love in their world, when I granted you the wonders of Blood life?' Her gaze was intense and ice cold. It would've frozen me to silence. But that was before she'd shared blood with her brother.

Before *she'd bloody told them...*

'You're not getting it.' Frustrated, I paced closer. I wasn't explaining it right: the vibrant buzz of Carnaby Street and the shock of recognition, which had forced me to see that our species were not divided in the way that had always been preached - with all the terrifying implications when your food turns round and looks you in the eye and then into your Soul... 'It's changed. *They've* changed. I don't reckon we have to choose between Blood or First Life. What if we're close cousins or something?'

Ruby's smile was mocking. 'A revelation, was it?'

I opened my mouth to answer but then stopped.

Sod it, I didn't want to share that bubbling, joyous memory with her. For the first time in our bloody exploration of a cruel world, I didn't want to share something, which Ruby would rip apart.

For the first time in a century, I felt truly alone.

Had Ruby ever needed me as I'd needed her? Was I love or only something to while away the years?

I made one final effort. 'I got you a gift,' I pulled out the Union Jack mug from the drawer I'd hidden it in, so I could surprise Ruby when we were alone, and she was awake for once. I held it out to her, like a peace offering. The last glimmer of hope flared that this ritual, at least, wasn't broken. 'I pinched it from this cool shop--'

'Why?'

Nonplussed, I stared at Ruby, the mug still held out in my stiff arm, ludicrous between us. 'I don't... What..?'

'Why did you steal, like a common thief? We have money now.'

I slowly crouched down, placing the mug back in the drawer; I patted the mug gently, before I pushed the drawer shut. When I straightened, I couldn't look over at Ruby. 'You've never... It's *their* money. This. All this is your brothers'.'

'*Ours*,' as I glanced up at her, Ruby stretched her pale legs out, one after the other. 'It was mine first, do you not understand that? You know the two most beautiful scents in the world? Blood and money.' Ruby threw herself up onto her elbow, laughing at my stony expression. 'Don't fret, darling Light. It's yours too now.'

With Ruby I'd always had this awareness of her, down to her very heartbeat and breath. I knew the sound of her footfall and rustle of her silk dress from streets away in the dark of the night. I knew she was going to speak, even before she opened her mouth. She was in my blood and I was of her blood.

It wasn't pathetic adoration, it was a bond forged by familiarity. A bloody century of it.

Yet now it was gone: I knew because I didn't recognise the words Ruby had spoken as hers. All that was left to me was silence.

It chilled me like I'd never be warm again; Ruby had killed me for a second time.

I scraped my nails down the wall, hearing the wallpaper tear and the umber leaves fall apart. They shredded, as my nails ripped. I embraced the pain.

I don't know how I got the words out but I did. 'But you see, no one owns me. Not even you.'

7

Look, us Blood Lifers aren't the only ones with bollocks myths: you First Lifers have them too. And the first one, which is branded on your grey matter? That you're above the sodding animals, solely because you tamed fire.

Here's where the bollocks lies: there's no taming something as crazy wild as fire. You know it, deep squirming in your gut. You can only borrow a slice of its blazing Soul. But mercurial, it'll burn you to blisters, or light your way to salvation.

That's why it fascinates you, as it dances in the dark.

Who can look away from the flames?

You were quieter tonight, sitting up for once in the high-back chair by the window.

I draped blankets around your shoulders and the checked rug over your knees.

The snow was melting on the creases of Ilkley Moor and dripping from the fingers of the birch and elder; the moon was shrouded behind the heavy mists.

Moth-like, you were transfixed by the wavering flame of my lighter. I knelt in front of you, playing the game you loved, or at least I guessed by your smile that you did: there's never more to go on now than that.

On, off, on, off...

Your smile. Bloody hell I'd flick my lighter all night to see that smile, rather than be cocooned in your low wailing or sodding stillness.

Does it help you remember me? Is that why you're smiling? This *bloody thing* as you called it? My gold lighter (flint and spring, smooth lid but barley pattern on its body), which I'd pinched off the suit on Carnaby Street?

I only kept it all these years because it became my talisman for the lightning strike moment, when I realised that losing our Souls, quivering piece by quivering piece, was a *choice*, rather than an inevitability of election.

There's no such thing as evil: there's only decisions, day in and day out. My lighter became the icon for the moment I twigged that if Blood Life was an evolution, then it was one I could share with the day dwellers. And love them.

I discovered a different way: not First Life and not Blood Life – my way.

See, rebel to the core. You woke me to that because you were my light. You still are.

Is that what you remember when you smile?

It was a Saturday night and I was working at the Heartbeat Club in a fug of smoke, lounging at the bar with my pint of Watneys Red and a fag. Yet all I could do was obsess over what Ruby and Aralt were up to, whilst I was playing in the shallow end.

Simply because the sun sleeps, doesn't mean the whole planet does too. Think of all those productive night hours; although of course *I* never did before those bloody twins.

Reckon I gave a damn, as if I was turned on by the scent of cash as well? Do me a favour. I learnt my lesson on that before I was elected and I didn't need teaching twice.

No, what Advance made clear to me was that First Lifers work in the daylight, whilst we snatch our shut eye, and at night, when you get your kip, we work or play in the shadows.

Once it was all about the play. But times change. Hadn't Ruby made that bleeding clear?

It's a perfect symbiosis or at least, it could be. The animal kingdom, however, is more brutal than that - First Life or Blood.

It was dark and close with heat in the club, reeking of youth and desire. The tables and chairs were like giant spools, dotted in the bar area. A dance floor spiralled in front of the live stage, which was jammed with gyrating First Lifers, in a rainbow burst of mini-dresses or Mod smart. Bugger, I hungered to drain every one of their bouncing, twisting bodies dry.

I wiped my shaking hand across my gob.

I still hadn't fed. I didn't reckon Ruby had noticed yet because since that night we... Since I'd dared to assert my own control and separate identity, I'd faded in Ruby's eyes. She hadn't even needed to say anything. I guess that was the point.

Suddenly this bleeder in suede jacket and fisher-man's corduroy cap, like he fancied himself another Lennon, knocked my arm as he leant across the bar.

My Watneys Red spilled onto the counter.

Mr Suede Jacket's gaze flickered across me and then away. 'Hey, sorry man.'

I pushed myself off my stool.

Everything had slowed - the band muffled - nothing but the *thud*, *thud*, *thud* of my own heartbeat in my lobes.

I could lunge at the bloke's jugular and taste the sweat on his skin, as I sank my teeth deep. He'd not even have time to... I blinked. 'Wasn't thirsty for beer anyway.'

I shoved the glass away, flicking the stub of my fag into the malty sea, where it crumpled. I padded my jacket for another.

And then...*that* voice. The one from Radio Komodo.

Do you remember this? You used to laugh about our first meeting and what a pillock you reckoned I was, lurking in the shadows by the bar in my leathers. How I just stared at you, like I could devour you.

And you were right, I could've done. I bloody wanted to.

Yet it's *because* you laughed that I never told you - and I won't ever get another chance to, unless I do it now - that it wasn't your blood but rather your sultry, fragile voice, which mesmerised me. It called to me across the divide of our species. It disturbed me in a way no one but Ruby ever had. It cut under the skin.

You were singing the same single, "Life's a Photograph", with your mouth so close to the microphone it was a part of you... *Everything's changing, so we've gotta change too...* You looked like some little Moon Girl, shimmering in silver: silver-spangled trousers, plastic biker jacket, with poppers and white ankle-length boots. I would've blasted into space with you in a bleeding heartbeat... *We're all memories, faded photographs...* The First Lifers were whipped up into a frenzy; the dance floor teemed with hormones... *But I'm alive, we're alive, so we've gotta live...*

I leant across to the barman, a hulking man, who was an ex-crim by his stance. 'Kathy..?'

'Freeborn.'

'Right then, after her set send her over.'

The barman nodded.

When you'd packed up and the next band had started, you didn't seem amused to have been summoned. 'You the Advance lad?'

'Well, yeah, I'm the Advance--'

'So? What do you want?' You raised your eyebrow with one impatient tap of your boot. You were cloaked in Chanel No 5. Your ebony curls were loose, tumbling around your mush. Your feline blue peepers, which were flicked with eyeliner, were coolly appraising me; their lashes were so thick they looked like they'd wing off around the room when they got bored. We Blood Lifers forget the paint you First Lifers hide your beauty behind, familiar instead with the naked skin, rather than the artifice. I found myself tracing the pretty patterns you'd masked yourself in. 'Something up with my face?'

'What?' I dragged myself back from my daze by the scruff of the neck.

I tried to lean casually on the bar as I lit up, but my elbow sank into the puddle of beer; I pretended not to notice.

You were just standing there, staring at me.

This wasn't how it was supposed to go. Not when I'd imagined it. And not between a Blood Lifer and a...

See, you were only a First Lifer, newly signed to the twins' label. In a century of discovery and revel, I'd never stooped to notice one of you. Except as a passing snack.

Yet now I had these pins and needles - weird little tremors - like I didn't know what to do with a body I'd had more than enough years to be versed in. But it was happening. There was no denying that.

Ruby had told me once that she'd kept this dim First Lifer as an experiment. More a pet than anything. She'd wanted to examine him, and I can imagine the kind of games she put that poor sod through. Eventually, however, Ruby had cocked up. She never elaborated because she wasn't one to admit failure easily (at least not to me), but she did tell me that the First Lifer - idiot as he might've been - had worked out Ruby wasn't quite human. Then that was that. Ruby had done him in because those are the rules: no evidence, no vampire hunters and no pitchforks. Vampire bollocks myth number...

But now here I was.

What was I bleeding doing?

All because I had this crater of emptiness, where Ruby should've been? And with some bitch, who looked like she thought I was as big a tosser, as I reckoned she was an evolutionary monkey?

Yeah, sorry, not really *the hearts and cupid* stuff, right?

'My face? You're gawpin'.' You sighed, shifting your chainmail bag on your shoulder with an impatient jerk. 'Is your gaffer..?'

'I'm the boss.' I straightened, drawing on my ciggie. When you laughed, the blood in my throat pounded.

'When the real gaffer wants to talk--'

'Your song, did you write it yourself? That's rare. A female creator in this industry. The lyrics...there's a line--'

'You going to give me a right nice, shiny medal?'

We glared at each other. Did you know two animals only look at each other like that, when they're going to fight? It triggered my flight and fight, and I don't sodding run.

I knew I'd insulted you but not how. This first contact was making my mind blaze; it'd been too long since I'd had to straightjacket myself in First Life convention. The skin was too tight. I felt like was I going to burst, bewildered with desire.

I slunk closer, so I could taste the scent of your sweat - my Moon Girl - sniff out the flowing strands of Soul underneath the painted beauty. 'I meant they're different... You're different to--'

'You're fair coming onto me?' You stepped back, eyeing the exit.

'No, what..?'

'I'm not into the whole Rockers scene,' you zigzagged your finger down, from my jacket to my scuffed motorcycle boots.

Confusion and humiliation, with something blazing at its core, which I wasn't going to bloody well accept (not this Blood Lifer and not again), shuddered through me.

I hurled down my ciggie, grinding it into the patterned carpet. 'That wasn't... As if I'd... And you know what? You were off coming into the third verse.'

Silence.

Your peepers were hard now: definite hit nerve. Yeah, bloody genius I was. I'd just risen in the rankings from insignificant to loathed. You crossed your arms, and I mirrored you.

'You ever tried not being a total prat?'

'Once. Didn't stick.'

You edged towards the door. 'Fab as this hasn't been, I must get on. My cousin's walking me home.' You tossed your nut at a bird with a thick fringe and Beatles do, who was perched at a spool table by the exit, glancing curiously over at us.

'I wanna take your picture.' The words had spilt out of my gob, before I'd even realised myself that I meant them.

I imagined my trusty camera snapping you from every angle, so I could possess your image to study without the accusation of *gawpin*. And then, before I could stop myself, the second image of tossing myself off over your smiling face, as Ruby shared blood with Aralt downstairs in his study.

See, I promised all *the nasties and wankery*, didn't I?

You were still heading for your cousin. 'Does it work with the other chicks? Pretending like you're David Bailey?' I darted after you through the hot jiving bodies, which stank of blood so strongly I gagged with the effort of keeping my fangs retracted. My own blood was up because this - what was happening between us? It was dead close to a *hunt*. I had to chain every instinct deep to stop myself from going for the kill. I grabbed hold of your arm. 'That the best line you can come up with? Think I'm a little fool?'

118

You shook me off, and I let you; it was more exhilarating this way. I wove after you through the crowds, catching you before you could reach your cousin. I was panting now, not out of breath but from the effort of controlling the bloodlust. 'It's for publicity, all right?'

'Yeah?'

'Reckon I'd want to spend time with you?'

'Happen you can give my agent a ring and set it up,' you admitted defeat with a weary sigh. 'I do take a good likeness.'

My quarry felled.

'Tomorrow evening?'

You frowned. 'Why evening?'

'That's when I work best, darlin'.'

You started towards your cousin again: a flash of silver. Stardust fallen to earth. Then you stopped and turned back to study me. 'You know you're a freak?'

I shrugged: one Blood Lifer lost in a sea of stinking humanity. 'No shame in flying that flag.'

For the first time your frown cleared and you seemed to see in the dark beyond the pompadour and the leather – see like a Blood Lifer - to the Soul and emotions buried underneath.

You First Lifers suck at that.

'You like Hendrix?'

'Of course.' I knew you'd have dead cool taste. It was in your scent. Your voice. And the way you were throbbing in my blood.

You stepped closer. 'What's your name?'

You hadn't even bothered to ask before. Now the hunt was really over. I smiled. 'Light. My name's Light.'

So I took your photo and it was one of the best nights of my life. You in gold catsuit and that bloody mask of make-up, which I craved to claw from your skin and find the woman underneath.

Flash, flash, flash...

In an empty room at the back of the Heartbeat Club. Your cousin and cigar-smoking agent hawk-like in the door. You in a strop refusing to say a single word.

Yet there was me, you and my camera, alone in a way I'd never been with anyone but Ruby and never cared to be, not since I was elected.

This new need to be wanted was messing with everything I knew. And everything I reckoned I was.

Your smile lit your peepers as much as your mouth; even though something told me it was a trick (and you couldn't mean it), I still treasured it.

You glowed, the same as any Blood Lifer - no, bollocks, it was different. Because this was *life* - true life - in a way I'd never stopped to scrutinise before. Only drain. It was real and I could smell it: courage, imagination and ambition.

Was this what it'd been like for Ruby, when she'd found me? Before she'd decided to elect?

Flash. The curve of your lips. The wisp of creativity.

Flash. Black curls caught behind your ear. The edge of ruthlessness.

Flash. Those blue peepers staring right down the lens, like a challenge. The scent of passion.

I'd captured your Soul, forever mine, and you didn't say a word.

Flash, flash, flash.

It must've been sodding hours I'd spend sprawled on my back each night in Alessandro's room, drinking in your record over and over, until the lyrics were branded onto my brain and then haunted my sleep.

Ruby would nudge me irritably when I'd start to hum the tune next to her in bed, without realising.

You were eating me whole. A delicious torture.

Whenever I was alone, I'd spread your photos out over the crimson covers, pressing my fingers to your face and trying to taste your spark, as the memory shuddered through me of that night.

Had you felt it too? This...thing? I didn't have a name for it. No sticky label.

Ruby would've called it a *perversion*.

Ruby still came to my bed but she hadn't touched me. Not like...that. It was as if she could sense I was less than the Blood Lifer I'd once been.

Bugger that, I was *more*, but Ruby couldn't see it. She was too caught up in whatever dodgy business the twins had going. I knew there was no place in her new family for me.

Did you lie awake thinking about me too? The dark things you wanted to do to me? Were we lying there at the same time, whispering each other's names?

Yeah, all right, I know the answer; I'm not deluded now. But then...that's what I fantasized about, whilst this empty, bunched feeling, built twisted in my gut. I had to see you again, even if you called me *freak* or didn't say a word and strolled on by, as if I didn't even exist.

The next Saturday, however, when I checked the lists at the club, you weren't playing. I'd booted the sound system, sending the guitarists scattering. I could've ripped the joint to shreds.

I needed a drink of blood so sodding badly I shook with it.

Ruby was noticing at last: the grimacing pain when I stood, the way I grasped onto edges of chairs to stop myself from blacking out and the constant tremble, which I couldn't hide any longer.

I stumbled to the khazi, kicking through into its muffled quiet. I sprayed freezing water onto my ashen mush.

A sudden low groan came from the corner of the latrines.

Bollocks.

Some berk tripping out on wacky backy had fallen, smashing his skull on the porcelain.

I crouched closer, licking my lips.

Blood was seeping from the wound in fat, purple clots and trickling down between the bloke's spaced out peepers.

I waved my hand in front of him: no response. Not a flicker. He was flying.

My whole body was quivering... The smell... The intoxicating splendour of it, burst like stars in showers around me; I could reach out and touch them, closer and closer...

Saliva dribbled, as my fangs shot out. I couldn't retract them. This was happening.

Christ in heaven, it was happening...

I gripped the bloke's shoulders, sliding out my tongue, further and further away from those teeth and deadly toxins.

Then I was licking, drinking from the gash, as if I was a panther. The blood hit my anaemic bloodstream, like it was my very first kill. The whole world was alive. And I was resurrected.

I shook with the high of pot infused blood; the kid giggled, whilst I fed from him.

Afterwards, I wiped myself clean at the sinks, before staring down at the still quietly sniggering mess, who was sprawled in his own piss.

I shook my nut, before swaggering back into the bar. The world was bright and small again in the brilliance of the blood's light.

Abstinence had neutered me, Ruby was right about that at least: we had to feed. The two drives were tearing me in two; I was blood but did I have to be death?

For tonight at least I was full.

I banged on the counter for the barman. 'Khazi needs checking. Something's blocking it.'

All right then, so most exciting lay there is: the jewellery heist. You'd have guessed that, right?

Look, any lay gets my blood going. It's not the money. It never is with me. It doesn't need to be high value diamond bollocks either, as that'll take you into a whole new league of headache on the planning side; I'm more for the cut and thrust of a good caper, clean and fast.

So jewellery: best payoff, minimum boredom. Not to mention those glittery trinkets speak to the Soul, even though what are they but pretty rocks strung on string?

That night, exploding with blood, I'd wandered the London streets searching for just the right hit because all I wanted was to share the moment with you. I knew, even then, lost as I was in the haze, that you weren't thinking of me and maybe hadn't since the day I'd snapped you. Yet still I couldn't stop myself.

I was addicted and I thought maybe...just *maybe*...

Hope - that's the true killer.

I had the idea this was what you First Lifers did, wasn't it? Courted with gifts? Or had the rituals changed so much since I'd been elected?

I knew a lad bound and wrapped in scarlet ribbons, or a horsehair whip, wouldn't be your thing. Jewellery though, I'd always relied on that to make Ruby smile. And I hungered to earn another smile from you.

Then there it was in the window, displayed on black velvet cloth: a silver choker, with sapphire disc, for my Moon Girl.

That's when the fun started.

Later, back in my room, I ran the choker gently through my fingers. I hadn't seen Ruby all night and it'd soon be dawn. I traced over the sapphire; its cold burnt.

Now I had it though, what the bloody hell did I do with it?

I paced up and down, glancing at your mug smiling up at me, over and over, from the photos, which were strewn on the sheets.

What did people even say in this new age?

'I saw this and...' I held out the choker loosely at an invisible you. 'Well, it's...and you're, well, you're blinding and...' I shook my nut in disgust, as I paced away. 'Look, I got you this, you fancy it, it's yours, all right?' I booted the bed, so hard the pictures became a trembling sea. Then I closed my peepers, holding out the choker towards your photo. 'Please accept this as a token of my highest regard... Laugh at me, will you?' I stared down at your mush, annihilated by your imagined mockery and my own frustration. 'Why don't you just sod off?' I hurled the choker skittering down the length of the room. Immediately, I regretted it. I rushed to scoop up the choker, twisting it between my hands to check it over: it wasn't broken. I breathed deeply, before holding it out again in front of me. 'So, you like sapphires?'

What you don't know, is what it took for me to find out where you were renting in Soho.

See, behind every important man in those days was a Secretary. Your agent's was called Jane (this daft bint with pasty legs), who spilled her boss' secrets for a bit of slap and tickle. I hope you don't reckon she got the raw end of the deal: I whored myself for you. Doesn't that just make you feel all warm and fuzzy inside?

Yeah, I'm the big romantic me.

Have the *hearts and cupid* shown up yet?

All right then, so I had this spiel all planned out, with the choker snug in my pocket, because no way was I going to look like a gormless wanker again.

My heart was wild stallioning, as I dived between the shadows, passing sex shops and illegal gambling dens. The night was alive with car horns and riffs of jazz drifting from coffee houses.

This is how it would play out: I'd knock, you'd ask me in and I'd say...

Then all of a sudden you were there.

You were coming out of your flat in high silver boots and a metal tunic, over a mini-skirt, which transformed you into a futuristic Amazon queen. You slammed the door and marched straight towards me, before I even had time to think of a new plan.

This I hadn't practised, in fact, hadn't even thought of in all my scenarios: *yeah, I was a sodding genius*.

You still hadn't seen me though, so there might be time to get out of it - for tonight at least.

I hung back and nearly let you pass. My palm was tense around the choker, like it was a relic.

Then came the fresh scent of you and it was too much: it overwhelmed me. You were devouring me.

I stepped out right in front of you, so close our faces almost touched.

I hadn't realised you'd jump like that. Then you looked pissed.

'*You*,' you gripped your bag closer, 'what do you want? I'm late.'

It'd never started like this in my head. 'Well I...' I began to draw out the choker. But then I frowned. 'Don't throw a wobbly, luv; Public Street last time I looked.'

'Then you're welcome to it.' You skirted round me.

For a moment, I listened to you march away.

'Hold up,' I dashed after you, but you kept on striding in those bloody high boots, towards the beat of the rock club on the corner and between the rush of the dirty traffic, 'come on, sorry, I was...'

'You following me?'

'No, I...' You stopped, raising your eyebrow. 'Yeah, a bit. I just... Look, this is for you.' I pulled out the silver and sapphire choker, which rested on my pale palm. Looking down at it, I wished I'd scrubbed my nails. I could see your peepers widening. But something was wrong because you weren't taking the choker. Instead, you were simply standing there, under the off yellow of the streetlight, studying me with this look, which I didn't understand. Was this what First Lifers did? It didn't feel right; it was more kind of sickening. I gestured with the choker towards you, but you shrank away. Then I remembered something, which

126

I'd seen other First Lifers do. 'Right, sorry, want me to put it on you?' I began to fumble with the clasp.

'No, don't.' You hurriedly stilled my hand with your fingers; your unexpected touch was like a silver roar. 'You can't just... Some'at like this, it's...too much. Don't you..? I can't accept it.'

The silver roar transformed into a howling blackness: the type, which made me hunger to feast on the world because maybe that'd dim the pain. 'Why?' I clutched the sapphire disc so tightly it sliced into my palm; I felt my blood meld with the rock, like a sacrifice.

Your voice was softer than I'd yet heard it. 'You know nowt about me and if you did...maybe you wouldn't want to.'

'What if I say I do?'

'Then you'd be a right fool.'

'That's my choice.'

'No,' you pushed me back with a firm shake of your nut, 'it's mine. Reckon this is a game? Little girl with a voice runs away to London for a record contract? Easy, is it? My life? What I want? I can't have someone like you--'

'That right? Someone like me?' Anger flashed at last and it was laced with a raw, remembered bitterness. You never forget your First Life and you don't forgive either. 'Suppose you'd prefer a bank clerk?'

'I'd settle for someone who wasn't a freak.' You bit your lip as soon as the words were out. I've always wondered if you regretted them, as much as they hurt me.

You immediately put your nut down, avoiding my eye, as your strode deeper into the centre of Soho. You didn't look back.

This time I didn't follow.

The choker was buried in the flesh of my palm; blood poured down my wrist. I wrenched the choker out, gasping with pain. Tipping my nut back, I hollered to the stars, with the rage and humiliation.

Then drawing my arm as far back as I could, I chucked that sodding choker in front of the wheels of a double-decker bus. I watched as it was pulverised; I wanted it to be ground back into the earth, so I'd never have to see it again. But you? I still yearned to see you and for the sweet torture to continue.

How can someone trap you with simply a smile?

8

You smiled at me in the early hours of this morning.

Will you ever understand what your smile means to me?

Because for that moment, as we lay curled together under the warmth of the covers, you were with me again: you saw me.

When I held you soft in my arms, you were Kathy and you remembered.

Your blue peepers studied mine, as clear as ever, and then came *that* smile. The one, which has always caught me helpless on your lips. And you know what?

For those few minutes before your peepers clouded, your smile wavered, and you were lost again - *that* was bloody *hearts and cupid.*

Another Saturday night in the dark buzz and clashing din of the Heartbeat, slouched with a smoke and a pint, flicking through the psychedelic pages of an underground magazine.

Bloody hell, these First Lifers weren't as blinkered or dull as us Blood Lifers conned ourselves, at least not in the world of these mags, which catered for the freaks out there. Free love and screwing the system right royally?

Just add blood and I was sold.

Here's the thing, the more I wandered this First Lifer world without Ruby, the more I realised my Author, muse and liberator didn't have a buggering clue what she was on about.

Instead (for some reason I didn't fully understand), Ruby was too frightened of the First Lifers, who were meant to be our prey, to dive headfirst into their world. Without the parent in the room, however, I'd been drowning in them. I luxuriated in the teeming, reeking humanity, with all its uncivilized barbarity. Sod that, *because* of it.

So I'd died? Not like I wasn't still here, kicking the hell out of the world. I breathed the same air. Pissed and shagged, just the same as any First Lifer. Were we really so bloody different?

That's why *A Clockwork Orange* blew my mind. Because there it was, in black and white screaming from the page at last: the self-awareness of this new age and the evolutionary jump to a subversion of everything that went before. It was enough to give me pause. It challenged all I knew about being one of the Lost.

Now you First Lifers were in my territory.

I downed my pint. I was meant to be helping Alessandro after closing with Advance's books. That was more of the twins' dirt on my hands then.

The more I dug, the more I knew in my gut something was off.

The money, power and empire-building? It stank.

Was that the true Blood Life? Elected from death, simply to live through a rerun of First Life all over again? The same treadmill but this time only as a shadow, or a pale imitation in the darkness because none of us were getting a bleeding suntan, were we?

This existence, which the twins were creating for us, seemed to me nothing but a sick charade of humanity, and greedy wanker that I was, I hungered for more than that: for something better, bigger – different. That was my own. And that I'd *chosen*.

If I was finally outside the bullshit shackles of school, work, government and sodding money too (the bollocks of First Lifers, who can't see the figures dance), then I'd earned the freedom.

But Aralt's little family? We had new chains.

I'd just slipped out a new fag and lit up, when it started. The music.

I didn't turn round, move or even bloody breathe because I wouldn't give you the satisfaction.

...Everything's changing, so we've gotta change too... It cut deep, bugger did you make me bleed... *But I'm alive, we're alive, so we've gotta live...* And you were, like every one of the bopping Mods in this swarming club: sweating bags of skin, pounding with hearts, veins and arteries, which coiled in blue and red, like the wax anatomical models under the glass cases in Florence.

Yet here I was, trembling with hunger and the agony of the constant fight to leash it inside, but not one of you even noticed me – the dead bloke sitting right in your midst.

What would you think if you knew? What would you do?

I realised I was flicking my lighter - *on, off, on, off* - and staring into its orange flame, as your voice kept on singing.

I wanted to turn around so badly but I bloody well wasn't going to.

It's a myth that blokes think about sex every few seconds. Yet we're still led by our todgers - that's just nature - and when we're in love, it sodding burns.

It's a type of madness.

I wanted the thought of you - that worm squirming deeper and deeper into my core as you sang - incinerated.

I passed my hand over the lighter, holding its shimmering heat against my palm. And then again, lowering my hand...lower and lower.

The burn felt good. It was the first time in weeks I'd had something to really concentrate on. When it became too white hot even for me to bear, I snatched it away. Then, however, I forced my palm over the fire again. This time I held it there.

The skin blistered, peeling in blackened strips. I shuddered but I didn't pull back. Instead I struggled to absorb the pain. This way I didn't have to listen to your siren song; I could feel nothing but the fire.

At last, I wrenched my hand back; beads of sweat trickled down my forehead. Then I shifted my lighter over again but this time onto another spot.

It took me a couple more moments to notice you'd stopped singing, maybe you had awhile ago, but I'd been too lost to the world, submerged under waves of pain.

Breathing out with relief, I glanced over my shoulder, and there you were - my Moon Girl - dolled up and blinding as always.

Our eyes met. You were staring at me from across the dance floor in shock.

Buggering hell.

I snatched my hand away from the lighter, but it was too late - you'd seen.

I'd wager you reckoned I was a true freak after that?

I started off the stool, but you'd already dived for the door and were gone, before I'd been able to slip the lighter into my pocket (my scorched hand now making its protest known), and fight my way through the scrum.

The hunt was on.

I darted after you through the night-time streets. I didn't even know what I'd say when I caught you. As if I could tell you I was burning myself because it hurt too much to listen to your voice, when I couldn't have you...

That sort of thing would've been romantic to Ruby.

I was beginning to realise, however, that you First Lifers weren't so obsessive. Every emotion amplified, right? Love is twinned with hate. Pain to passion.

When I glimpsed the flash of your silver ankle boot turning down a side street, I prowled after you, hunched against the light summer rain. My blood sang.

All right, cards on the table, I had my first stiffy in weeks, which hadn't needed my own vigorous help getting there. Pursuing you pushed every one of my buttons. I was complete. Exhilarated. And alive in a new and yeah, sexual way. Reckon I'm going to apologise for it? You know me too well for that.

Two chicks in trucker jackets fell out of the doorway to a coffeehouse, which swung to the rhythm of jazz, jamming over a beat poet's declaration of war on his parents' generation. Squiffy, the birds hung onto my arm to steady themselves; they stank of light ale and cheap fags.

I shook them off, weaving on down the side street after you. I could scarcely see you now; the waves of your hair bobbed in and out, bleeding into the crowds.

That's when I heard the muffled scream and scuffle. It was unmistakable to us Blood Lifers: a kill in an urban area.

Of course we all have our signature styles or quirks.

I once met this Blood Lifer in Berlin, who had a fixation with strangling his kills, not enough to stop the heart but just enough to silence them. I don't know if that made him touched or highly efficient.

So I heard this sound down a narrow alley and out of curiosity, I glanced down it as I passed, in case it was Ruby, or one of the other wankers from Advance, catching a bite on their night-time wanderings.

Instead, I saw it wasn't any Blood Lifer I knew but some dandy nancy boy, all white cravat and tight trousers, as if he was auditioning for the role of vampire in some crap flick. It definitely looked like I needed to go run through the list of bollocks myths with him.

Then I realised who the dandy's kill was: *your cousin* - the bird with the Beatles mop. She was trapped trembling up against the wall and a rotting poster for a long ago jazz show, with the Blood Lifer's hand slammed against her mouth.

I took a quick shufti, checking there weren't any bloody marks on your cousin's neck. No puncture wounds, so she wasn't dead. Yet. The dandy must be still at the playing stage. His hand crawled down from your cousin's waist, lifting up her mini-skirt, before circling towards her muff.

I started towards them but then I stopped myself. Confused by the conflict, which I'd never had to war with before in this Blood Life, I backed away towards the main road again.

Who the hell was I to interrupt someone else's dinner?

Me turning round, right? I wish I could mould myself into more of a hero for you, like I know you reckon I was. But if this is my last chance, then I need you to see me - the worst of me - as well.

It was easy to let you believe this played out like I had a sodding Soul of gold. But at that moment, it hung in tarnished tatters: I was no bleeding knight. I never was.

I backed off, as your cousin began to weep.

Look, there's a code of sorts: never interrupt someone else's kill and never steal it, like in a lion pack. If you do, you'd better be prepared for an almighty barney. Or to cop it.

I turned away.

Then I thought of you and how you'd feel when you discovered one of your family had died. The grief. The funeral. Your loneliness. The same pain, which I now felt and the same as I'd experienced in my First Life.

Unexpectedly, for a fleeting moment, it was *joy* tingling through me. I thought *good, I bloody well hope you feel it.*

Just as fast, it was replaced by...well, it wasn't guilt, rather a chilling devastation that you could ever experience the same anguish as I had. Then a desperation to protect you. To make sure you never did.

I'd never suffered such a bewildering see-saw of emotions.

That's when I couldn't go through with it. For the first time ever, I couldn't leave another Blood Lifer to their kill.

I squared my shoulders, before I legged it down the dark alley. The wanker ignored me, when I stopped behind him. 'I want a quiet word.'

The dandy glared round at me in astonishment. He examined my leathers, as if I was a stinking specimen of beetle. He knew what I was though because a Blood Lifer always knows another Blood Lifer. It's in the scent: death can't mask itself.

When she saw me, your cousin must've recognised me because her teary peepers widened and she started to struggle.

The dandy leaned on her more heavily. 'You're young,' even his voice lisped, 'so I will forgive you this slip of etiquette. Pray leave now, there's a good fellow.'

I shook my nut.

The Blood Lifer sighed, adjusting his cravat. 'What? Busy here.'

'She's not yours, mate.' I glanced at your cousin, who was shaking like a rabbit in an eagle's claws. 'I can't let you, all right? Clear off.'

The dandy chuckled. 'Now I really have heard everything. She's your pet?'

I shrugged.

His peepers hardened. 'So sorry. But I'm famished.'

The dandy twisted back to your cousin, with one hand at her throat now; his fingers bit hard enough to bruise. He leant closer. His fangs would be shooting from his teeth at any moment...

I hurled myself at the dandy, knocking him off your cousin and flinging him rolling, with a *clang*, over a metal dustbin.

As he scrambled up, he snarled with rage and frustration at the loss of blood. The hunger would drive his fight: his fists, boots and bite. His fangs sank so deeply into my arm that they went clean through my leathers and skin to the blood.

I hollered, kicking him off.

Then the poofy git had me around the waist.

I glimpsed your cousin's terrified mug, from where she was huddled behind a dustbin. 'It's all right, luv, just hold on a tick...'

I was hauled back by the dandy, as I desperately tried to wrestle his arms from around my chest. He was squeezing the life from me - *bloody hell* - he was stronger than he looked.

But he had no street smarts.

I nutted him, hearing the satisfying *crunch* as his nose broke. I watched as the scarlet flowed. He roared, and then we were rumbling in earnest with elbows and knees, punching at joints and throats and every other point of weakness. He clouted me a good shiner; I could feel it purpling up, as he laid into every inch of me.

But this? Everyone's got to have a talent. Ruby had taught me well how to embrace pain, as just part of the cut and thrust. Now I could turn that to my advantage.

I grinned, as I grabbed the dandy, chucking him against the bricks and pummelling – *bam, bam, bam* – until my knuckles bled. Then the

dandy let out a deep snarl. He belted me back –
snap - breaking my ribs.

Suddenly the ludicrousness of two Blood
Lifers, elected into this...whatever it was...but
centuries old and so very beyond First Life,
standing in the street and giving each other a hiding
in front of some little groupie, gripped me, and I
doubled up with painful laughter.

The dandy stared at me like I was off my
bleeding trolley. He panted, wiping the blood from
his nose.

After a moment, I got a grip of myself. I shook
my nut. 'Oh just sod off, will you?'

The dandy hesitated, before he straightened his
now crimson spattered cravat and limped away
down the alley. Then he turned back, pointing at
me with a shaking finger. I was right - thwarted
bloody Laurence Olivier. 'You, sir, are no Blood
Lifer.'

I flipped the two-fingered salute at him. He
drew himself up to his full height in disdain, before
sweeping off into the night and his own fantasy of
what Blood Life meant.

*I really should've told him about the bollocks
myths.*

'Thanks.'

Surprised, I glanced down at your cousin. I'd
forgotten about her.

She crawled up still shivering, whilst tugging
down her mini-skirt, as if this could wipe clean
what I'd seen.

Yeah, like I could wipe clean what I'd done? I
was breaking every rule here: leaving witnesses
alive, rescuing chicks and interrupting kills.

But then, when did I give a damn about rules? I
cut them up into pretty pieces and let them blow
away on the wind.

What had your cousin really seen, when it came down to it? Some smarmy bastard, no different to a human rapist. Just like our barney could've been two maniacs having a right old go, like First Lifers after chucking out time.

I slumped against the damp wall.

The rain was heavier now. Warm drops dripped down my neck and washed away the congealing blood. Once the heat was off the battle, the pain was kicking in; it jolted electricity up nerves, straight to my brain. Buggering hell, this was the part I always forget, or else nothing can brand it deep enough to curb the impulses, which come first.

I fought it down, running a bloodied hand through my sweep of hair. 'I reckon that bloke was off his nut or something. You all right?'

Your cousin nodded tentatively. 'Are you?'

First time I'd been asked that, maybe since my papa was alive. I shook the thought away. This wasn't the time. I must've looked a right mess then. 'Yeah, tickety-boo.'

'Load of cobblers. You're coming with me.' Before I knew what was happening, your cousin had slipped her arm around my shoulders and was leading me out of the alleyway.

That's when I realised I needed to lean on her for support. It was bleeding humiliating: I'd never needed that from a First Lifer before. Yet your cousin didn't comment or laugh, like I'd expected. Instead, she kept on holding me, whilst I hobbled next to her.

'You're Kathy's cousin?'

'I have got a name, you know, not like I'm her dog.'

Despite myself, I smiled. 'Sorry. So?'

'It's Susan. And I know who you are.' She didn't say it like that was a good thing. I hadn't reckoned she would.

I'd dead buggered up this courting thing; there were too many steps I no longer knew. All right, I'd never known them to begin with.

As we walked, I noticed Susan was taking me into Soho. There was your scent again. Growing stronger.

Your apartment.

Susan had brought me to the one place, where I knew I wouldn't be welcome.

For a moment, I drew back, resisting. Look, what man wants the woman they - dream about, toss off over and obsess on - to see them all duffed up, like a nancy boy, as well as the freak you'd already made it clear as day you reckoned I was?

Yet the pull and the fast beat of my heart, told me I didn't care if you saw me carved to shreds at your feet because you'd still see me and I'd still see you. Watching you only from the shadows?

I was so done with that.

When we reached your scarlet front door, I managed to ask Susan, whilst trying to sound nonchalant, 'You live with Kathy?'

Susan nodded, looking like she wanted to ask something herself. But she didn't. When she struggled to both support me and turn her key in the lock, she knocked.

Those moments before you swung the door open nearly did me in. Then you were there, my Moon Girl: no makeup now, simply that dead beautiful face, just like I'd always desired to see it. You shone.

I straightened, trying not to let the hurt show.

When you saw me, however, your expression hardened. You slammed your arm across the doorway, blocking it. 'Well he's not sodding well coming in. I don't care what's happened to him. Hasn't he got a home to go to?'

Yeah, you were sugar and spice.

Susan frowned. 'Don't be such a nitwit. He saved me. He's a hero.'

I registered the surprise and doubt in your peepers. I kept my own gaze fixed on the floor because I didn't want you to read anything different in mine. You lowered your arm, however, before you nodded.

When Susan helped me into the hall, you shifted your weight to round my waist and then I saw your peepers soften, as I flinched. Your touch was intimate and unexpected; it made every clout a thousand times worth it.

As Susan clicked the door closed behind me, I knew at last I'd found my way in.

9

You remember that Victorian blanket box, which you came back with from a junk shop in Ilkley in 1969 and then stripped of its varnish, before painting it kaleidoscopic? Well I dragged it out of the back of the garage last night and had a sort out.

I wanted to make a rummage box for you out of your ivory scarf, photos, your LP, chainmail bag and Jimi Hendrix poster. I figure it'll help you remember longer: who you are and who I am. Our life.

That way, I'll hold onto this – different life – by my fingertips a bit longer too.

I'm slipping here without you, I can admit that now and I know where the darkness leads; I lived it long enough, didn't I? I don't want to go back there. Even though it'd be just like going home.

Funny thing, memory.

First Lifers lose it, like a fading photograph.

Yet every moment of my Blood Life has remained as crystal clear as the second I lived it.

That's not cool: it's a curse to have all those memories bobbing around in my brain, like a sodding computer, waiting to be processed.

They're only what *I* remember. They're not the truth. Just one man's witness.

Lately, I've felt like there are too many moments pressing in my skull. I wonder if this is what happens to Blood Lifers when they live long enough. They're not touched but rather they remember too much: every face, scent and taste. All at once. I wish I could black them out, the bad ones at least. But be careful what you wish for, right? Yeah, every time I look at you, I...

Be careful what you wish for.

SEPTEMBER 1968   LONDON

The acid face of Hendrix stared down from the walls of your flat, like a prophetic god, in the yellow light thrown by your mushroom lights, as we sprawled on beanbags and "Are You Experienced" span on your record player. The sonic, breath-taking guitar battled in psychedelic rock'n'roll with drums, howling into birth a new world of freedom and danger.

We were drowning in it.

Our hands were clasped. Our feet were tapping. Our mugs were plastered in daft grins.

And *this*? Yeah, this was happiness.

You know as I see it, you weren't my Moon Girl anymore, in fact, you hadn't been for weeks. You were dressed dead casual in jeans and hippy drawstring top, with an ivory scarf knotted snug at your neck: your *sexy little thing*, I called it. You didn't know it then, of course, but it drove me wild, the way it drew the eye to the jugular, yet coyly hid it at the same time. I'd kiss up and down your neck, light and hot, sliding my fingers under that sexy little thing. And the sensation when it tightened...

I've got a stiffy just writing it - look at the effect you have on me, Christ in heaven, even now.

Don't be narked but that version of you, which you kept for private - behind closed doors - no glued on spider lashes or synthetic hair, was the lass I'd fought to burrow down to, ever since I'd first seen you. The humanity, which had beckoned to me, when I'd heard you on the radio in Alessandro's room. That my Soul had twinned to.

The chick shimmering in silver up on stage? She was Advance's creation, and I was fast coming to realise that there was always something rotten inside one of those, no matter how pretty the trinket.

Earlier, we'd been to a late showing at the flicks to see *Barbarella*.

You'd picked the movie but still, the first virtually nude woman up on the big screen and whether it was set in the forty-first century or not, I'd offered to take you out of there. That was no way to court a bird; I was definite that couldn't be one of those grey areas of convention, with which I was still struggling.

You'd simply laughed and called me a *prude*. Futuristic erotica was this new age's mating ritual? All right then, so you're out of the dating scene for a century, and all the rules of the game get bleeding changed on you.

When I'd settled back again, we'd watched this Barbarella chick rescuing her time, whilst giving us blokes plenty of flesh to wank over. It seemed like a fair exchange to me.

But the best part? The dead blinding part? The way your fingers had curled around mine, as your nut had nestled onto my shoulder, in silent intimacy in the dark; I'd hardly dared breath, in case I'd broken it.

Freak or not, I was yours now: you'd claimed me.

We could sit quietly together, just watching, as if I was no different to any other First Lifer, pulsing with blood in their seats around us.

Ruby would never believe that this new world imagined such fantasies. She refused to go to the flicks: *cold empty shadows*, that's what she called them. She had no time for moving lights, false pictures with no blood in them; if you couldn't bleed them, then they were beneath her notice. But me? Me, Ruby had started to notice again, just in small ways.

Ruby would search me out and make demands when I was least expecting it. Or she'd startle me awake. Then watch me through cool peepers.

I'd been a jammy bastard that she hadn't already twigged something wasn't pukkah about my blood abstinence. But now with you as well..? It was only a matter of time before Ruby smelt you. I could smell Aralt on *her* couldn't I? Even on her glowing red hair.

Yet the difference was Ruby wasn't even trying to hide it. It was as if she wanted me to know - rub the pup's nose in it. Whereas me? I'd bathe, scrubbing my skin until it near bled, like that barmy bloke, who I'd been forced to shank during the Cuban Revolution.

Look, don't get the hump. I wish I could've held onto every embrace. Your scent cocooning me. I

145

still shared a bed with Ruby, however, and that devil could've plucked me apart.

Yet the greatest problem was that I still needed blood.

Without it we're not alive, and to hell with it if I was dying twice.

Every day that went by, Ruby was catching on, glancing at the way my hands would betray me with their trembling.

Remember the berk spaced out on wacky backy in the latrines? I couldn't rely on stumbling over flukes like that when I went for a jimmy, every time I needed a feed. All that mind over matter crap's clap-trap because the strongest will in the world can only hold out so long, when it comes to the stuff of life.

So I got creative.

Right, so all the *nasties and wankery*? Don't roll your eyes. I know you're going to, however, because on the way to yours through Soho, there were all these sex shops. And one night I collected some cards for...

This skanky bint was off her nut. Her skin was crusted with pimples and her room stank of cum and vomit. But she was the one who said *yes* - for the right fee - and I was desperate.

Ruby always let me have money now, like I was her wife (or maybe her whore), so I could buy what I liked. Rather than nick it. I'd rejected it before but had started silently pocketing the money without a word, which meant I had enough to pay for the blood.

The First Lifer stuck this needle into her thin vein, selecting the one closest to her muff because the others were already collapsed. Despite everything, I started to salivate, as she drew out the blood. You know what blew my mind though? She watched, when I squirted the blood into my gob and then swallowed in my near starvation, as if it was the sweetest (rather than the rankest), blood I'd tasted in decades. Her expression, however, didn't change: it was blank, like she'd seen it all before.

Maybe she bleeding had.

She was still a teenager, yet even a freak drinking her blood from a needle didn't surprise her.

I saw the bird once a week, taking just enough to keep the tremors at bay. I never asked her name; she never asked mine. And I never told you. In two lifetimes of bad choices and sodding carnage, that's a lie, which never let my conscience rest. I let myself believe it was about survival because that's the get out of gaol free card. Or so we tell ourselves. But never telling you? That was all on my head.

The soundscapes of Jimi Hendrix's "Are You Experienced" soared, as we sprawled side by side on your bean bags.

'Susan got it. The secretarial post.'

I grinned. 'Blinding.'

You tore at the rough edge of the shagpile, dragging frayed edges out – hard - between your twisting fingers. 'Would be if her new boss weren't a right pig.'

Stiffening with that automatic tension when a predator's close, yet a swirl of confusion too because this time the adrenaline surge wasn't for me, but rather for a First Lifer. Everything I'd been taught told me that wasn't right. But I still couldn't stop myself. 'What's he..?'

'Not like he's any worse than the rest, I guess.'

'Want me to..?'

'What?' You stopped worrying the carpet, trapping my fingers between yours instead. 'You our white knight now?'

Mockery.

You were always good at that, with an added hint of seduction, just the right side of annoying. You could play me so well, ensnaring me somewhere between rage and lust, which for a Blood Lifer is bloody heaven.

Let's face it, neither you nor me would be content with boring, ordinary lives, whatever the hell they look like.

It's not only us Blood Lifers, who walk and crave that thin line between pleasure and pain. I'm not simply talking about the kinky stuff either.

Do you remember the nights (and if you remember nothing else, Christ in heaven, you must remember those nights), when you'd keep me on the edge for hours because you said you loved to watch me stretched out, shuddering under you, in that hazy zone where pleasure and pain meld sublimely? What divides the screams and moans, which everyone the world over makes when they come, from the sounds of torture?

You did that to me with your words. I don't know if you ever got that.

Disgruntled, I shrugged. 'Armour wouldn't suit me. I'll stick to leathers.' I kissed the tips of your fingers; they were soft, but your long nails grazed my lips. 'You got a gig this weekend?'

You nodded. 'Recording next month and likely...' You stopped.

'What?'

'It's nowt. But this - what I do - it burns me with exhilarating fear because I know I'm fair lucky. I don't want it to end or... Not with everything I've done. Everything I've been through. It could be me in that office with a pig of a--'

'Never you. That could never be you.'

You rolled off your beanbag onto me, your body hard against mine. Then we were snogging, lost somewhere in the wild roar of the music. My mind opened to this new age, the stars bursting and the rhythms beating through my blood in time with the power of the drums.

At last I knew what this *thing* was.

You'd possessed me, invading every bleeding inch of me, until all I breathed was you.

But now I knew its true name – this was *love*.

You snuggled closer onto my chest; your arms hugged tight around me, limpet-like. 'I wish you didn't have to go. Wish we could be here like this. Forever.'

What had you just said?

I tried not to tense, as I stroked a dark curl back from your cheek. 'Do you?'

'What?'

'Forever?'

You smiled. 'What are you on about, freak?'

See that was the moment. Had it been like this for Ruby? A sudden awareness the time had come?

Yet Ruby hadn't even known me, not like I knew you; she'd only tasted my Soul. That was enough, however, for most Blood Lifers. I'd tasted your Soul too; I'd been hollowed out by it and now I was filled up with something real. This...love.

Did you love me as well? Maybe. Dunno. But I did know how *I* felt and that was enough.

Election was meant to be for the cream of each generation. You had beauty, talent and ambition, with the streak of ruthlessness, which made a leader. You deserved Blood Life.

Then we'd be together fully and forever. Not in that fairy-tale bollocks way but as long as anyone could wish for on one planet. I'd always known something had been different - this call to you. Different to the taste of every other First Lifer.

The vistas stretched before me of the world I'd reveal to you, just as you'd introduced me to yours. I remembered the decades of exploration with Ruby and all the wonders she'd shown me. I shook with anticipation that I could be your Author, muse, liberator. And love.

I sat up, pulling you with me onto my lap. You stared at me, with a look of surprise. I tried to smile but I was too nervous. 'If you could... If there was a way to live for centuries and--'

'Like a vampire?'

I stiffened. 'No, not like a sodding vampire.'

'You want to go out somewhere tomorrow evening? Take the Mini and--'

'So when you said you wished we could be like this forever..?'

You frowned. 'I was just playing, ninny. You're serious all of a sudden, what's..? I'd rather live fully every second. Who'd want to go on and on with no end? Always out of step with the world? Sounds lonely to me.'

I hugged your small body closer; I found I couldn't loosen my arms. 'But if you were with someone else? Like, you'd found someone who... It was me and you, together..?'

'The vampire and his bride?'

'Not bloody vampires.'

Irritated now, you dragged my arms away from your middle and I let you, as you pushed off me. You swung to the record player, lifting the needle off the Hendrix LP. The sudden silence was like a bleeding black hole.

I stared at your tense back, when you didn't turn round to me.

I'd done that all wrong, hadn't I? How had I buggered it up so badly?

Ruby had opened my peepers to the splendours of Blood Life at my election. She'd exhilarated me with the glorious possibilities of my new world and the superiority of the species, into which I'd evolved. But daft berk that I was, all I'd been able to conjure up for you was shadow puppets of Halloween nasties.

I'd screwed up the moment - the *only* moment - and I knew it.

You'd never want to be elected into this Blood Life with me.

Yeah, it was lonely.

At last, you twisted back to me. Your peepers were serious and dark. 'But you wouldn't be human, would you? I'd never want that. I could never love something that was... Isn't this life enough for you?'

'You are,' I answered softly, 'you are, luv.'

MAY 1866   LONDON

I checked the numbers again. There was no doubt: Overend, Gurney and Company, London's wholesale discount bank - the banker's bank - was about to collapse.

Junior clerk as I was, I could see the ripples from the rumbling earthquake in its wake spreading out with photographic clarity: the panic and run on banks spreading to Liverpool, Manchester, Norwich, Derby and Bristol, and then all the other companies failing, like dominoes in a row.

I'd written warnings to the directors, especially Mr John Wesley Erwood, ever since they'd employed me on the written recommendation and good word of my uncle. That, however, had nearly got me bloody fired.

Junior clerks weren't meant to get above themselves; it was bleeding presumptuous and should've been already beaten out of me. I should've simply got on with my job, bowed and scraped - *yes sir, no sir* – and kept my peepers to the ground, rather than lifted to the lofty heights of high finance. But I've always been a curious bastard. Not one to stay in my place.

The one talent I had was for numbers.

Numbers had danced in my mind, in glimmering cascades, before I even had the words to describe them. And these ones at the bank? They'd never added up. Not when the bank had millions of pounds more liabilities than liquid assets, yet still couldn't see the danger. Not when the stock and bond prices collapsed. Not when the Bank of England failed to play ball.

I slammed the hefty, leather accounts book shut, tapping my fingers thoughtfully on top. I'd requested to work late in a dusty backroom, which was lined with the bank's ledgers; their secrets for the last decade were hidden in the numbers. Gradually I'd unearthed the truth in their patterns. The fading light streamed through the single high window.

The answer I'd discovered in that room of numbers, was that the world was about to come tumbling down on all our heads. Yet no one realised it because the reality was masked by the directors' fraud – and *that* was the buried truth.

Every night I came here, I was working myself up to something, which took more courage than I reckoned I possessed.

The directors were conning the world and I was the only one, who could do anything about it. If I didn't, honest men and their families would suffer; I understood too well what poverty and misery could follow, when livelihoods were lost.

I knew I'd have to reveal the lies.

Real hero, right?

Prat more like.

I was innocent as a babe in my First Life. But I was fired by the flames of the righteous for all the little people, who'd be caught in the whirlwind, when the banks turned bad.

Clueless I was but still, that's when I started my plan to worm close to Mr Erwood, (the stuffed walrus). I made sure I was in the position to overhear snatches of muttered meetings, which I could then match up with the dodgy numbers that paraded - day and night - in my brain. Those numbers never let me get a moment's kip.

They became like a second conscience.

Luckily, the bigwigs never worried about my presence because a *nobody* hasn't got lobes. They gabbed in front of me, no different to a master yaks about his mistress in front of his servants: they're invisible and what would they know? What did *I* know? More than they did, and I was going to show them.

I was a man on a sodding mission. I burnt with it.

Most of all, I had to prove they knew (those fat cats in their gold-gilt offices), who were scrabbling to safety, whilst the death knell had already sounded for the common man, with his life savings invested: those poor sods would be bloody buried alive. But the banks and their directors, who'd caused the catastrophe? They'd survive (of course their type always do).

I guess, just once, I wanted to even the odds.

But love will rot you through every time.

Mr Erwood had a daughter: Grace. I reckon she only came to the bank, with her tiny shrew of an aunt as chaperone, to torment us clerks. No, hands up, to torment *me* because I was the poor git assigned to escort her.

I don't know why her papa chose me, but it could've been partly because I'd been sticking to his side like a bloody limpet and partly because he couldn't imagine anybody, who'd be less of a threat to his unmarried daughter: this ambitious but friendless clerk.

He wasn't a good judge of character that one.

Grace wore the latest Parisian fashions. Her cloud of blonde hair was always perfectly arranged and smelling of the sweetest violets. She was alien to the male environment of echoing marble halls and clusters of blokes trying not to be caught out in their furtive glances, whilst hiding their stiffys behind clutched bundles of files. Grace would flash just a glimpse of ankle, as I'd help her back into her crested carriage amidst blankets, pillows and footwarmers, like an Arabian princess. Then she'd give me that coquettish smile of hers.

I had no way of hiding *my* stiffy in my tight trousers after that.

Grace – my first love, sweet torturer and for three years the only lady, who haunted my dreams.

But the real hell of it? She knew it.

Cat and mouse, Grace played with me (out of boredom I knew); I was only a little something to pass the time. The bleeding crime was that I let her because it felt so good to have someone to worship.

Ever being loved back by someone, just seemed too distant a hope.

That evening when I strolled out of the backroom, the numbers crashing through my brain and pounding so hard a headache had formed, something made me stop and make the decision, which I'd been building up to for weeks.

Bravery isn't as easy as they show it in the flicks. It's a slow burn, stoked by incremental choices. When you decide to risk everything, few First Lifers can do that in a moment, unless it's drilled into them. That's what military training's all about, or did you reckon pulling a trigger was to do with finger strength?

That night? It was when I finally knew I was ready. To throw away everything I'd built up over the last three years. I would find those incriminating papers, take them to the beaks and explode this bank and my whole life along with it. And that did take balls.

Stupidity but balls.

I knew the papers were in Mr Erwood's office; I'd watched him perusing them, his heavy features furrowed in a deep frown. I'd have to filch them. There's a first time for everything, right?

Adrenaline and fear surged. I stalked along the cavernous corridors, which were deserted now after hours - *clack*, *clack*, *clack* - each footstep was sharp against the marble, even in my stealth.

I drew in my breath, when I saw the wide doors to Mr Erwood's office were open. Then *movement* in the dancing light of the lamps. I crept closer, my back to the wall.

When I reached the door, I peered round into the dim room. Like a vaulted cathedral, the ceiling domed high above me, veined in gold. Mr Erwood's vast oak desk crouched in the centre. His papers were laid out, as if awaiting a clandestine meeting.

My blood pounded because it was *Grace* pacing back and forth in front of the desk, floating in a dress of lilac tartalan muslin with matching sash, so light it was almost transparent - a fairy ghost that shaped her into a perfect doll. Her arms, however, were crossed impatiently.

I drew back, but it was too late: Grace had seen me. 'Do come in, Mr Blickle.'

I reluctantly edged inside, eyeing those papers - those pretty numbers - which proved the world was about to change unimaginably. They were just there. But out of reach.

Grace was studying me in that way she had, which made me shiver: half haughty and half inviting.

You got me right, when you reckoned I was a dead pillock, watching you from the shadows in the club. Maybe Blood Life doesn't change us as much as we like to think.

Uncomfortable, I noted Grace's aunt wasn't with her.

Grace seemed to read the question in my peepers, as I shifted my feet. She smiled. 'Aunt's not feeling quite well. So she has left me here. Alone. I am awful bored by myself, waiting for papa and his dreadful friends. Why they barely say two words to me, can you imagine?' Grace stroked her soft hair back, before raising her eyebrows.

'I...need these papers and then I should leave you...' I made a grab for the sheaf on the desk but as soon as I had, Grace's fingers curled around my bicep, giving it a light squeeze. Any other day, her touch would've paralysed me with desire but today it caught me off guard. I simply stared at her.

Affronted by my response, Grace withdrew her hand. A sullen pout settled onto her mush. Something darker flashed in her peepers, which made me step back from her. 'Stay with me, until my papa returns, will you not? It is late and I do not wish to be alone, *Thomas*.' *My name on her lips.* For the first time on any lady's lips. I froze. A smile curled Grace's mouth because she'd known what it'd do to me. When she saw what she'd achieved with a single word, which her touch alone couldn't, Grace's blue eyes sang victory. She bustled to a drinks cabinet, which was shaped like a globe. It marked out Britain's bloody empire: money and power proudly displayed. She slid it open, pouring amber whiskey into a tumbler. And *that's* how the bitch did me, at least how I figure it, because she held out that heavy glass to me (solid with affluence and influence), as she said, 'Taste it.'

Easy, wasn't I? Grace was my tempter and destroyer. But I was weak - I can admit that now - because I had those bastard papers tight in my daddles and could've walked out right there and then.

How would things have been if I had?

Moments like that - we all have them - are turning points. Bollocks, they're simply choices: decisions we make every day. We can't go back or change a single bloody one.

So you have to deal with it. Deal with what you decided to do. You and no one else. That fight you took on or didn't. The time you walked away or stayed to the bitter end. The love you stuck with or gave up on. Every one you and you alone.

No one takes responsibility – First Lifer or Blood – but the hard truth is yours is the ugly face behind every shred of pain. The paths you took or never walked. No one and nothing to blame or praise, apart from yourself.

We're all alone with that reality, when everything's said and done. Alone every breath.

So I could've walked there and then with the papers. But fool that I was, I chose to stay because a bird, who I reckoned I was in love with, had taken notice of me for the first time. She'd found out my first name and then had offered me a forbidden drink from her papa's own booze. I was tempted - more than I'd ever been in my life - to take a sip of this world, which I knew I'd never be a part of, before I brought it crashing down.

When I rushed to Grace, taking the tumbler from her with shaking hands, she watched me with hungry, admiring eyes. The whiskey was smooth and warm. Suave as I was in those days, however, I choked on it. I wasn't one for alcohol back then: I'd seen what degradation gin could lead to. It was Ruby who later introduced me to those delights.

Grace smiled, as she pressed me down into her papa's brown leather chair.

The throne itself? Sod it, I was sweating now.

I resisted, but Grace's hands on my shoulders pushed harder. Insistent.

At last, I sank into the soft leather, as the last rays of the sun bled over the dying day, through the high arched windows: the eyes out from this cathedral of finance.

'Don't you look grand?' Grace caressed my collar.

Gazing over the shining desk, my palms pressed on its cold surface, I felt like a cardinal: this was power. For the first time a new, odd sensation swelled. It confused me - this biting need, which was twisting my gut, for something *more*.

When you've had so little (and what you did have has been snatched away from you), it doesn't take much to corrupt the good in you. Although, as I don't go in for sticky labels, maybe it's more that it doesn't take much to be taken as a mug.

When I caught Grace's scent of violets, my lust was lit. The blood rushed down below to my tackle, as if at some unspoken signal. I surged up from my chair.

Bloody hell, this was it at last.

I was going to crush Grace in my arms and ravish that bowed mouth. Just like I'd wet dreamed, ever since Grace had swept down from her carriage and into these corridors to torture me. But I'd caught her unguarded and unmasked: Grace's expression wasn't admiring, as it'd been only moments before. Instead, there was mocking laughter in her blue peepers.

Instantly, Grace readjusted her features, catching her smile behind her hand, as she turned back to the drinks cabinet. But it was too late. Because I'd sodding seen.

I was cold. The room had drained to grey.

I realised right then my own ludicrousness for playing at king and something I'd never be, with someone I'd never have. Worse, that I'd never be more than the outsider looking in.

Yeah, everybody laugh at the clown.

All passion ruthlessly slaughtered, I felt sick; I loathed the bitch.

Grace glanced back at me, her peepers still shining with mockery.

I snatched the papers off the desk, before storming out of the office with Grace tripping at my heels.

'Where are you going so fast? Do you not wish to play some more?' Grace was trying to catch at me with her betrayer's fingers, but they burnt red hot, each one a brand of my idiocy. 'Thomas, please, you are no fun at all, Thomas...'

Bang...

You know how life kicks you right in the balls sometimes, yet when you look at it dead close, you're actually the one who put in the boot yourself? That's when it hurts so much bleeding worse.

I bolted out of the director's office, like I was in the midst of a caper, with a bundle of the director's nicked papers clutched to my chest, his beloved only daughter (and no chaperone), in tow, hot after me and panting my first name, as if we'd just been up to some serious hanky panky, when I collided with the monolith that was Mr Erwood.

I bowled backwards. The files flew up like white rain. Grace stumbled into an ungainly heap, her dress riding up to show her layers of petticoats and a single glimpse of her drawers.

'My word...' The other directors were huddled, like a group of schoolboys, gawping goggled-eyed.

Grace's peepers flashed with humiliated rage but then immediately filled with spoilt tears. They fixed on me and in that moment, I knew what it meant: *I was buggered.*

The other blokes seemed to suddenly remember their chivalry; they rushed to Grace's shamed aid.

I heard Grace's muffled sniffles, as I forced myself to raise my gaze to Mr Erwood. His mottled, Dundreary whiskered face peeping out of his starched collar was crimson, shaking with outrage.

Bloody hell, I was going to cop it.

'Take her home,' Mr Erwood curtly ordered.

I heard the shuffle of Grace's light footsteps, as she was escorted away. Her whiney voice melted to honey, once she warmed to her new male company.

Now I was alone with her papa.

Everything told me to leg it. My body, however, wouldn't obey me. I shrank back against the wall.

All right then, so here's the thing, I wasn't a brawler back then, not once I was out of the schoolyard. That came later with Ruby. I guess the talent had always been buried under there; Ruby simply unleashed it. But as a First Lifer? I took the beatings, I didn't dish them out. It was just the way things were, that's all.

Mr Erwood had noticed the papers now, which were lying in snowy mounds across the marble floor. At first he frowned, as if I really was merely a junior clerk. The nobody, who'd been forced on his consciousness, like an irritating flea, and who'd disappear again just as quickly. Then, however, realisation spread like a dark sea. And with it, a hissing fury, which was greater even than when he'd seen me with Grace, because a flea like me trying to despoil his business was worse - to a bloke like him - than me despoiling his daughter.

Priorities, right?

I'd tried the hero bit - to save the world. I'd spectacularly failed. Now I knew I'd pay a bloody high price.

Mr Erwood didn't say anything. Instead he crushed me, like a man would crush a flea.

Mr Erwood raised his silver-headed cane and brought it down across my nut. Then he hauled me closer to him with one hand and brought the cane down again. And again and...

My blood sprayed over Mr Erwood's pristine white cravat, patterning it with crimson; even through my haze of agony, I saw him grimace at the inconvenience to his threads. I clutched my hands over my nut, struggling away from him. That surprised Mr Erwood because what flea fights back?

I was dizzy, stumbling to my knees, when I saw the shadow of Mr Erwood's cane swinging above me again.

This time, however, I grasped hold of the wood as it arced down. I stopped it, inches from my cheek.

Mr Erwood shook me off, clouting me across the jaw and dropping me sprawling over the cold marble.

Then I felt, like fire, blow after shattering blow across my back, followed by the *snap* of ribs and spine. I tried to crawl away, sliding inch by inch, by my fingertips. I was caught in a daze of blazing pain. I was driven by the one thought of escaping it.

But there *he* was, with that sodding cane, blocking me.

The hiding continued: me bloody at Mr Erwood's feet, unable now even to move.

The thought squirmed in me that he didn't intend to stop, not until there was no breath left in me. This was it then. How it ended. I was going to cop it, beaten and alone on this cold floor.

It's strange that when death comes, you don't have any astounding revelations. The most you think is: *is this it then?*

And I was bloody pissed about it.

It was right then - right when I reckoned I had no more life left on this world - that's when *she* came.

I was stretched out on that marble, with blood trickling into my peepers, so I couldn't see her. *But I heard her all right.*

First the doors *banging* open down the corridor and then I felt the blows from the cane suddenly stop, followed by the cane's *clatter*, when it was hurled against the wall and lastly, as Mr Erwood followed it.

'Good God...' Then Mr Erwood's *scream*, which was high-pitched like a little girl. That was the last noise he ever made. And I'll admit that was bleeding satisfying.

There was this silence, and then footsteps coming towards where I lay, broken and defenceless... The *swish* of a dress... When I blinked the blood away from my peepers, I could see scarlet silk sweeping the floor...

A *bird* had done this? Like a bloody avenging angel.

She knelt next to me, a long veil of red hair brushing against my bruised mug, as she peered at me.

I didn't have the strength to do anything but lie there. I knew I was buggered, after what this creature had done to Mr Erwood.

Yet I wasn't scared; for once in my life, there was no fear worming under my skin. The threads of my life were already unravelled. My heart was hardly beating; it was no more than the trembling of a butterfly's wing in my chest. I'd laugh if I was still able to because what more could she do to me? It wasn't like she could hurt me any worse.

That was when she said something, which made me understand how wrong I was – about everything. 'You are going to die, dearest prince. After that? We will talk more formally.' She stroked my hair back from my forehead gently. 'Because then all these petty things, which seem important now, will fade to nothing. I give you my troth. Have courage, for you and I will be twinned eternally, blood to blood. Close your eyes; I shall see you when you open them again.'

Before my peepers fluttered closed, I thought I saw her teeth elongate, as she stretched her mouth wide, like a python.

10

OCTOBER 1968   LONDON

'Darling Light, see how the flame dances?' Ruby
wove the scarlet candle in front of my peepers, in
the dark bedroom; shadow imps cavorted across
the bed's heavy curtains, as an incense infused lake
pooled at the candle's wick.

Then Ruby caressed her fingers down my
naked body, which was stretched out on the bed.
My hands clutched at the wood of the four-poster,
which had been stripped of its sheets because it's
sodding hard to get out hardened wax. Ruby
laughed when she saw how intently I followed the
light's ghost trail.

Look, there'd been no way out of it, you've got
to believe that. I'd rather bleeding well not have
been banging Ruby too and all this – *play* – was
more her cup of tea than mine. It always had been.

But she was still my Author, and we had decades of history, right?

There's no way a First Lifer can understand the bonds of Blood Life. Death and then resurrection are bloody big deals. They're not something you can just shrug off.

Yeah, it's a poncey excuse.

The truth? I didn't yet have the bottle to fly solo.

Rebel to the core? Who am I kidding?

Still, this was Ruby noticing me again - testing me more like it - and with months of scrubbing your scent off my skin, I didn't have any choice but to make it convincing.

Ruby slunk even closer. She was lethally beautiful in black lace corset and suspenders. I hadn't filched or bought them with my shameful allowance, so they distracted me for a moment.

Ruby never indulged in stuff like that for herself. So who'd got them for her? *Aralt*?

Then Ruby's hand was teasing my todger, and I wasn't distracted anymore.

Ruby licked down my cheek and round my lips. As she kissed me, she tipped the wax, burning pretty crimson patterns down my chest and stomach: marking her property.

I gasped and arched. I could take this. It wasn't any different to the hundreds of other times we'd played this game.

Yet this time it *was* different because now there was you and the way your hand curled gently into mine, rather than pinning me down hard into place, like Ruby was doing, with that gleam of dominance in her peepers. Now I had a new way. And this?

I didn't sodding want it anymore.

The realisation hurt more than Ruby's games.

Ruby smiled, stroking my hair. Then she tipped the wax once more. She straddled me, moving the wax lower and lower down my agonised body. She bent to snog me again.

And that's when it happened: I cocked up.

One simple movement but it said everything.

That's when I couldn't stop myself turning my mouth away from Ruby's kiss.

Ruby sat back, staring down at me in shock. Then she hurled the candle so hard it smashed against the wallpaper behind my nut.

'Buggering hell...' I covered my mush against the flying spots of burning wax. I could hear Ruby's breathing, like a lion about to savage its kill. I carefully lowered my spattered arms. Ruby was still just kneeling over me, glaring down. 'Look, I...'

'Peace be quiet.' I saw tears sparkling in Ruby's peepers: it kicked me in the gut, in a way I hadn't expected. 'We were twinned eternally, blood to blood. But still, I'm losing you, am I not?'

I peeked up at Ruby, not daring to speak because when you've been together as long as we had - crossed continents and centuries, survived wars, rebellions and disasters – you know the lies in each other's words, so what's the bloody point?

Ruby slowly pushed herself off me. 'But to lose you to...the disease of humanity and this base time? To have to live with a shadow of the Blood Lifer you once were...the *man* you were..? You think I know not you've been blood abstaining? That I cannot tell the signs in one of my own? Such beggarly behaviour brings down shame on our line.'

Furious, I threw myself out of the bed and opposite Ruby, scratching off the wax and enjoying the pain, as it ripped tender pink skin underneath. I didn't want her branding of ownership on me. Not any longer. 'Sorry I haven't lived up to your name.

And what is it again? *Plantagenet*? Yeah, see the lesson about keeping my nose out still hasn't seeded.'

I reckoned for a moment Ruby was going to fly at me, like a flaming arrow, across the bed and throw me against the wall. Instead, she shook her nut. 'Why does it matter who my Author was? He's gone, and we're his legacy.'

I leant across in one final effort to reach Ruby, in the bond of blood shared and the burn of a love, which had been brighter than any fire, as we'd revelled in the Bedlam, alone against the world. For those long days and dark nights in the Great War and the years after, when Ruby had sat quietly tending to me, pressing First Lifers' necks to my lips. For a lifetime together.

'We were good, weren't we? Before we came here to your family. They're sure as hell not *my* family. That's what's ripped the heart out of--'

'You would blame me?'

'I warned you that I don't play well with others, or that they don't with me.'

Ruby let out a long hiss of exasperation. I bloody well knew how she felt. 'My brothers are the best of--'

'That right? Assassins? Who despise the British, and were murdered by the Black and Tans? Yeah, this *babby's* been doing his homework. So tell me they still don't want to blow our bloody heads off? All reformed, are they?'

'Being elected does that for you,' Ruby raised her eyebrow, as she prowled towards me around the bed. 'Prithee, why do you still think like a First Lifer? Petty divisions fade and die, as First Life has faded and died. I pray you, live more years, and then you'll understand.'

But here's the thing, I wasn't sure Ruby was right.

Hate's a powerful emotion, and all are amplified: the bad, the same as the good. Obsession surges through me, just as passion does. It's no different to how I experienced it in my First Life, only it's brighter. The emotion worms through us, off-kilter and on a grander scale, like a dream half-remembered when you wake up with a morning glory and a head full of crazy. It's still there, deep inside.

As I dragged on my black jeans, Ruby watched me through narrowed peepers. When I wrenched on my t-shirt, she demanded, 'Where are you..?'

I shrugged.

Ruby darted forward, so fast she was blocking the door, before I'd even taken a step. 'Let us hunt together; it has been too long. You can show me this street, which has so bewitched you. Carnaby, is it not? We'll eat this city whole together, my dearest prince and regain your birthright,' she circled her long finger around my lips. 'We will anoint you with blood and wine.'

I caught her finger between my hands and gently lowered it. 'I don't think so, Ruby.'

I might as well have cut out her heart, there and then, by the expression on Ruby's mush.

Yeah, wanker.

After that, I'd ducked out as fast as I could, seeking refuge from Ruby's rejected fury in Alessandro's room.

Surprised, I'd stared around at Advance's account books, which were cascading over the desk and wooden floors. Flicking one open, the streams of numbers absorbed me, like an exhilarating game of chase.

Because this?

Aralt didn't see it (clearly didn't want to), but this was where I was *king*: buried balls deep in the numbers and giving my mind free rein for once.

Aralt wielded effortless control because he preyed on others' weaknesses, sniffing them out like blood. Yet he never saw their strengths. And that? Was *his* weakness.

All right then, so by now I knew Advance was nothing but a front for something dodgy. Even the gigs and LPs.

Sorry love, I never wanted to tell you before, not bald like this. I'm certain you guessed at it. But this is me turning round, so there's no hiding it, even after all these years. Christ you deserved so much better with that voice of yours.

I wish I'd been the one to give it to you.

See what those reams of numbers whispered to me was that Advance was there to make cash (and it did), but it was also a money laundering scheme.

It was hidden in plain sight but also had gaping black bloody holes in its finances. They gave Alessandro nightmares each night because he was too honest to understand his Author had to know they were there. The thing was, I'd partly sussed out where the money was being siphoned to, and *that's* what was giving *me* bleeding nightmares.

When I glanced round for Alessandro, I saw his legs in tweed trousers, poking out from behind the bed. He was crouched in the tiny space against the wall, rocking backwards and forwards. He was muttering something under his breath. Over and over. I sighed.

Alessandro was one of the snowflake patterns. Not one the same. But now with you I've grown intimate with that rocking and muttering, haven't I? Sometimes it feels like it's all I've got left of you because when you stop, you lie so still I'd give anything for you to start up again.

What are you thinking about when you rock? *Come back to me.*

I'm here. Keep listening to my voice. And come back to me.

Alessandro was curled foetal. When I slipped down next to him, he flinched, like I was gearing up to clout him. We sat in silence like that for nearly half an hour, until slowly Alessandro unfurled. He glanced out of the corners of his peepers at me.

'It's too much,' Alessandro murmured, 'too much.' Then his pale cheeks pinked, as if suddenly becoming aware of what he'd been doing, in an awful moment of lucidity. He mumbled, 'I'm sorry.'

I shrugged. 'It's all right. I'm bloody with you on that, mate.' I flashed him a grin. Alessandro stared at me and then he grinned too. 'Come on,' I dragged him up, before we clambered over the bed. 'Let's stick something on.'

'Kathy again?' Alessandro suggested with a furtive glance, diving for his orange paper record racks. The racks were now permanently ranked around his walls, transforming his dormitory into a proper bloke's room for the first time. It was a small change but it'd made me smile when I'd seen it.

You can liberate someone's body from the prison of First Life, but it takes a hell of a lot more to free their mind.

Alessandro began to flip through to find your record.

I quickly shook my nut. The image of Ruby's devastated expression was still too raw; I wasn't that much of a tosser...not that I'd forgotten the stench of Aralt on every inch of Ruby's skin.

Alessandro glanced at me, surprised. I realised I was frowning. Alessandro shuffled to the lipstick transistor, twisting it on instead to Radio Komodo.

The Kink's "Really Got me Going's" gritty, distorted guitar blasted out, loud enough to hide what I had to say. It was time to dig down below Advance's glossy red surface to the rottenness underneath; I wanted to know where that money was disappearing. If the Plantagenet siblings intended to make me a part of this, then I wasn't about to be a mindless puppet.

I edged closer to Alessandro. 'When I was coming here I saw this older bloke, up in our private area. He was marching around like he owned it, wearing this...you know...white coat...scientist type...'

'Silverman.'

'Right, so what's he then?' Alessandro shifted from foot to foot, tapping his fingers up and down on the aluminium chair. 'Come on, this is me here. I'm Ruby's, just like you're Aralt's. That makes us family. You can tell me.'

Alessandro nodded. 'I know. But Aralt's rule states--'

'Sod the rules. I've told you before, we're the Lost: we take what we like and we do what we want. Or are you still locked up in an institution? Did you never bloody escape?'

Alessandro was breathing hard. He was wearing this glazed look, like he was imagining being back there right now, abandoned by everyone he loved, with the label of *idiot* around his neck. And I'd caused that, heartless bastard that I was.

But how I figure it, sometimes you have to push, if something's important enough. Plus it was for the lad's own good. It wasn't like anyone else was volunteering to show Alessandro what was what.

At least, that's how I justified it, even with everything that happened after. We all make our choices: I reckoned I was doing the right thing. What that meant, however, got screwed up, even before I was elected into Blood Life.

I gripped Alessandro's shoulders. 'Who's Silverman?'

'A biologist. He's a specialist.'

'In what?' I caught a flash of ugly lizard, leering down from the walls, as its mouth salivated blood and I knew, clear as day. Alessandro's obsession – and Aralt's. What this whole set up was built around, like a bleeding house of cards. 'Komodo?'

Alessandro nodded, running his hand through his neat hair. His glance darted to the door, as if Aralt would sweep down on us in bloody vengeance.

I remembered what I'd seen, as I'd stormed away from Ruby, blinded at first with grief and rage at the death of our love but then how I'd spotted this bloke, who was out of place in scientist get up. He'd also been where he *shouldn't* have been.

I realised this scientist had lurked in the shadows for weeks now, without it sinking into my consciousness. I'd caught glimpses of him out of the corner of my eye, down corridors or coming out of meetings with Aralt. You know the way you miss the most important things because they're hidden under the everyday? Now my emotions had been heightened by my pain, until every detail shone out to pinpoint clarity, I'd noticed: the way the geezer had crept silently along the edge of the corridor, his greying nut down, as if deliberately trying not to draw attention.

Here's how I was fixing it: what record company needed to research anything, let alone in secret?

So I'd followed the scientist down a warren of hallways to a section of Advance, which I'd never explored before.

When the bloke had opened a locked door and edged inside, I'd caught a whiff of pungent chemicals. I'd dashed closer.

Just before the door had slammed closed, I'd seen a sliver of what was inside: a white room, which was decked out like some sort of laboratory. Needles. Vast crimson vats, which I could taste - even from that distance - fizzing on my tongue. And what did the bastard have strapped down to a steel table?

A starkers First Lifer, shackled at wrists and ankles.

'Tell me about the experiments,' I ordered softly.

Alessandro started forward, his small fingers gripping my arms, like bleeding claws. 'Aralt expressly told me not to--'

'Ask him myself, shall I?'

'No, no, no,' Alessandro dragged me back. 'It was the Komodo. That's what the whole thing has been for. The venom. Of course, then they started to bring in these First Lifers and...' He wrung his hands miserably.

'Told you I'd be a Dutchman, didn't I? So what's it really all about?'

Alessandro collapsed onto the bed. '*Our* venom. How to split it: the part, which paralyses and that which kills. Truly, though, I don't know why, cross my heart and hope to die.'

'But you will know, 'cos you're gonna find out.'

Alessandro jolted off the bed. 'Can't, please, can't.'

I placed my hands on his shoulders again. 'You told me that to be alone and trapped was worse than death. But what I can't figure out is how *this*,' I gestured round at Alessandro's tiny room (improved though it was), 'your life, such as it is here with Aralt, is any better? You don't owe that tosser nothing. And I promise, if you help me, I'll take care of him. I'll free you, good and proper. Then, if I'm still breathing, I'll show you the world, as you should always have been shown it. Understand?'

Alessandro shook his nut. 'But how..?'

'Let me worry about that. For now, you figure out a way to hold up your end.'

I skulked down the carpeted corridor towards Aralt's study, like bloody history repeating itself. I was going to sneak into the lions' den and unearth into the light, whatever secrets were festering deep in Advance's dirty heart.

All right, so last time I'd played at heroics like this, I'd got done in by Erwood. But I was learning that Blood Life wasn't so different to First. You could fight against it, run or hide, yet in the end the same Soul still clung to you and babbled in your ear, until you sodding well listened. This was who I'd been and who I was: a daft berk with a death wish.

I was passing Donovan's quarters, the buzz of the Small Faces' high energy guitars bleeding through, when his rosewood doors swung wide, and I was hit by the full blast of the music. Then I was grabbed by my jacket and hauled inside.

'Hey man, where are you going? Stick around, it's really happening in here.' Donovan slammed me against the wall, with a shrill laugh.

The git was tripping; the sweet fug from a thick joint, which he was clutching, choked me. Donovan took a drag, before offering it to me.

I shook my nut. I didn't need to add being stoned to this night's heady mix of danger. See one lesson had seeded from first time round at least: I wouldn't allow myself to be sucked in by the world's temptations.

But then unlike Grace, Donovan wasn't my type.

Donovan shrugged, slipping his arm around my shoulders. He pulled me further into his suite of rooms, which were an explosion of colour and life, as much as Aralt's were a paean to the cold space age: a rainbow of pop artist posters and black and white portraits of celebrities. Donovan seemed as in love with this age, as I'd fallen tackle deep.

Donovan caught me staring at the posters. He puffed on his joint with a grin, which turned his mouth up wide around his canines.

'Man does all this bug my bro,' Donovan gestured round at his room. 'But you know what I say?' Donovan threw himself down on an inflatable PVC chair, which was cast in sickly orange by the Lava Lamp next to it that oozed translucently. His pupils were dilated. *He was so sodding gone.* 'We take our poses on the stage. Dress up. Choose our props, set, lighting and music. First Life's just the opening act. But us? What's so groovy is we get to live the grand finale. And how I see it? Why not go out with a freaking bang?' He stroked his fingers down the Lava Lamp, tracing the bubbles. 'Try watching this when you've taken something to expand your mind...it's far out...'

I eyed the door. How many hours left before dawn? Before Aralt came home? I took a step backwards. 'I need to--'

'Sit down.' A sudden steel, as Donovan fixed me with a gaze, which said *no bleeding way* was I getting out of that door anytime soon.

Here I was meant to be redeeming myself for a former life's mistakes and instead I was trapped with this nancy boy and his mind altered wanderings. I should've guessed this was how it'd go.

There's no such thing as redemption: that's only so much claptrap to keep the night-time terrors at bay, when the old conscience comes aknocking.

How great's a photographic memory then?

I glanced around but I couldn't see another seat; I wouldn't put it past these wankers to make everyone kneel at their feet. Sighing, I began to crouch down.

'Watch this, it'll blow your mind.' Donovan staggered up to an abstract sculpture, which was pushed against the wall, like a giant brown puzzle. Then he hauled it apart with quick motions, chucking the foam pieces down into bizarre seats.

You First Lifers never stop amazing me with the different ways you invent to conceal the truth: seating as art, radios as lipsticks, false hair, eyelashes and bodies...

You're so frightened of this world and the one fundamental truth of all - you're born, you live and then you bloody die – that everything in-between you hide, mask and transform, as if that makes it easier. It sodding doesn't, you know. Get what I'm fixing at?

Only when you stare at what lies beneath - right in the eyes - can you face living. And dying too.

That's what I'm doing right now, even though this hurts, every bleeding word I write. Hurts worse than anything I've ever felt. I've got to face it though because you deserve that. No, you deserve so much more than I can give. Yet it's something, and that's got to count, right?

Can you still hear me? Hold on, love. Just hold on a little more for me.

'Chairs are so bourgeois,' Donovan shrugged. 'Everything should either be art or throwaway.' All right then, so there I was perched on one end of this sphere, Donovan draped on the other, as he swayed to the music. 'You're gonna dig the gigs I booked for Saturday. Are you having a cool time in that crazy scene?'

'Beats a pointy stick.'

'Right on,' Donovan flashed me that smile of his, which was predatory in all the wrong places. It made me itch to bolt again. I held myself still, however, with a struggle. 'See my brother, he's the money man. That's why I leave him to his numbers. Me? I'm the creative.' Donovan leant closer, his fingers trailing over the back of my hand. 'The music? It's my lifeblood. The most righteous thing about this backward country. It's like, in Ireland I was into the bloodshed. The rush and the roar. But Aralt? Freaking cold heart, mind and Soul to the cause. He was a scientist of death. I was just along for the thrill. Having a blast, man. But I'm his bro, so where else would I've been? Here,' he stabbed his joint at me, 'what's family for, if we don't share?'

I risked another small shake of my nut.

'No?' Donovan stared down at the stub, which was rimmed with a lipstick ghost, like he was accusing it of something, before tossing it away over his shoulder.

Then Donovan's hand caressed up my arm, as he slid closer along the sphere, until our groins were touching. Donovan was rock hard – that wasn't something I wanted to feel. I started up, but his fingers stiffened around my arm.

I suddenly remembered your cousin in the damp alleyway, trapped under that dandy, who had one hand clamped tight over her mouth and the other crawling down her waist, before inching up her micro-mini...and how I'd hesitated to help her.

It was strange this conscience bollocks. Things had been so much simpler with Ruby: slash and burn the world and dance in the flames.

'You're barking up the wrong tree. I don't swing that way.' I kept my voice as low and level as I could manage.

I tried to stand again, but Donovan dragged me down closer. 'Hey, that's OK. There's no need to split...'cos I do.'

Then Donovan was snogging me, his snaking tongue forcing its way deep into my mouth and down my throat, until I tasted his bitter lipstick.

Even in the moment, there was still a part of me detached enough to recognise the way Donovan kissed, like a touch memory. After a century with Ruby, I knew every variation of her and here it was, like they'd been swapping notes. Or learned from the same lover.

Then there was no time, however, even for those thoughts because despite my struggling, Donovan was pinning me back onto the sphere; my legs were pushed out either side and my arms were dragged above my nut.

Those Plantagenets were something else: stronger, faster (Ruby would've said purer Blood Lifers), but *worse*, that's what I'm looking for.

Don't get narked, like I cheated on you twice: first with Ruby and now with her brother. I promised all the *nasties and wankery*, but this was anything but consensual, you figuring that?

Donovan's fingers were worming down the waistband of my jeans, and then I felt them dextrously undo them, as he edged inside the denim towards my...

That's when Donovan pushed himself off me, like we'd just been having a casual chat and announced, 'Snack time.'

The spaced out bastard wandered to his desk. Donovan glanced back at me with a smile, as if I was going to thank him for this treat.

I wouldn't have let any of the others see how badly my fingers shook as I did up my jeans, as soon as Donovan turned away from me again and leant over the desk.

Then Donovan yanked something – *someone* – over the top by their short, straw-coloured hair. Donovan dangled the limp body of a bound and gagged First Lifer, who'd been stripped to only his white underwear. Bleeding hell, the poor sod wasn't moving. Yet he hadn't even been bitten yet. It was like he'd been sedated.

I jumped up, glancing once again at the door. Could I make it before Donovan stopped me? Maybe whilst he was distracted by his new toy...

'Want a bite?' Donovan offered the First Lifer's pale jugular.

I saw the slow throb of his arteries and felt the painful pull of his blood. I wet my lips. I wondered if Ruby knew her brother was offering to blood share with the man, who she'd elected. And what she'd do to me if I accepted.

'I prefer to hunt, mate.'

Donovan wagged his finger at me. 'You're the type. Me? Delivery and convenience every time.'

When Donovan sank his fangs into the First Lifer's throat, I watched the movement in his own, as Donovan swallowed down the blood in deep sucks. I shuddered, hungering to dive to him and savage the other side. To taste blood like it should be tasted: from warm skin, rather than dirty needle.

Nothing'll ever be the same as a kill. The death drives the desire; you can't have the one, without the other.

First Lifers are no different: pain and death excite passion because they remind you that you're always going to experience both. If not today, then someday. For us Blood Lifers it's even more intimate because we already have. We've died once (and that's not something you bloody forget). It covers you like a second skin and you wear it every moment, until the instant of your second death.

When I sidled towards the door, Donovan didn't look up. He was too lost in the blood. I should've slipped away there and then.

Yet something about what he'd said got to me: *delivery*? That and the way the lad had lain there, like he was awaiting an operation, reeked of Silverman and the white room with its needles.

When Donovan finally raised his nut, his gob sticky with scarlet, I asked, with an effort to sound casual, 'How'd you get it delivered then, you lucky git?'

'Secret.'

I could see the blood was pounding through Donovan - a burst of surging heat - mingling with the wacky backy, in a tripper's heaven. It'd be piss poor if I couldn't ferret the information out of him in that state. Even if it was like tugging on a shark's tail. 'Aralt, right?'

'Yeah, how'd you..? Groupies man,' Donovan laughed, as he swayed, steadying himself with one hand on the desk. 'It was Aralt's idea for our Blood Lifer bands to pick out the tastiest, slip something fun in their drinks and then send them back to us. Perks of being the boss.'

'Just to feed on?'

'Hey,' Donovan dropped the boy's corpse across the desk – *bang* – the steel back in his peepers; sod it, I'd gone too bloody far, 'this is a drag. No more questions. Come here.'

Donovan opened his arms wide, like I'd rush back into his powerful embrace.

Not bleeding likely.

I could feel the door knob hard behind my back; its sharp outline was all I could think about. I tested it with my fingers without Donovan seeing. 'He's a good bro for letting you have them all. Come on, what's the big deal? We're tight, aren't we?'

'All? My bro was never one for letting anyone but himself have it all. He feeds me one or two scraps and the rest...' Donovan stopped, peering at me suspiciously. 'Why are you over there? I said, come here.'

'Love to but... I've gotta hunt.' I thrust the door open in one twist, diving out into the corridor. I was expecting to feel Donovan's hands hauling me back in, but he didn't follow.

This time nothing would stop me from finding out what the hell was going on.

I legged it down the deserted corridor to Aralt's study; bloody blinding, no one was in. I slid inside, slipping to the storage unit, which skirted the desk and tried not to think about that prat sharing blood with Ruby over it, until she was overdosed.

It still smelled of both of them, under the rich blood, which laced the entire room.

Life's like that: it bites you where it hurts. The bad memories kick themselves to the surface faster than the good. We're secret masochists at heart.

I didn't know what I was searching for, I only knew I had to look, like the stupid berk I was (and always have been I guess).

The top compartment of the unit was an internally lit Plexiglas band. Beneath that were box drawers and sliding aluminium doors. I scrabbled through them, discovering finances, formulas and scraps of data, which all formed a picture of something big. It was still too scattered and fragmented, however, to leap to life.

Yet.

The pattern was there and it was off, like it'd been at the bank a century before. If I could just study it a bit longer...

I glanced up at the door, as I reached for the next file.

Voices.

Then footsteps coming closer.

I was in his Nibb's study, surrounded by a tempest of paperwork, in a way that would only have looked comical to me: Aralt wouldn't get the funny side.

I snatched the papers up in handfuls, throwing them back, snapping shut boxes and crashing aluminium doors round, before chucking myself across the room.

Visions of Overend, Gurney and Company's marble floor, my spit and blood pooling, as my peepers closed, possessed me... *You are going to die, dearest prince...* Yeah, so your own death's hard to shake. And my second one was seeming a lot closer.

Some blokes just don't learn from their mistakes.

Aralt slammed through the door, his arm hooked around Ruby's waist. He was nuzzling into her neck. Ruby was laughing, and I could tell by the way she quivered, shuddering in waves, that she was high on feasting again. They stopped abruptly though, when they saw me bang centre of the study.

'And what is my darling Light doing in here, all by his lonesome?'

Aralt wasn't looking at me. He'd disentangled himself from Ruby and was sauntering over to a UFO-shaped drinks cabinet, where he poured himself a whiskey. He swirled the amber liquid around the glass. 'You're taking ages to answer there, babby,' he said softly.

Here's the thing, it's easier to think of lies, when your bloody life doesn't depend on it. I remember a time too as a First Lifer, when they'd come tripping from my tongue, as easily as breathing.

A century spent with Ruby, however, when our Souls were bared, and we were each other's truth (at least I'd thought so), had weakened my ability to fib. Reckon that's a small thing?

Ask the autistic bloke.

It's our natural defence because either everyone must tell the truth or everyone must lie. Now I'd found myself in a land of falsehood and it was me with the serious design flaw. Still, I was getting better every day I shared the same fetid air with these lot. After all, I'd held my own with Donovan, hadn't I?

'Looking for Ruby. Where else was she gonna be? Not like she'd be with me, is it? The bloke she actually elected?' I tried to act the sulky teenager, sticking my hands in the pockets of my jeans with a sullen pout. I reckon they half believed me.

Ruby stretched on her back over the length of the desk, her hair flowing out, like a flame. 'Dearest prince, you have been naughty indeed.'

Aralt stroked down the silk of Ruby's stomach, taking small, careful sips of his whiskey. His black gaze didn't leave my face. You know that feeling when someone's mentally ripping you apart?

I glanced at the door, but Aralt was already stalking towards me. He stood so close our noses were nearly touching. 'Remember that wee conversation we had?' I tried to twist my head away. Aralt, however, grabbed me by the chin, yanking me back. 'Ruby's not your ma. She's not even your bird anymore. Stop making such a holy show of yourself.'

Aralt turned away but then just as fast, cracked the whiskey tumbler down across the side of my mug.

I felt the skin split, and the blood pour from the gash, as I fell to my knees.

Through my quickly closing peeper, I saw the wanker swagger back to the UFO cabinet and casually take himself a new glass. He poured himself a second whiskey, trailing his hand between Ruby's knockers.

And Ruby? She was gazing up at her brother, like he was head of the pride. As if I wasn't crouched in a mess of my own blood and bruises, with a lacerated face sliced to sodding pieces.

That was it, the moment I knew beyond any doubt: we'd been twinned in blood for over a century. Yet now that bond was broken.

I'd been replaced.

Ruby would always love Aralt more than me.

11

Funny how you First Lifers divide everything with your sticky labels, as if it's not enough for a house to have four walls to be called a *home* or even to be with the one your heart bleeds for.

I never got it until now. Not until these last few quiet years with you.

We've spent so much of our life running, and that's all on me. I've tried to make it into one big adventure because I can be full of bollocks too, if it'd help you. Was that how you felt? You never told me. And now it's too late.

I'd work nights. It didn't matter what city or job and no matter how dirty or low the work because I wasn't exactly official, no matter where we went. I wasn't in the taking what I wanted, when I wanted business either - not with you at my shoulder.

When we were travelling through the Philippines, it was brutal cage fights, like the blinding martial arts matches in Japan. In Las

Vegas, I'd help casino owners sniff out card counters. It wasn't like I didn't know every trick in the book. They weren't the sort of bosses to worry about paperwork, although it'd felt wrong to be sitting on that side of the glass and not to be the one pocketing my winnings. You, however, had been very firm about that.

If there was nothing else going, I'd work bars or take a bouncer gig, like that time in Mississippi. But you hadn't been keen. Look, it'd been the accent. The American birds had been dead into it; you'd got shirty about them stuffing their numbers into the back pocket of my jeans.

When we were settled long enough to make it count, you took the type of office roles, which I'd sworn would never be for a woman like you. Another broken promise. It seems I'm better at breaking them, than keeping them.

I did show you the world though, didn't I?

You never mentioned your singing again and because you didn't, it meant I couldn't. Yet there were so many times, especially in the quiet of twilight, when I'd see that distracted look on your mush and I'd break inside not to say...sod it, *something*. Like *I* had the right? So I didn't.

I couldn't listen to your record, and since you never sang either, the silence drove me mad.

I reckoned - just once - you'd burst free. Then I'd hear the beauty of your sultry, raw tone, even if you were only cleaning the bathroom or thought I was still sleeping, as you pulled on your stockings in the morning.

Peace is overrated.

Occasionally, we'd pass a pram with some gurgling tyke, and I'd see this expression behind your peepers, like sadness or...regret. You'd mask it quickly, which you First Lifers are so good at. I knew a part of you yearned for children, grandchildren and the whole package deal fantasy, which everyone's fed from the cradle. That deep down you craved a *normal* life. Except that's no more than a sticky label again.

It's no different to how I've always wondered if electing was like having a child. Whether Ruby had seen *me* in that way. How can it ever be an equal pairing, when it starts with one having such power over the other? When an Author tries, like a parent, to create their own reflection? Which then led me to question how anyone would want to subject another being to childhood and that abject powerlessness.

If I'd elected you, then you'd have been *my* act of procreation; I'd have been birthing a new member of my species. But you didn't want that. It was *you* who denied me the chance.

How do you reckon I felt, every time you looked at some kid and got that expression in your peepers, when I'd have given you anything but I couldn't give you that...gift of humanity?

Not that First Lifers are so special, of course, before you go running away with that thought. Like you're a shining example to the rest of us..? If the Lost seem like monsters, then we learnt everything we know from First Lifers.

I've more of a conscience than many First Lifers. Sure I've killed to survive. There are, however, bleeding worse things.

Just watch the news.

I know plenty of Blood Lifers with more of their Souls intact, than the bastards I met in my First Life. And I've met First Lifers, who seem to have none.

If there's something after death or second death, I don't have a bloody clue how they'll sort us all out. But it's not going to be a neat little reaping; it'll be messy as...well, Hell.

Still, when everything's said and done, I need to say sorry.

I'm sorry you lost everything. Sorry I buggered up your short First Life. Sorry you didn't even have a home, not before I brought you to Ilkley Moor again and I don't even know if you can really tell you're here.

How much do you know or sense?

I reckon you do realise you're home. I can feel it deep in me, like something moving.

You're home and...sod those wankers at the Blood Life Council: when you die, what more could anyone do to me that I give a damn about?

As a First Lifer, I never had a real home, not since I was very young. And as a Blood Lifer? Who'd choose to live out their span in one tiny box, like cats marking their territory, when we could prowl the earth every inch our own in the night?

Wherever we rested for a day (or settled for weeks or months) was our crib but never - no matter the trinkets I filched and discarded as fast - our home. We were beyond that. At least, that's what I'd reckoned.

When we came to stay at Advance in 1968, however, I realised something about Ruby, which she'd kept buried secret from me in all our years of nomadic wandering.

You see *I* never had a home. But *her*? It'd been right there at Advance with her brothers. And before that? With Plantagenet.

Every time Ruby had disappeared on me without a word *that* was where she'd been: playing happy families. Without me.

In a world of outsiders that's got to make a bloke feel like the biggest outsider of them all.

But then I found you.

NOVEMBER 1968   LONDON

We were curled together on the red baroque rug, as I stroked my fingers through your long, black hair in the quiet of evening.

The moments with the stillness and silence have always been the most perfect ones to me. In Blood Life, you're never in the eye of the storm - you *are* the storm. So I took the calm, with you, whenever I could.

This disease of humanity? I guess I was riddled with it.

Then *bang*, *bang*, *bang*, as loud as a thunderclap. You startled up.

'What is it, luv?' There was something in your peepers, almost like you'd been expecting this knock in the dark of the night; the same something, which'd made you say you couldn't have someone like me – Rocker, bad boy, freak – in your life. 'It's just the door. You want me to..?'

We both pushed ourselves up, but you brushed me aside, like I was a ghost. Then you paced out into the hall by yourself.

Here's how I figure it, you die once and come back? Then an ancient part of your brain, which is attuned to danger, fight or flight, grows or ups its game because it'd be a right berk not to.

So when I saw how you were acting all of a sudden? I got real quiet and crept to the door out to the hallway.

There was this dark silhouette framed on the step, all bulky suit and hat. You weren't moving. You were like this fairy statue next to a giant; I knew dodgy when I saw it and I could taste it sour now.

Not all your nightmares are mine.

The ones that shake you side to side and make you rake your nails bloody down my mug? They could be yours - this one moment - the same as any of my night-time horrors.

Do you want me to lie to you about this? I wish you could tell me, or that I was able to decipher your *tap, tap, tapping* on the white covers. But love, I'm lost here, so all I can do is tell it how I remember it. What else is there now?

I pushed the lounge door wider. I knew this was it then - this wanker - the reason you'd reckoned I'd not want to know you: the *real* you.

'All right Kathy?' My voice seemed to trigger you to life. You turned towards me.

The figure next to you emitted a low growl, as it burst by, shouldering into the lounge. You trailed at the man's heels. He reeked of stale bitter and fags. When he spun round on me, I could read the threat in his peepers. He backed me further into the room, but you patted my arm, as if calming a bleeding guard dog.

'Who the bloody hell is this?' The man snarled. 'You living tally ower t'brush with him?'

You quickly shook your nut. Too quickly, for my liking. 'No, father.'

Father? I eyed the shambling wreck, as he glowered at me blearily. His single-breasted suit was bulky and creased under his overcoat, like he never wore them except at weddings. He crumpled his hat between weathered fingers. I could see a breath of you in his hard features: the black hair threading to grey and watery blue peepers.

He tossed his head at me dismissively. 'Then get thee gone.'

'Not a chance, mate.'

'This is between--'

'Not a chance.'

Your father glared first at me and then at you, whilst scuffing his dirty shoes backwards and forwards through the shagpile. Then he nodded. 'Get ready lass, you're going home.'

You started; a pink flush spread up your neck to your cheeks.

Here's the thing, when the bloke first barged in here, breaking into our safe cocoon, I hadn't understood the skin of tension, which had sent warning howls from my ancient brain, through every nerve of my body. But now the scent of fear was overwhelming. Your distress and the menace on your father's face was impossible to miss; it would've been even to a First Lifer.

Suddenly I was overwhelmed with the hunger to rip out your father's throat and let him watch himself bleed out at your feet; my bloody sacrifice for everything I sensed he'd done to you. There wasn't any need for words: it was all there in the fear, which is something we Blood Lifers sodding understand.

You stepped away from your father, twisting your ivory scarf in these little nervous jerks – *twist, twist, twist* – like you were struggling to breathe. 'This is my home now. I don't have to go back.'

'Happen you do.'

I knew your father was going to move towards you, moments before he did. Blood Life heightens every sense, and then the hunt sharpens them with a thrill, which is as great as enslaving the world. Don't knock it just because it's hard to imagine. And yeah, maybe it corrupts, but power's a bleeding turn on.

So when I realised your father was preparing to belt you, I blocked him. Then I eyeballed him, like the bastard's never been eyeballed.

Your father was so shocked, he merely stood there, like he'd been stuffed and mounted

When I heard you behind me, however, you were bleeding pissed. 'I fair don't need you fighting my battles.'

Your father chuckled; his peepers were mocking.

You really know how to cut off a bloke's baubles, you know that? Like a deflated balloon, I stepped aside. Stalking to the corner, I kicked the beanbag loudly as I passed for good measure, realising as I did it what a teenage tosser I looked. I leant against the wall with my arms crossed, trying to regain some pride.

'You mun know you don't belong here? And not with...*him*?' Your father's voice was softer. He ran his rough finger down your cheek. You flinched. 'Why did you run? Stop acting fair maungy. There's nowt here for thee...for people like us. But you have family. Think on.'

You pressed back against the wall. 'I have.'

Your father smashed his fist close to the side of your nut.

When you jumped, I struggled not to dive at him, fangs out. Trinkets crushed, however, I didn't intend to be your white knight, if you didn't want rescuing. There was also no bloody way I was going anywhere, until you were safe. It was typical of how you made me feel: my every impulse and emotion turned on its head, see-sawing between contradictions.

Guess that's what life's about, right?

Your father ripped the poster of Jimi Hendrix, which he'd felt under his hand, off the wall in disgust. He waved it in your face. 'This? You choose *this*?' He crumpled up the poster, tossing it hard at you.

This time you didn't flinch. 'Yeah, I do.'

I thought your father was about to throttle you; his hands were so close to your throat and that ivory scarf of yours that I tensed every muscle hard enough to spasm.

You, however, didn't move or look away from your father; I've never admired you more.

Ruby had got you First Lifers all wrong. When your backs were against the wall, some of you had the same bottle as any Blood Lifer - you simply had to take the time to see it.

Then the moment passed. Your father slammed his hat down on his nut, like a goodbye, before he stormed out, banging the front door closed after him. It rang in the silence of the flat with deafening violence.

I studied your immobile expression. Buggering hell, I never was one for times like this. Did you want me to rush to you and hold you or to sod off?

I hovered half way between the two, when to my surprise you crumpled, slipping to the carpet. That's when I finally got how much strength it'd taken to hold up your puppet strings taut enough to deal with your father.

You'd have made a blinding Blood Lifer. Why was I never able to convince you of that?

I ran to you (castrated or not), and drew you up into my arms. For one bleeding wonderful moment, you held onto me like you needed me, with your cheek on my chest. I knew you could hear my heart thudding, just like I could always hear the pound of yours.

Then you pulled back, however, your face twisted with rage and...

Smack – you slapped me hard in the mush.

Before I'd even registered the pain, you'd dragged me closer and were kissing away the hurt. You snogged me as if you never wanted us to part.

I was alight with you, bloody aflame; you were going to burn me to ash. You twirled us round, in a crazy dance of entwined bodies. Then you were pushing me down, and we were ripping at our clothes and each other's, lost to the world. Nothing existed but our lines, curves and pleasure. We shagged right there in the lounge, which your father had desecrated, as if our union was exorcising his haunting.

Afterwards, we sprawled naked on the baroque rug in that intimate silence, which I bleeding loved, with your nut resting on my chest and listening to my heart again. Your hand stroked my arm; it sent tingles, like static electricity, shooting all the way to my todger.

Then you said, real quiet like, 'Don't leave me.'

I stared down at the black crown of your nut. 'Don't you get it yet? I'm yours. I'll always be yours.' Then I heard something, which I never wanted to hear from you again because it made me vibrate with pain: these sniffling sobs. Your salty tears were wet on my chest. What a prat I was. I told you I was rubbish at these moments, right? 'Luv? What did I..?'

When you raised your mush, I couldn't read the look in your peepers. 'I'm sorry. If you're hurting, you fair hurt others. I didn't mean to--'

'I don't mind.'

'That's not the point, don't you see?' You sat up, pulling your knees under your chin. I pushed myself onto my elbows, watching you closely. I didn't get where this was going and I tingled with terror that you were about to chuck me out or return to the steely indifference from earlier in the summer, when you'd acted as if I might as well have been a spectre. First Life conventions were tight over me again. I couldn't play this game, when all I knew was Ruby. What had I done? You stared at me with serious peepers, as if you could read my thoughts or at least some of them. 'Dus't a' reckon I want... I don't own you. I want us both to be free. Together.'

You know what the Inquisition is?

The problem was Ruby remembered it from first time round, so lucky me, she could make sure my interrogation was extra bloody authentic.

My Author, muse, liberator and her brothers (the bane of my sodding Blood Life), were ranked across from me behind the plastic table, which had been buried under gammon, crisps and a halved grapefruit that looked like a bleeding hedgehog, the last time I was in here for Ruby's *welcome home* party.

Aralt had already removed his suit jacket. He'd carefully folded it over the back of his chair, and I knew what *that* meant. Kira was leaning, with crossed arms, in the shadows at the back of the room - the enforcer for the proceedings.

Kira was the one, who'd dragged me out of bed as soon as the sun had set, and before I'd had time to fully wake up. I'd cursed her with a string of sleepy expletives. She'd only allowed me to stumble into my pair of jeans, before she'd hauled me down here, in my befuddled state, as if before a court of judges and bloody executioners. I'd blinked at my accusers in outraged confusion, as I'd tried to field their barrage of questions.

I dared to glance from underneath my eyelashes at Ruby. She had this strange calmness about her, which was unsettling. You know that look a barrister has when they've got something on you but they're holding it back for just the right moment to go for the jugular? Yeah, it was that look.

I could tell they were circling round something. I didn't, however, have a bleeding clue yet what it was.

Had Alessandro got himself caught by asking too many nosey questions? He wasn't exactly Mr Social Skills. I could just see him blurting the truth out and then not knowing why the twins had turned on him.

Why had I trusted something so important to Alessandro? Maybe because he was the first bloke I'd ever felt was a true friend.

Of course I could be a trusting mug, and instead Alessandro had squealed on me. Aralt was his Author after all. Ties of Blood run deep.

Or worse, had it been tortured out of Alessandro's small body?

Something caught in my throat when I imagined Alessandro in agony. I had to work hard to block the image out of my mind. I had enough of my own worries. But even so, I found myself blinking back the tears, which were forming. I couldn't let these gits see they were getting to me.

Now here was a turn up for the books: discovering that the thought of another Blood Lifer's hurt actually bothered me.

Before we'd come back to London, I couldn't have cared less what happened to anyone - First or Blood Lifer - apart from Ruby. She was the start and end of my world. Society? All a lie, mate. Friends? A needy joke clung to by the terminally lonely. But now? That bloody conscience was clawing its way back in. And with it? These new feelings and the need for something *different*, even to what I'd experienced in my First Life. It was fresh and raw. I didn't know how to handle it; it was painful in its intensity.

Somehow, however, I reckoned this circus put on in my honour wasn't about Alessandro or Silverman's experiments.

I examined Ruby, hoping she'd give something away. It was disturbing how her peepers shone and her fingers trembled.

I tried to clear my mind, so I could concentrate on my lies. Or else I'd be burnt alive.

That's when Aralt asked it: the question I was dreading. 'Who's Kathy Freeborn?'

Breathe, bloody breathe.

Their gazes were boring into me.

I shifted from one foot to another on the cold wood, feeling strangely vulnerable without my boots, as I noted Ruby's python smile. 'You should know, you signed her.'

'None of your cheek. We know you've been riding her. Stop acting the maggot.'

I stared down fixedly at the floor. 'Dunno what you mean.'

'Thou liest! I can smell the tiny trails of her, dirty on your skin,' Ruby pressed her palms hard on the top of the table, as she leant across it. 'You rub, rub, rub but your bawd is in your Soul, stuck like a cawl and will not clean off. You've taken this conceit and you will die by it.'

'You saved the skirt's cousin,' Donovan was watching me through lowered eyelids, which were painted lilac to match his velvet jacket. 'This poncey Blood Lifer came to us complaining his kill was stolen. Not cool, man. Not cool.'

I glanced between the three of them. So this was it then, what Ruby had been gloating about and waiting for the perfect moment to kick me in the goolies over. This was about *you*.

I was buggered.

I shivered in the cool of the twilight, hugging my arms close across my naked chest.

I tried to set my expression to total indifference. 'So I'm banging some bird? It's just a bit of fun.' I saw a muscle twitch above Ruby's mouth. A quick gander over the twins told me they weren't buying it either. 'She doesn't know what I am. It's not like she--'

I made a dash for the door, snatching the moment.

All right, so this once I chose *flight* over *fight*; you've got to pick your battles. And against three Plantagenets and the bitch they'd elected? Yeah, I was as good as done in.

Caught off guard, the siblings only managed to half-stand, trapped behind the table, as I grasped at the door handle. Kira, however, was after me like a bloody bullet. She snatched me by the hair, agonisingly ripping it at the roots. She yanked me backwards, like I was her latest trophy, ready to be skinned.

I twisted, struggling, but Kira's grip was iron. 'Bloody hell...'

I heard Ruby laugh. I flushed.

'I rip out his heart now, da?' Kira looked hopeful.

'Hey chill there, my sweet terror.' Donovan slunk out around the table to Kira's side, easing her fist off my hair and tearing thick chunks with it.

I gasped.

Donovan's fingers teased down my naked chest, twisting my nipple but I refused to register his touch.

Then Kira flung me face forwards across the table, slamming me right in the guts, like an offering.

Ruby smacked her hands hard together. 'Darling Light has been bad and needs a beating.'

'*Secret*,' Aralt cradled his hands, like he was a bloody emperor, 'are you so fecking gone in the head, babby, that you don't get it? First Lifers mustn't know we exist. Especially now. You'd risk everything because you've scored some skank?'

'She's not a...' Kira pressed my back harder into the desk. My cheek bruised against the cold plastic. I struggled to get out the words. 'I tasted her Soul, and she's blinding. Better than most sodding Blood Lifers.'

I couldn't see Ruby but I could hear how silent the room had suddenly become.

Bollocks - that's never good.

Then the creak of Aralt's chair, as he sat back. 'Let the wee gobshite up.' When I felt the pressure on my back reluctantly ease, I pushed myself off the table. Ruby was glaring down at the carpet, like she wished she could set it alight with her gaze – or me. Yeah, I knew it was me that she wanted to consume with the flames. 'So you fancy yourself in love? You do know it's just a boy's fevered daydreams, not a man's truth?' Aralt was considering me with dark peepers. Then he shrugged. 'You are...what? Over a century old now? Donovan here has elected Kira, and I elected Alessandro. Yet we're less than half your age. Perhaps it's time your Author let you fly from the nest.'

Ruby started from her seat, but Aralt gripped her arm and dragged her down. I wanted to break every one of those fingers – slowly - knuckle down to tip, for the way he was holding her.

Love, it's a strange thing because it didn't matter what Ruby had done to me, it didn't stop me protecting her. Or trying to. But what good was I now, when I couldn't protect myself?

I had the sudden urge to laugh, remembering the things Ruby and I had done on every continent of this earth; how we hadn't feared anyone. We'd never answered to anything but our own wants and the dance of the call of blood and each other. That was until Ruby had brought us to this place. Her *family*. Where suddenly our freedom was leashed under the whip, and the fears were painfully real again.

What had happened to Ruby's promises of liberation?

Aralt seemed to have noticed the fleeting laughter across my mush because he frowned. 'What's..?' Then he composed himself and smiled. 'Sure it's a gift from me. It's time you stopped being a dosser and became an Author yourself instead. It'll make a man of you.'

And there it was – the ultimate control.

Aralt had already taken everything from me: my first love and Author and even my freedom. But now he wanted more.

Aralt sought to decide who I elected as well. The most glorious act of creation, which there is on earth: evolution from one species to another, through the process of dying and rebirth. The transformative twinning of two creatures for centuries, in the black shadows of night and blood. To me it meant being set free from men's rules and wankery. From the cruelty of life's society, which I'd never felt part of anyway. And Aralt wanted to sully all of that with an order..?

To me, Aralt's version of Blood Life was a repellent perversion. It revolted me to the gut.

I never told you that your election was offered twice. I couldn't have explained this to you. Any of it. Not with what came after. You've no idea how much I ached to.

But life's not fair, and this was one of those times where you get booted in the balls.

I glanced at Ruby. With everything we'd lived by - soaring through the world under no one's thumb - I knew she must feel the same as me. She bloody had to. Her brother's hand, however, was still clutched around her arm; I could see the bruises forming.

Why wasn't Ruby shaking it off?

I backed away. 'Thanks. But I'll have to say no. Humanity suits Kathy just fine.'

That did it. Aralt surged up, pulsing with outrage. 'You think that's what this is? Take what you want, when you want? All bonds banjaxed. Hierarchies toppled. Yet everything's grand? I wonder at how Ruby has allowed you to behave for so long; I would've taught you by now. First life ties are melted, but you were resurrected into the darkness of a second desperate and brutal world of blood. It unites us closer than any weak human love. We are family. We beat through each other's hearts. There's no escape from that.'

I smiled for the first time since I'd been hauled in here, half-dressed and barely awake, leery of what awaited me, because now all the dreams were chased away. So I bloody smiled. If I was going to go down, then I'd go down swinging. 'Here's the thing, I've always been the take what I want, how I want and when I want, kind of bloke. I don't play well with others, let alone - what was that bollocks? - *beat through their hearts*. So this desperate,

202

brutal world of yours? I'll have to say *no thanks* to that as well.'

Then Aralt was nothing but a blur of fangs and suit, as he launched himself across the desk at me, and I was falling backwards under the weight of him. The wind was knocked out of me, when he decked me.

There was no point fighting back. This was no alleyway brawl. This was the head of my dysfunctional family teaching me in his dead special way, and if I didn't take it, Aralt would simply keep going, until there was nothing left of me but a bloody mess. Or pass me over to Kira to take her up on the offer of ripping out my heart. So I lay there unmoving, as I was battered by Aralt's fury.

With a boxer's precision, Aralt worked my bare chest down to my gut and he knew it hurt - he got off on it - pausing between belts, whilst he considered the reddening skin that was deepening to purple, before moving on and then back and working the same area over again.

I groaned and then bit my teeth hard together. I wouldn't give Aralt the bloody satisfaction.

It wasn't a good move, however, because Aralt seemed to sense my defiance. That's when he dragged my arms above my nut and started in on my mug: right cheek, left cheek, right cheek...

I started hollering then because a bloke can only be so much of a stoic and I never pretended to be a hero.

I felt my cheekbone *crunch* and *smash*. I could taste the tang of blood, trickling from my broken nose. Christ in heaven, broken noses were the bleeding worst - the pain's like nothing else.

My peepers were closing; I knew they'd be purple and black. Aralt was only a shadow now above the slits of my swollen peepers. At each swing of his fist, I could see my blood spattered on his pristine white cuff in a pretty crimson pattern. I had the sudden memory of how I'd stained Erwood's cravat: do bastards like him and Aralt always paint themselves in the blood of nobodies like me?

I saw the shadow's arm pulled back, readying for a right old belt and braced myself the best I could. Then someone was grabbing hold of Aralt's fist and heaving him off me, like a crushing stone had been lifted from my broken ribs.

Then I heard Donovan's voice, 'Cool it, man; he gets the message. Don't freak out.'

Followed by Aralt's cold tone, 'When are you gonna think with your head and not your langer, for once in your fecking life?'

'When that's more of a gas.'

I heard Aralt sigh but I didn't have the strength to raise my nut. Then someone lugged me up under my arms and I realised it was Kira, holding me like a doll, as blood spilled from every gash: my teeth, mouth, nostrils, peepers...

I was bloody black and blue and couldn't move without the tightness of pain. Ruby was examining me, as if I was an interesting exhibit: a nice little show put on for her benefit.

I guess the instinct for protection didn't cut both ways.

Aralt asked, 'You still won't elect this bird? But she doesn't know what you are?'

I swallowed a mouthful of my own blood, before I managed to spit out, 'Not a clue, I swear.'

'Your oaths are no use to us. Do you think we'll trust you? You're a chancer: I smelt it on you as soon as I met you.' Aralt was breathing hard. When he stepped closer, Kira held me straighter. Now this is what you never found out; the moment I tried to explain as best as I could but which you never forgave. Not totally. Because it's the one, which shattered your heart, and I'm so sodding sorry. 'Break up with this skank. And make it good 'cos then you're never to see her again. Or else I'll kill her slow, as you're too nancy to do it yourself.'

'Don't bloody well touch her or I'll--'

Aralt's fingers shot out, crushing my larynx, until the stars burst. 'You'll..?' I fought for breath, but that throttling hand was stopping every whisper of oxygen. I tried not to panic, whilst my body instinctively fought and clawed at Kira. Sharp shanks shot through my lungs. Aralt only let go, when blackness started to consume me, and I grew limp in Kira's arms. As I gulped in air desperately through my sore throat, feeling like I was ascending again into consciousness, Aralt wiped the trickles of blood carefully out of my peepers. Then he moved his mug so close to mine it was all I could see. 'You're lucky this bitch brings in fierce amounts of cash for Advance, or else I'd have fed on her myself and made you watch.' He smiled - long and slow. His sharp canine teeth glinted in the light. 'Break up and don't see her again. I don't offer second chances: I'm not your Author.'

'What's happened? Your face? You're right...' You reached out your hand to my bruised cheek, but I pulled back, like it'd burn me. Or I'd burn you. Surprised, you frowned. 'Well, come in then; don't stop out there.'

I shook my nut, whilst clutching my jacket tighter against the cold shower of rain.

You stared out at me from the warmth of your flat. It'd take so little - one step - to walk inside there with you, like nothing had happened.

I could hear Hendrix's "Love or Confusion" drifting from your record player; it tasted of every time we'd held each other close without moving, cocooned in the music... And there was you in your ivory scarf, smelling of your own scent, which I'd know anywhere in the world and just...being you and everything I hungered for, desired and needed like...the blood.

No *hearts and cupid* but the truth - and that's more than anyone else offers cradle to the grave.

You *were* my blood. Inside me. My Soul. Yet I'd have to rip you out because it was the only way I could figure to save you.

That's when I finally understood that love wasn't owning or possessing; you'd been right. It was freedom. I couldn't hold onto you forever. I had to free you from this desperate, brutal world, which I'd found myself in. Even if I couldn't free myself.

Yet to do that I had to break your bleeding heart. And with it, my own.

You were just standing there with those blue peepers, which I daren't look into because then I wouldn't be able to get out the words. The rain pelted down harder, stinging my sore mush, but I welcomed the pain.

You were starting to fidget now. 'Light, you're fair frightening me.'

'I can't.' Still I couldn't look at you, as I spat out the words mechanically. 'This. You. I'm sorry.'

The silence drew on, as I shivered in the dark.

Then you flew at me in a flurry of fists and tears, each blow an agonising stab on my tender body. Nevertheless it was your touch, and I never wanted you to stop. Every second we were close

206

was one more I wasn't alone, and you weren't lost. At last you sagged, as if drained of even the energy to belt me. We stood slumped, the rain driving down on us.

'I knew,' you said flatly, looking up at me, 'what you were. A freak. So why am I surprised? What else should I've expected from a man like you? I should never have listened to you. Never have let you in.'

You cut me then. Deep enough to bleed. But I bloody deserved it, so what could I say? Christ I burned to tell you, reckon I didn't? You never wanted rescuing. For once, however, I had to save you by hurting you.

Yet it felt so wrong.

You turned away without glancing at me again. You marched back into your flat, slamming the door behind you. Hendrix was cut off mid-sentence and that was it.

I was alone in the dark and rain, with only my thoughts and sodding regrets.

I sagged against the wall. And yeah, I'll admit it, I cried, the tears smarting my cuts.

That's when Ruby stepped out of the shadows. 'Faith, dearest prince, that was well done. Now you're free again. Come, do not be melancholic; things can be as they were between us. I will help you. You have a new home. With your family.'

I wiped the wetness quickly from my cheeks. I didn't want Ruby to see the tears or share my grief with her; I'd be damned if she'd be the one to comfort me.

As Ruby tucked her arm snugly around me, supporting me back down the alley through Soho, I felt truly dead inside - in a way I never had since my death.

12

DECEMBER 1968   LONDON

'You need blood. Truly you must feed,' Ruby licked luxuriously up the First Lifer's long neck, before pressing it towards my dry lips, as I lay stretched out – unmoving - on our bed. 'That way you'll heal more quickly. Then we can hunt and play together, like we used to. Will that not be fun?' Ruby stroked down my cheek.

I didn't reply.

'Nay, turn not your head from me. Eat.' Ruby gripped my chin, twisting my mouth back to the bird's jugular. I could smell the powerful aroma of the blood. It was thick and vital, pulsing fast: *thud, thud, thud...* 'Faith, let us share blood. Then we can be one again. You must trust me.'

Ruby kissed me in light flurries across the faded bruises, all the way down from my closed peepers to my chest and up again.

When I glanced at Ruby cautiously, her fangs sprang out, before she sank them deep into one side of the First Lifer's neck; the poor bint's black lashes shuddered with the onset of paralysis, as Ruby sucked.

Ruby pushed the marked throat closer to me, until warm skin was touching my lips again, making them twitch with desire. I could taste my own blood cramping through me.

I knew how this was meant to play out: what my role was, dictated by biology, evolution and training. This was the moment when I brought out my teeth, drained the other side of the First Lifer and united with Ruby in bloody communion. But you know what?

Bollocks to that.

This Blood Life hadn't transmuted the world from base metal to gold (like Ruby had promised), but to hot ash instead. And I'd been buried alive in it.

It'd only taken me a century. Yet now I was awake to Ruby's tricks and indoctrination - I was never one for cults.

What's a second life, if you simply live it over? Another chance, if you don't do anything different? The same controls, establishment and fears, only they haunt the night, rather than the day? Don't you reckon that's bloody ironic?

You'd told me that you wanted us *both* to be free. I couldn't have put it better myself. Yet there was only one way I knew to do that: the only sure, eternal rest way.

I could've run. But where would I've gone? This was all I knew. All I had. There was no sanctuary outside Advance's walls. No family, friends and now no lover either. Aralt had made sure of that.

Ruby had noticed I wasn't drinking. She surfaced, wiping the crimson from her mouth. She stared at me for one long moment, before she hurled the First Lifer, in a pile of limp limbs, against the far wall. She hooked her fist back, but I was too weary to care. 'By this hand you will drink and stop acting the wretch.'

I simply turned my nut again, staring at the gilt Victorian mirror, which I'd nicked from a junk shop when we'd first arrived; I'd taken it because it'd reminded me of the one my mama would check her hair in, before she'd been lost to me. Time's funny like that: you can live as long as us Blood Lifers and still be caught off guard by how much can change in a few sodding months.

I didn't say anything because there was nothing *to* say. I was waiting for second death. And Ruby knew it.

That's not an easy thing for a bloke to admit.

It was the only freedom I could see. I wouldn't play by their rules. Not again. His life is sometimes all a bloke has left in his control. When everything's been taken away from you, choosing to end this shell of existence is the lone act of defiance in your arsenal. And I wanted to blow them to bloody pieces.

So I refused to eat. Blood? It's life for us. Without it? It's game over.

Ruby let out a shriek, Christ in heaven, like I'd never heard before, ripping at her long red hair, as she swung round in circles. Like she was ready to annihilate the world.

I cringed, but I still only continued to lie there.

Then Ruby fell quiet. Surprised, I saw that tears were streaming down her cheeks.

Ruby dropped to her knees next to me, clutching her ruby pendant with sudden fierceness. She shoved it close in front of my peepers. 'Have you never wondered why I wear this?'

'Always. But why would you tell me?'

The sound of her slap, echoed for stinging seconds, after Ruby had marked me with her handprint. Her eyelashes were matted wet. 'You will not just lie there and die,' Ruby gently traced down the pink of my cheek, as if to soothe the hurt, before she glanced back down at the pendant. 'I wear it because I want to remember - every moment - what this Blood Life gave me. What I know I gifted you too. *Freedom*.' I didn't understand when Ruby frowned. 'My father was a powerful man at Court. As a daughter, I was his to be owned and traded to a foolish knave, who would have allowed his house and estate to fall to wrack and ruin, if I hadn't run it for him, whilst he whored and fucked his mistresses.' I jolted at Ruby's dispassionate tone. Yet her gaze was still fixed steadily on mine; she'd never spoken a word to me before about her First Life, and when I'd once tried to kiss and wheedle it out of her, I'd only got a hiding for my pains. 'Then this...Plantagenet came to me and offered liberation from my slavery to men: father, brother, husband...every one of them...forever. I would no longer be their chattel or a womb to fill and breed hearty sons to be sent to fight and be slaughtered. And if I bore a daughter? Yet more chattel to be sold and bred from.'

With tentative fingers, I reached out, stroking the cold surface of the pendant. I remembered how Ruby arched under my caress of that place beneath it, from collar bone to collar bone, which had been our secret shared intimacy...until I'd seen Aralt doing the same move.

Who'd taught Aralt that?

Ruby glanced down. 'This jewel was part of my dowry: the price of my slavery. It was my mother's. Famous in its day. My toad of a husband did not wish me to wear it. Yet I still did, for I would have what was mine, though I needs must share his bed.' Ruby's peepers glinted: I even experienced a momentary flash of sympathy for the poor git, who'd married her. 'I flaunted it. Toyed with him. And forsooth, it drove him into a near Abraham. I wear it now because it reminds me of my independence. That I will never be caged again.'

'Sure about that?'

Like Ruby wasn't as caged in this building as me..?

Ruby's gaze darkened. 'When I tasted your Soul, I knew that just as I had been, you were trapped and enslaved. So I freed you. You were called to Blood Life because it's where you belong.' I closed my peepers; I couldn't continue to look at Ruby, not with that pleading expression on her mush. The one I'd never seen on her before. It twisted my gut, in a way I'd never have guessed at. 'You will feed.'

Still I said nothing, willing my body not to move.

'Look at me.'

I didn't open my peepers. Bugger it, this was hard. Why was Ruby making it so difficult?

The ghost trail of Ruby's palm lightly over my eyelids. Then I heard the *sweep* of her silk away from me and the *bang* of the door, as she slammed out of the room.

I thumped the covers, as waves of nausea wracked me. I allowed the effects of cold turkey to show now I was alone. It was bleeding agony.

'Are you quite well?'

Opening my peepers painfully, I sighed. 'What do you want?'

Alessandro was peering in at me anxiously from the doorway. 'I've been hoping to see you for weeks, but you never came to my room. Then when I asked where you were, Donovan finally said...'

Alessandro pottered closer. He gasped when he saw my half-healed cuts and bruising.

We don't heal so well without the blood, which is what regenerates, as much as gives us life.

I tried to smile. 'Pretty, aren't I?'

'Is it still kids play?'

I turned my nut away from Alessandro, shifting on my side with a grunt. 'Put a sock in it; I've got a whole lot of nothing to get on with here.'

Alessandro frowned. 'What's going on?'

'You wouldn't... Just spit it out, whatever you came here for, all right?'

I heard Alessandro's quick pace to the bed and then felt his light touch on my shoulder. I fought not to flinch. 'I found out for you...well that is, not everything, of course, but some of what you wanted to know. I did my best. That's good, isn't it?'

'I don't--'

'About the Komodo.'

Shocked out of my personal black dog, I twisted back to Alessandro, ignoring the pain, which was spearing through my chest and shoved myself up onto my elbows. 'Nice one! You're bloody blinding. Close the door.' Alessandro rushed to push it shut, glancing at the chick's corpse as he passed and then perched next to me. 'So what the buggering hell are those tossers up to?'

'Experimentation on First Lifers. It's something to do with splitting our venom, like I believed. I can't for the life of me, however, work out why they'd wish to do it. I couldn't discover more than that I'm afraid.' I collapsed back onto the bed, deflated. All right then, so I'd been clutching at this unexpected information from Alessandro, which amidst my own grief at the loss of you, I'd forgotten he was even digging for, like it could call me back to life. It was as if I needed it for permission not to die. Amidst everything, screwing the twins and their dodgy plans for...whatever *this* was...sod it, was worth a thousand times more than the petty vengeance of taking my own life. 'Ask me why.'

'What?'

'Why I couldn't discover more.' Alessandro was grinning now.

'All right, I'll bite. Why?'

'Because Silverman only has *one* of his labs here. Not his main one. His chief lab's somewhere more private, where he can work uninterrupted. Select First Lifers are taken to him for...'

I scrambled up, giving all thoughts of death or blood starvation the two finger salute. Reckon that sounds more like me? Give me a crisis every time. 'The groupies?'

Alessandro nodded. 'I've been poring over the delivery records, trying to unearth the ones, which don't fit. There's one that matches the pattern tomorrow night.'

'Guess who'll be catching that ride?'

'But here's the truly ingenious part,' Alessandro edged closer. His peepers were lit by both an excitement and a fear, which I realised with a kick was for me. 'Silverman's lab? It's on Radio Komodo.'

Right, so this is how it was. Alessandro had explained that there'd be a black van parked behind

Advance's offices at twilight, all ready to take its human cargo to Portsmouth. I figured one more passenger wouldn't hurt.

First though, I found the card for the skanky bint, who plied her trade in the tiny flat above the sex shop in Soho. I promised her five times her usual fee if I could see her right away. She was dead sweet, when she saw the state of me; I guess she felt an affinity because she recognised the signs of withdrawal.

When the girl drew her blood for me, bugger it looked good sucked up thick and dark like that in the needle, as she dragged her cardigan closer around her against the cold: I wasn't there for her other talents, after all. Her cool expression didn't waver, even though I was panting, as I squirted the blood down my throat in desperate gulps. Finally, the shaking subsided and I started to mend.

When I gave her a quick nod of thanks, she acknowledged it with the first smile I'd yet seen; it was so brief, maybe I imagined it.

At twilight I spied the black van. It was just where Alessandro had said it would be: parked up the alley behind Advance. Good on the little bugger. A bit of barmy in the mix makes a blinding snowflake pattern.

I scanned up and down the street. The Plantagenet siblings were nowhere to be seen. I darted for the back of the van, wrenching at the doors. Thank Christ, they weren't locked. I swung them open, diving inside, before edging them silently shut behind me. Covert ops could get to be my thing.

When I backed up, I stepped on something warm and soft.

Buggering hell, *Susan*.

Susan was hogtied like a pig for slaughter. She seemed tiny and lost, in a red and purple jersey dress, in the dark of that manky, oil puddled van.

I crouched down next to Susan, examining her neck: no bite marks, which meant she was alive. For now. Unless the bite marks had healed over already...bloody evolution. When I tweezed open her peepers, I saw her pupils were dilated, with the spaced look of the deeply sedated. She stank of her own tangy piss.

This whole setup sang of bloody Aralt tying up loose ends in a pretty bow. I realised I'd saved your cousin once, only to lay her open to this.

Are you?

It's all Susan had asked that day in the damp alley, when I'd rumbled with the dandy over her honour and had been left limping and wounded. Yet it was the first time anyone had asked if I was all right, for over a hundred years. And meant it.

It was the first time since my parents...

I hadn't let myself think about that because you mustn't (not once you're transmuted into Blood Life), or everything falls to pieces. This strange little First Lifer, however, had wrapped her arms around my broken body and supported me back to her home, like I wasn't a... Like I was no different to her. As if I had a place there.

You'd wanted nothing to do with me. I don't blame you. It was Susan, however, who'd taken my weight on her tiny body, trusting this violent stranger enough to insist I was allowed into your home. Then she'd patched me up with her gentle hands, as you'd watched. All because I'd saved her.

Yeah, I'm a sodding hero.

It makes me feel dirty to think it now. That's the kind of daft bint behaviour, which got you killed in this city.

I stared down at Susan's motionless body, bound on the floor of the freezing van: all because I wasn't the hero she'd reckoned.

In that moment, I decided I would rescue Susan for real this time, even if I had to burn Aralt, Advance and the whole bleeding Blood Lifer world around my ears to do it. She'd cared if I was all right or not. And that made me feel like I should care too.

I reached under Susan's arms. 'Let's get you sodding well...'

I started to lift Susan up. Then, however, I carefully dropped her back down again. I patted her softly on her moptop nut, as I huddled close to her for warmth, whilst I waited for the van to pull out.

All right then, so don't get shirty, or at least - hands up - I *was* going to save Susan. Get her out of harm's way. But if I'd done that, then what would I've used as...*bait's* too strong a word.

Me turning round? Bait, yeah, I needed a First Lifer, the same as they were expecting. Susan was my passport onto Radio Komodo. I didn't know if I'd get another chance at this...whatever *this* would be.

Tosser, right? But Susan was that First Lifer. And there was nothing I could do about it.

What was strange, was how hard that hit me in the gut. It hurt worse than I thought I could feel about a First Lifer. Except for you and you were different, weren't you? Feeling something for you when you were... What, the woman I loved and would've elected in a heartbeat? That I got. But now feeling it for another First Lifer..?

Still, I had to take this chance. And I don't regret it. The only things I regret are those I didn't have control over: the decisions I slid into, opportunities I let slip by or the times I was manipulated.

Christ was I manipulated.

But this? It wasn't one of those times.

This was all on me.

At last, the van lurched, and we were pulling away across night-time London and then down towards the coast. I tried to occupy my mind on the journey by checking on your cousin. I listened out for the steady beat of her heart. The way her blood coursed through her, slow with the drugs. The way her breath would catch - once in a while - in the back of her throat. I cradled her nut in my lap, stroking her hair, like some kind of nancy.

I guess that's what they call guilt then?

Trapped in that little metal box, shaken side to side as it swerved and deafened by its growl, I could only tell we were nearing Portsmouth when we slowed: there was the sudden hiss and slap of the sea and the ghost wail of horns in the black.

I was struck with the photo clear memory of striding through the London Docks with Ruby, my red-haired devil, at my side. The cacophony of sailors' songs, goats bleating from ships' holds and ropes splashing into the water, as we'd wound our way to my first kill. Then later, when we'd boarded the first ship I'd ever sailed in, on route for our Grand Tour. I'd been intoxicated with excitement for a life, which I'd hardly understood.

That was before the darkness had begun to bite. Before I'd lost Ruby. When I still thought she'd always be mine alone, as I'd be hers. Yeah, when I'd been a lovesick fool and killing was still as innocent as only a clean death can be.

Well, this was it then. One more glance at Susan's bound body and I was up, hurling myself at the van's back doors and slamming out into the bitter night, before I could think too much about what I was doing.

I hit the road hard, grating my mush, palms and knees...tumbling over and over in a dusty mess. Why does it always hurt more than you remember?

When I dragged myself up, I saw the van swerve away down towards the harbour. The lights of the City curved behind, as the ships rose and fell on the waves, like hulking whales in the shadows.

Hobbling after the van, I forced myself to gain speed.

Sod my fractured ankle. Sod everything but Aralt and screwing him as much as he had me, Susan, Alessandro - even Ruby. As much as he had you. Sod everything but getting all our lives back.

It wasn't the noblest battle speech but it got me to the dock wall.

I crouched down and peered round. The van was stopped now in the quiet, by an ancient fishing trawler, which was miniature next to the giants boxing it in on either side.

Then the door was flung open, and Kira was jumping out of the front. It had to be that bitch, didn't it? It was nice to know Aralt kept the business in the family.

When Kira marched round to the back, she threw a seabag over Susan. Then she lifted her, as if Susan was a light catch of the day, over her shoulder and tipped her into the boat. I flinched, imagining the *bang* as Susan landed.

When Kira embarked, she started the shuddering engine. I crept down the slimy slope, leaping into the back of the trawler.

See here's the thing, I'm mostly a winging it kind of bloke. Yeah, that's a surprise, right? I figured I had about a minute - if I was fluky - to get out of sight.

I had a quick shufti, staggering as the boat swayed under the steep, salty swells. I dragged up a corner of a slippery, canary yellow tarpaulin, which by the stink of it must've been used for covering the fish because Christ - the *smell*. I buried my nose in my sleeve (well, beggars can't be choosers). I dived underneath the tarpaulin, shrouding myself in the stench, as I wriggled lower.

Then there was nothing but the *chug, chug* of the engine and the rocking *creak* of the trawler. Enough time to think about the unknown, which I was riding to as willing victim. Enough time to think about you.

The intimate closeness in our silence. Sitting with our fingers so tight around each other's you couldn't tell where your hand stopped and mine started. No longer my Moon Girl - *my* girl - like I was yours. I tried not to think about the look in your peepers - cold but defeated - as you'd turned away from me on your doorstep that last time.

I tried so hard not to think about that last time, until my brain near burst. And you know what?

Lying there, where the dead and dying fish waited their turn to be sold and gutted, gave me enough time for the adrenaline to build, pulse and bubble through what was left of my weak blood. To rejuvenate every bleeding inch of me. I sparked with it; I could've lit whole continents.

All right, so I was going to die. Probably. But I was alive again right now. And if I was about to go out a second time, then this was how I wanted to cop it: not like some wounded baby bird starving slowly. But bloody alive and kicking.

I pushed the edge of the fishy tarpaulin up and squinted out. First at a square of sharp stars and the bright moon in the deep black. Then further, at the back of Kira's nut and the pull of her pilot's jacket, as she steered. I felt the boat jerk, when we slowed. I couldn't see the seabag with Susan rugged in it: Kira must've stashed it somewhere near her feet.

Then the metal side of a ship's hull loomed out of the dark – *Radio Komodo*.

This was bloody well it then.

When Kira cut the engine, we bobbed closer, clanging against *Radio Komodo*.

I heard the slither of a rope thrown over the side. Then I ducked down, as Kira stepped back through the boat and – *splash* – that must be the anchor. I risked another gander.

Kira's wiry form was half-way up the rope-ladder, with your cousin in the seabag gripped over her shoulder; if they pulled up the ladder after them, I'd be stuck impotently kicking my heels in the trawler, like a right berk.

Bugger.

I forced myself to hold back and not go charging up there for a good two minutes at least. It felt like I'd lived another bloody century in that short span. But the ladder was still just hanging there.

I struggled out from under the tarpaulin, clambering along the lurching trawler in the cutting wind.

I assessed the ladder suspiciously, as if it was a rattlesnake.

I took a deep breath and started to climb. The rough rope dug into my shredded palms, as it swung and twisted, like a bleeding fairground ride.

When I reached the deck, I hung low enough to suss out if I was likely to have my head blown off; jammy bugger that I was, no one was on guard. I guess they didn't imagine anyone would try and board a radio pirate station manned by Blood Lifers, secret labs or not.

Blood Lifers are arrogant wankers like that.

I crouched, scuttling crab-like along the deck, even though there were no windows to avoid. We don't like suntans, remember? I noticed there was only one small lifeboat, which was good news: it hinted there weren't hordes of Blood Lifers aboard. If there had been, I'd have been snookered. There were probably only a couple of them working shifts. And Silverman, of course: I mustn't forget that scumbag.

There were two routes down - one aft and one stern - whichever the hell was which. Russian roulette. My type of odds. I chose one, edging down the steel steps, and there she was: Susan was slumped to the side of an empty cabin.

Was that relief surging through me? Making me giddy as a bloody teenager? I had to get a grip on these new emotions. They were damaging my Blood Lifer image.

Susan was untied and out of the seabag at least. She was still, however, lost somewhere in fairyland. After a quick examination, I couldn't hold back a sigh, when I realised there were no fang marks on her throat, like the world's most lethal love bite. They hadn't had time to heal. I hoped.

I'd wager you reckon all I cared about was my bloody plan?

Clap-trap.

That suckling conscience...or Soul...or whatever the hell it is, which boots me in the goolies when I screw up, *that's* what was relieved that for once in either life I hadn't gambled and lost. What made it burn deeper, was this time it'd been *your* cousin, who'd been the stake.

So I stopped everything and took Susan out of there. I was done playing with her, like she was no more than an object, just as Kira had used her.

What made Advance any different to Ruby's wanker of a father and husband?

I took Susan gently in my arms, carrying her up the steps. There was still no one on the deck, so I ducked to the lifeboat and hid Susan in the bottom of it. I struggled to release the boat down onto the heaving waves, listening for the soft *splash* as it landed. If I ever got out of here, I'd row Susan safely to the coast - as long as I wasn't burned like a candle by the sun before I got there.

If I didn't escape from here..?

I watched the lifeboat, as it started to float away, carried on the currents. Susan would simply have to take her chances, like the rest of us.

Now it was time to see what Aralt and Silverman had been researching in their fascist experiments. Why they'd been fighting to change our natural place in the world - a lesson Ruby had beaten into me well enough over the years - by splitting our venom. Wasn't that the venom's very genius? Its predator's perfection: paralyse the victim so they couldn't escape and then explode the heart to hide the kill?

I ducked down the steps again, this time noticing the shadowed stairs, which led deeper into the hold.

See this is how I figure it, folks bury their nasties: underground, basements or holds... It's the same with your subconscious. You stuff down everything dark, as deep as it'll go. Those nightmares, which you can't face when you're awake? You dream them, rather than admit their reality. Of course that doesn't make them any less real, but everyone likes to pretend. For First Lifers, that's what the night's for.

So I reckoned whatever nasties Silverman had set up would be hidden in the hold.

As I stole towards the stairs, I heard Kira and Silverman, deep in conversation, coming down the passageway. I threw myself down the stairs. It was shadowy, reeking of stringent chemicals and something else: First Lifers and *blood*...

When my senses adjusted into night vision, I stumbled back, knocking over a bubbling flask on a long worktop, which instantly burnt through the wood in furious spits.

Christ in heaven, what was this..?

Vats of virulent chemicals lined the walls. And between them?

Now this is the part, which I've always skirted over (even to myself), because I'm a soft git sometimes and I hide from the nasties of this world, the same as anyone.

And you?

You only got the candy floss version. I never wanted you to know what Blood Lifers are capable of imagining...planning...doing...

You love me. Yet if I'd put the same image in your mind as I had, then maybe you wouldn't have been able to see past it. Or see me. Just like now you can't, lost in your long-ago nightmares. I'm still haunted and I'm a Blood Lifer. Maybe I should've trusted you. But I couldn't risk it.

So I'm telling you now, when I know it's too late to make a difference either way. At least, however, the truth of it will be out, rather than eating me from the inside.

Naked First Lifers lined the walls of the hold. They were both male and female but they were so shrunken, paled to ghosts, that it didn't seem to matter which they were anymore. Feeding tubes looped them into place, in and out of their bodies, like bloody lacing; one to keep them alive and one to drain their blood from them in dark umbilical cords, out into a central vat. That was the smell: overpowering fresh blood. It made my body tremble with its call. The worst of it? They weren't dead or even dying, like they should've been if they'd been bitten. Yet they weren't alive either. Not fully.

I stumbled closer, waving my hands in front of each of them in turn, in increasing agitation. I punched this one bloke hard in the gut, but there was no response. It was like they were all in a sodding coma.

Repulsed, I collapsed back away from them.

When my hand touched the worktop, I felt the sharp prick of a needle. Twisting round, I studied a rank of syringes, which were filled with this thick, transparent stuff: like saliva. *Evidence*. I nicked one, pocketing it.

That's when I finally got it: why Aralt was so hooked on dividing our venom.

Our pure venom - here in these neat little syringes - could be used for its various properties. The part that paralysed had been injected into these poor sods. I'd wager there was also one somewhere for pure death. And who knew how Aralt was planning to use that? I shuddered at the thought.

To Aralt, Blood Lifers weren't perfectly evolved. Instead, our double whammy of paralysis and death was a flaw to be fixed.

Aralt's Blood Life hadn't unleashed a connection to the earth and nature, red in tooth and nail, rather the scientist of death, which he'd been in First Life. He was set on improving what his election had granted him. The same as the First Lifers racing to lunar victory.

Aralt planned to subjugate the world.

I forced myself not to shiver, as I ran my fingers down a feeding tube, which was gushing warm nutrients and water into one First Lifer's gut. Another tube glugged the waste away, as blood was sucked in a dark red line from jugular and wrists. Dead cold efficiency. No need for hunting or the kill. When this method was perfected and rolled out, we could feed by simply strolling to the larder. Advance would hold the patent to the distilled venom, making Aralt...anything he bleeding wanted.

I trailed my fingers lightly over the First Lifer's lips. I could feel the weak flutter of breath.

It'd been a woman once, although hard to tell when she'd been shaved bald, and her dugs were shrivelled and painful to look at. She was the same age as you, I reckoned. I wondered if she had a bloke desperately searching for her: his bird, the one who held him in the quiet and laughed at the same moments in the dark of the flicks.

This was what they'd been planning to reduce Susan to, purely because I'd dared to love you.

All on me.

Christ this conscience business was enough to make a man bloody cry.

And the worst of it? The image of a silent, deserted world, with no life but us Blood Lifers - us select few - who were deemed worthy to wander the streets. Streets that were now ours alone, whilst the lonely sun baked a world without humanity because First Lifers only existed in our harvested factories.

Disgust isn't the word, love.

How I figure it, First Lifers and Blood Lifers are two sides of the same coin, even though you don't know it. One can't exist without the other. Dark to the light.

I love you, how many times have I said that? Yet how I felt about this wasn't about that. Or even about you.

I loved (and realised I'd always loved, even in those crazy, wild days with Ruby), your First Lifer world: Billy Fury, my leather jacket, the Triton on a hard, fast road, Florence's piazzas, as evening sets over Duomo's terracotta dome, the aroma of spices, "I was Lord Kitchener's Valet" and the exploding joy of Carnaby Street.

All that dead and silent, so we could feast in comfort? That creativity, spirit and life vanished, and in its place zombies with tubes and blood on tap, like sodding beer? A Blood Lifer World imagined and dictated by Aralt?

This new vision wasn't progress. Eden. The next step. It wasn't buggering evolution.

It was the end of the world for both our species.

'Sorry,' I murmured, not knowing as I said it, if these shells could even hear me (but uncontrollably feeling the need to say it anyway), as I smashed the flasks and booted at the vats until they shattered and the chemicals bubbled out.

I dodged back into the doorway. The First Lifers didn't even flinch, as their feet melted to the bone. But I reckoned they could still feel the pain under the paralysis. They just couldn't get out the screams.

There's always something worse than dying, and there's always someone in First or Blood Life, who'll find a way to inflict it.

When I flicked my lighter, the flame jumped. For a moment, I was mesmerised. Then I bent down and lit the boiling flood.

A sheet of fire roared across the hold. It climbed the walls, up the tubes and flamed the First Lifers' motionless bodies, like burning lollipops.

Still the humans didn't utter a bloody sound, as I smelt their crackling skin and that - right there - is the worst of it. When I'd whimper in the night and you'd nudge me awake, hugging me closer into your warm shoulder, *that's* the recurring dream, which I'd never repeat to you. Because it wasn't a dream. It was too real, and I deserved every sweating, restless night and will do, until the day of my second death.

We all have our ghosts.

When I gagged and backed up the stairs, there he was - Silverman himself. He was leonine in his lab coat, which gave him an austere air of false authority.

Silverman was storming down the corridor towards me, staring aghast at the black smoke, which was curling from the hold. '*You*, what on God's earth are you doing?'

'I don't reckon any of this has got to do with God.'

I launched myself at Silverman's stuck up, shocked mug. I belted him back against the round window of a DJ's booth; on the other side, some Blood Lifer with wavy hair and a straggly beard, was still transmitting.

The DJ was so lost in his tunes that he was oblivious to the life or death struggle inches on the other side of the glass. "Sgt. Pepper's Lonely Hearts Club Band" was leaking from his booth.

Silverman grappled me, twisting me round and banging my nut against the window, as he tried to jab his thumbs into my peepers.

The smoke was drifting down the corridor in choking clouds, stinging me, until I could barely see through the tears. When I choked, Silverman clocked me round the jaw and then kneed me in the groin. I went down but rammed Silverman against the opposite wall with every shred of fury for what I'd seen in the hold: those First Lifer experiments and food banks.

Now my fangs were out. My blood up. When I bit into his thigh, Silverman hollered. He ripped desperately at my hair, stomping down on my foot, so hard I felt the bones crack. I didn't release my grip, however, as I tore into Silverman's flesh, tasting the powerful kick of his blood.

I'd forgotten the glory of a right royal barney, even amidst the horror, fear and the knowledge I was aboard a burning ship in the middle of an ocean - all alone - because right now this felt *bloody good*.

When at last I let go, Silverman punched me across the temples, until I could see the stars, even though we were below decks. But he was down, bleeding out from his wound.

Then we were wrestling on the wet ground, lost in the chemical fog.

The toxins were infecting my lungs: I was struggling to breath. Vampire bollocks myth... Bugger it, we need oxygen, that's what's in the blood, all right? It's why the heart pumps it round the body. I had to get out of this corridor if I wasn't going to cop it.

Silverman, however, had pinned my arms behind my nut. He was twisting my wrists with painful knack.

Lucky for me, as you know, I don't play by gentlemen's rules. So I nutted Silverman, hearing the familiar yelp and *crunch* of a breaking nose. Silverman was a determined bugger though and didn't let go. His grip, however, loosened just enough for me to wriggle one wrist free and down to my pocket. I snatched out the syringe of paralysing venom. My lungs searing hot, throat hoarse from trying to gasp in air that wasn't there, I was in the realm of last bloody hopes, when I rammed the syringe hard into Silverman's throat.

Silverman's peepers widened. He scrabbled at the syringe, but I'd emptied the whole sodding lot before he could yank it out. Now that's a bloody overdose.

How's that for poetic justice?

Silverman backhanded me one more time, before he stiffened and fell back, one eyelid twitching, as he stilled. I pushed him off my legs and then crawled closer.

'You're a bloody monster,' I stared down into Silverman's peepers, which were still open and staring as vacantly as the First Lifers, who I'd discovered having the life sucked from them in Silverman's lab. I reckoned he had as much chance of hearing me, as they'd had. 'Know what? I can smell burning, can't you? Best of British to you, mate.'

I patted Silverman on his motionless nut, before throwing myself through the dense fog of smoke, up the steps and onto the deck. When I rushed to the rail and stared out over the churning ocean, I could just see the lifeboat - a tiny speck carried away on the waves.

I was about to take my jacket off to jump into the water but hesitated because...it's a blinding coat.

When you get to wearing something for such a long time, it becomes your second skin. So I was figuring I could still make it even in my leathers (after all, I've always liked the thrill of danger), when Kira's arm caught me around the throat.

Kira dragged me back across the slippery deck, my boots kicking ineffectually and sliding out from underneath me. I clawed at her, but this night witch was made of iron. My tongue wagged in my mouth; Kira was crushing my larynx.

'Donovan was wrong. He should have let me kill you.' Kira chucked me across a pile of heavy ropes.

I gasped, rubbing my bruised neck. I ran my hand along the coils, looping one behind me.

That lifeboat would be bobbing further and further away. If it was out of sight, I'd have to burn too on this ship or swim into the unknown. I didn't fancy being caught in the waves, as the sun came up.

Still, if this was my last stand, I'd promised I'd go down bloody kicking. I felt lighter than I had in weeks. I'd chosen how I went out of this Blood Life: now that's liberation.

I forced myself to smirk in the way I knew had always annoyed Ruby the most. 'Everyone makes mistakes, darlin'.'

Kira hissed. She bent to grab me by the collar to haul me up. Her fist was already cocked. That's exactly what I'd been waiting for.

I caught Kira around the throat with the rope, twisting it in one quick motion, which I'd learnt from the Blood Lifer in Berlin, who'd strangled his kills. I'm nothing but adaptable. I dragged Kira down between my knees, pulling harder. I ignored the horrible little sounds, which she was making, as she scrabbled at the rope and then as she beat at my chest. Her feet were flapping up and down. I throttled her until...

Here it is. The biggest bollocks myth of them all. Because when I killed Kira there was no explosion of dust, blood or dramatic screeching.

There was simply a body, alive a moment ago and now dead for the second time. Blood *Life*, right? We're as fully alive as you First Lifers and we die the same.

I'd just murdered a member of my own family. Kira's blood was on my hands, the same as every one of the First Lifers I'd ever killed. Except those had been about feeding. And Kira's death? Had been a betrayal of my own species.

I was sick from it.

If there'd been no corpse, it would be like our existence didn't count in the same way as a First Lifer. Like we were that bit *less*, just as Aralt, Silverman and their followers reckoned we were the superior *more*.

The truth is more complex because isn't it always?

I had to push Kira's dead body off me, not quite knowing why tears were pricking the corners of my peepers.

Dense smoke was now billowing up onto the deck. I dashed to the side of the ship, clambering to the edge. There was the lifeboat - a shadow in the night. Sod the rope ladder. I dived straight into the freezing water, striking out for the boat and battling the force of the rolling waves.

I swallowed mouthfuls of brine, shaking uncontrollably, as I was swept under the swell. But I was driven - possessed. I wasn't going to be beaten, not after everything I'd seen and done. The lifeboat grew larger and larger, like a beacon.

Do you want to know, however, what got me there, when I was close to sinking down to the seabed?

I thought of *you* and your pain if Susan never got back to you safely. My legs were numbed to hell by then, but that thought made me kick harder. I pulled my arms more briskly through the skin of the water.

At last I was there, heaving myself up over the side. I gasped and spluttered in a sopping heap on the floor of the lifeboat.

That's when I looked back. For the first time I allowed myself to focus on something beyond simple survival. I turned to watch Radio Komodo as it burned. The shadow of the high, orange flames danced across the waves - bright in the dark - as the ship slowly sank.

When I heard Susan groan behind me, I wrenched myself away from the sight of the world I'd set alight and could now never return to. It's not as if I wanted to. Not after what I'd witnessed. Torching it, however, had set the seal on it.

I dropped down beside Susan. She was beginning to come round for the first time. Her dress had ridden up; her knickers were on show. I quickly straightened her out so she was decent and then on impulse, stroked her cheek because that'd soothed me when I was a kid.

Susan stared up at me. 'What's..?'

'You're all right. Everything's sorted now. I've got you.'

I grabbed the oars, feeling their tug against my raw palms and shooting up into my wrenched back and neck, as the blades ploughed through the rough waves. We started towards land, away from the burning hulk of Radio Komodo.

13

DECEMBER 1968 LONDON

When you caught a shufti of my bedraggled mug as you opened the front door, you nearly slammed it shut again. I didn't blame you, just to make that clear. Then, however, you saw Susan leaning on my arm. Susan was shivering under my damp jacket, which I'd wrapped around her in an attempt to keep her warm against the bite of the night air. Her jersey dress stank of brine.

Instantly, you swung the door wide instead, dragging Susan inside.

I sloped in afterwards, relegated again to the role of the invisible man. It made me wish Kira *had* ripped out my heart (like she'd always promised), because the way you did it was more painful.

You set to work, pulling out towels and blankets to drape around your cousin and then chucked my jacket to the floor, as if it was the cause of whatever had happened, rather than being the comfort.

Maybe you had a point there.

Irrationally protective, I snatched up my leathers, nursing them close to my chest, as you banged on the kettle. You slammed down the Union Jack mug, which I'd filched from Carnaby Street and brought to keep here, as if somehow it meant I could stay – *clink* – like the rattling of a bloody sabre (and no, I hadn't missed it was only one cuppa being brewed).

You left me standing there - cold and damp - like you reckoned if you ignored me for long enough, then I'd vanish – *puff*.

I simply stood there, however, studying every inch of you because I'd been certain I'd never get the chance to again. What'd happened to your long black curls? The ones I'd fantasized about - so many times - in the agonizing weeks without you, when I was wracked with blood abstinence? Dreams of how I'd run my fingers through their softness, as we lay on your beanbags listening to Hendrix? You'd hacked them off, that's what. Nothing was left now but the shortest Pixie cut.

Moon Girl was no more: you'd killed her.

You didn't speak. Not a single sodding word. You didn't look at me, even though I watched every move you made. If this was the last time I saw you, then I didn't want to miss the smallest detail.

I was knackered. I didn't reckon there was anything still keeping me upright, apart from the edge of adrenaline. I wouldn't let myself sit down, however, not in front of you and not after I'd... Not after what I'd done. So I leaned against the wall and started to talk instead. I gave you the sanitized candy floss of what was going on or at least as much as I dared.

Look, that's not an excuse: it's an explanation.

I told you Advance was an evil corporation run by dodgy characters, who were up to the sort of stuff that'd usually land a bloke at Her Majesty's Pleasure. That the boss was worse than Caligula, if he'd had a twin and necked LSD like there was no tomorrow. That when I'd found out the danger of my situation, I'd broken up with you because I was in deep and wanted to protect you and your cousin. That you were both in danger now because of your link with me.

In other words, I glossed over it. Just like every First or Blood Lifer always does, when it comes down to the true nasties of the world. I spun another bleeding cover up. What else could I have done? Would you even have believed me if I'd spilt the bloody truth? *Freak* as I was?

When I'd finished, you just stood there across the lounge without moving. Your mush was so cold. It made my breath catch. I might've been a century out of practice but I still knew I was buggered. 'You brought her back. Now you can go.'

You meant it, bollocking hell did you. But when did *I* ever listen? 'Reckon I saved her so you can both die now? You've gotta leave.'

You shook your nut. 'I've fought too hard for my life here. Dus't a'reckon I'm going to run from these men?'

'Anyone would.'

'I'm not anyone.'

You were pig-headed; it was the streak of ruthless courage and ambition, which I'd tasted in your Soul. That made you so ripe for election. Or death. Because in First Lifers it swings either way.

When I stared into your blazing blue peepers, I knew I wouldn't convince you. The only emotion radiating from you towards me now was hate. That bloody hurt. 'All right.' I shook my nut, ducking towards the door.

Susan rose up, however, chucking off her blanket. She waved at both of us in disgust. 'Are you both fair touched? Light *saved* me. That's twice now. And *you*,' Susan stabbed her finger at you, 'love him.' You flushed, turning away from me. I wished I could see your expression. 'Stop being such a maungy bitch. Who stayed up with you when you fair cried your eyes out over him? Why hide it? Look,' Susan marched to the door of her room, pausing in the frame. 'I'll pack and go stay with a friend in Manchester. You two sort it out.'

Then Susan disappeared inside, slamming the door, and we were left alone.

I was more frightened in that moment than when I'd been on the burning ship, with the stink of roasting flesh and Kira's brawny arm around my throat. Have you ever understood what you do to me?

You could flay me with a look.

We circled each other, like two lions sussing each other out. Not knowing if the other would attack.

At last you shrugged. 'This is what it's all been about? Advance? Why you..?'

'I never wanted to--'

'Shut your gob.'

In the silence, I couldn't meet your eye. Every decision and choice were no man's responsibility but his own; sod it, I knew that. 'I'm sorry.'

You edged closer to me, step by careful step, reaching your fingers up, like you were going to trace down my chest. I was desperate for your touch; I could feel it ghost-like. Your hand, however, hovered inches away from me, as if I was infected. For the first time after the horrors I'd witnessed on Radio Komodo and Aralt's vision of a Blood Life future, I felt as if I bloody well was.

Your voice was soft and close to tears, but none spilled. 'You promised you'd never leave me.'

And there it was: the killing blow.

I howled inside with rage at everything the Plantagenet siblings had stolen, broken and contaminated. At your pain, which I could never take back.

You were right though. It was me alone, who'd made that promise. No one else.

Yet now I'd endangered you again, and the only way to make you safe was to send you away. You'd once said, however, that hurt could be passed on. And I intended to pass it on with bloody credit.

I couldn't risk myself saying more than, 'Please go with Susan.'

You just shook your nut.

'Christ in heaven...' I booted the wall hard enough to jolt the throbbing hurt from my smashed toes right up my leg and then grabbed you by your shoulders, not caring that you tried to flinch away. 'Please?'

You stood there – frozen - like you were made of glass, only gazing at me with those large blue peepers, before you asked, 'Do you love me?'

I was surprised to realise it was *my* mush, which was wet with tears. I dropped my hands from your shoulders, gripping your fingers tight between mine instead, as I'd done in those treasured, quiet moments. I couldn't think about that. Not now. Not after everything. 'I've always sodding loved you.'

Then you kissed me gently on my bruised cheek. 'You fair think I'd leave without you?'

You'd reckon that on the way to the scaffold or the front line, some deep thoughts on life, the universe and everything would spark. Or maybe a moment of revelation or clarity, when the fragments slot into perfect place. Or else there'd be some bleeding peace at the end at least. But then life's not neat like that. It's mundane for the most part. Confused up to the final gasp. The interesting thing is that it's no different the second time round.

I waited for Aralt at the bottom of the wide staircase, by the doors out into the clear winter sunlight. He was barely keeping nocturnal hours anymore; like other Blood Life adaptations, our night-time living was to Aralt nothing but a weakness to be overcome. I was sure he had scientists somewhere working on that too.

As I tested the handle – *up*, *down*, *up*, *down* – tapping my foot with nervous energy, I tried to think only of you: my Moon Girl fallen to earth as *my* girl. I conjured the purr of your voice. The brilliant sparkle of you up on that stage. And those long nights, when I'd obsessed over your photo. Then, however, how much better the reality of your touch had been than I'd ever dreamed, as I'd tossed off whispering your name.

After all, I might as well make my last memories on this maddening earth blinding ones, right?

Yet I found, like water, that I couldn't hold onto them. Instead I kept blanking out, as my mind wandered to the buzzing of the flies, which were collecting in the ceiling's corners, the sensation of the cold metal handle or the stink of noxious smoke, which was still sticky in my nostrils.

I lit up one last fag, drawing in deeply: a condemned man's final request.

Then I heard footsteps on the stairs but not a single pair: Aralt wasn't alone. When he came strutting down, I saw Ruby magisterial on his arm, Alessandro scampering close behind and Donovan yapping at his heels.

'It stopped mid-broadcast, man. Not cool,' Donovan tried to grasp at Aralt, but Aralt was still heading down the stairs without slowing. 'You gotta sort it.'

Yeah that was right, a couple more steps...

I tossed the fag away, rubbing my hands together.

'What has befallen my dearest prince?' Ruby was staring at me in surprise. She stopped, assessing the damage; I must've looked a bleeding mess - but then Ruby didn't know the state of my adversaries.

I pressed my back against the door. I could see Alessandro's pale face, as he cringed back against the wall, his hands instinctively clutched over his ears. *Christ, if he started to rock...*

I forced myself to breathe. 'I know.'

'Know what?' Aralt jumped the last two steps, before swaggering towards me.

'About Radio Komodo. And Silverman.'

Donovan was glancing between us. I couldn't read his expression, but there was enough confusion in his peepers to make me wonder if he'd been played worse than I had. I hadn't been betting on that. But Ruby? There were no surprises there. Her expression hadn't changed - although of course she knew the truth when she shared a bed with her brother. I guess that was one thing Donovan couldn't give Aralt.

I was part of one hell of a screwed up family.

'Don't hold out on me,' Donovan sidled closer. 'It's dead air and--'

'Shut up ya pile of nancy,' Aralt's gaze was intent on me, as he flicked my chest. 'You've been fierce bold nosing into my business. What do you know?'

For the first time, I allowed myself to smile. This was it, when I brought Advance's cardboard empire toppling, just like my life had been tumbled down. This nobody had teeth. '*Everything*.' Aralt took one careful step back. 'You wanna control the First Lifers. And for what? Blood on tap? Are we predators or businessmen?'

Donovan spun to his brother. 'What's he talking about?'

'Not now.'

Donovan slammed Aralt against the wall, his fangs shooting out. 'This was mine, you said. Promised. After everything, Advance was gonna be *my* baby. What have you fecking done?'

Aralt squirmed. Bloody hell, it was blinding to see that. 'Nothing. It's... You're my brother.'

Donovan pushed himself off Aralt. 'Am I now? Used to be.'

'Don't...'

'I reckoned you already knew, ' I said softly, not looking up at them, 'seeing as Kira was on board. Wasn't she *your* Night Terror, Donovan?'

Bugger, did that hit the mark.

'You bastard,' Aralt stared at me, as if a kicked puppy had sunk its teeth into his ankle.

'*Boom, boom, boom...*' I replied dispassionately.

Aralt's jaw tensed, the muscles ticking. Before he could fly at me, however, I heard Donovan's small question, which stopped him, 'You used Kira?'

'You don't understand. This was important--'

Donovan yanked his brother back by the lapels of his expensive suit; Aralt grimaced as it creased. 'She's my elected. Still you ordered her to keep secrets from me?'

'I didn't need to order.'

Donovan flinched. 'We fought a war together, but now you'd have Kira tell your petty lies?'

'Petty?' Aralt flung his brother's hands off him, shoving him back. '*This* is a war. Are you blind?'

Bewildered, Donovan stared at him. 'Kira's mine.'

'Yours?' Aralt snorted. 'How could *you* satisfy a woman?'

Donovan stepped back in the silence, before stalking to the stairs. Ruby grabbed for the sleeve of his jacket, but he shook her off. He didn't look round at Aralt again. 'We stood side by side, even as our home burned and us with it. But whatever *this* is? You kept me in the dark. Like a stranger. Look, I'm gonna split before I have a total freak out and if I do...' Donovan legged it up the stairs, pausing at the top in the shadows. 'We're not blood brothers anymore. And that's on you.'

Then he was gone.

There was a long moment. Then Aralt dragged his fist back and slammed it into the wall. The plaster crumbled, but his knuckles were bloody; I hoped they were broken.

I smiled because an enemy's pain is the most delicious type there is; anyone who pretends different is a liar. Aralt had lost his brother, the same as he'd made me lose you. I don't normally go in for all that *eye for an eye, tooth for a tooth* stuff. But right then? It felt sodding smashing.

It felt slightly less smashing the next moment, when Aralt looked up from flexing his hand and caught my smile.

I read the murder in Aralt's expression. He squared his shoulders, like the head of the pride once more, before he prowled towards me. As I figured it, this was bloody perfect.

Time for the heroics then.

I steadied myself, testing the handle and gripping its cold iron harder.

'Pray let me correct Light's behaviour. I'm sure he did not...'

Aralt didn't even seem to have heard Ruby. And here's the thing, when I glanced at her, there was still this sparkling defiance in her expression, as if I'd been a daft berk for ever thinking there'd have been a hint of apology for her scheming. Yet at the same time, there was also that glorious fire, which made me remember - in one flaming moment - every decade of cruel carnage and love.

And that was the moment Aralt swung for me.

I felt my lip split and the burst of my own blood on my tongue. I heard Alessandro slide to the floor and start to whine.

'Who told you?' Aralt's voice was so soft it sliced with danger.

I shrugged.

Another belt, this time to the kidneys. I needed Aralt closer and more off balance. If I could wear him out through giving me a hiding, it wouldn't be long...

'How'd a wee gobshite like you..?'

'Must've underestimated me, mate.'

That earned me a kick in the goolies. One more step and...

'Me. It was me.'

Bollocks.

Alessandro was staring up at his Author with wide peepers, terror vibrating through him, until he quivered with it. Still he didn't look away.

'Shut up, Alessandro,' I tried to grab at Aralt to distract him from Alessandro, but it was too late. The noble bugger had put himself in the firing line to save me. And there was nothing I could do about it.

'You told him?' Aralt asked shocked, as if he couldn't compute that his tame little Blood Lifer could ever have an independent thought; my rebel nature had rubbed off on Alessandro, even after Aralt's training. 'You fecking told him?'

'All this...was meant to be about Komodo you said...but it wasn't. You lied.'

Lightning fast, Aralt hauled Alessandro's small body up from the floor by the front of his vest, pinning him on his tiptoes. 'That's what grownups do when the babbies can't be trusted.' Aralt traced his hand over the neat line of Alessandro's hair. 'Who's he to you? I'm your Author. I saved you.'

Alessandro's simple reply nearly broke my bloody heart, 'He's my friend.'

'You don't even know what that means - an idiot like you.' I could've flung myself on Aralt and ripped the tongue from his cruel mouth. If I hadn't known I had to keep clinging onto that door handle, I'd have done just that and to hell with everything else. I wish I hadn't seen the look in Alessandro's peepers. Aralt glanced at Ruby, who was standing very still on the stairs. 'Just because some of us,' and then Aralt turned his attention to me, 'don't know how to deal with those, who they elect...'

It was the way Aralt smiled at me - this thin smile, like from one predator to another – which meant I knew...*I bleeding knew*...what he was going to do. But I couldn't do anything about it fast enough. And Aralt realised that too, which was the sodding point.

With one quick, efficient motion, Aralt snatched his silver fountain pen out of his pocket and rammed the entire length of it right through Alessandro's chest cavity, skewering his heart.

'Christ in heaven, *no*...'

Red stained out through Alessandro's white shirt. Blood gurgled in his throat. He whimpered - just once. His peepers widened with startled pain, before they emptied, with what I tell myself is freedom, not simply a blankness because that's what I need to keep going every time I remember that moment. In vivid detail.

All because of me.

Because I caught Alessandro up in my spy games, vendettas and vengeance. Now instead of me, he'd been the one doing the dying. And I couldn't take it back...couldn't ever take it back.

When Aralt let go of Alessandro, his body slid down like a broken doll, crimson trickling from the corner of his mouth.

How could you murder someone you'd elected, who was twinned to you by blood?

My friend.

The words swirled in my mind, heavier than any others. Neither in First or Blood Life had I ever had one of those before and Alessandro hadn't either: sometimes it takes a loner to understand a loner.

But now Alessandro was gone.

Ruby was frozen, with an expression close to fear but more like the horror, which I remembered from when we'd edged, hand in hand, through the macabre La Specola, with its wax men flayed and gutted and our ape cousins stuffed on the other side of the glass.

That was when Aralt did something, which blew what tiny shreds remained of my reason, planning and thought to pieces: he wiped his hands together fastidiously, as if disgusted to have been dirtied by Alessandro's blood.

Then the blood in my own ears was roaring and I was roaring too. Nothing existed but that moment. And that pain.

I was going to sodding kill the bastard.

I didn't care if I went down with him because it was me, who got Alessandro done in. Just as I'd sacrificial offered myself up for slaughter at Erwood's hands.

My choices. My decisions. And I bloody well knew it.

I hurled myself at Aralt, punching right at the throat. For a moment, he was caught off balance, struggling to breathe.

Shocked, Aralt stared at me but then he recovered, throwing me round and jabbing me in the ribs. I felt them break: one, two, three... I gritted my teeth, fighting through the agony. In the red blur of rage, nothing mattered anymore. Aralt grabbed hold of my arm, twisting it with a brawler's dirty skill; he threw inverted punches with his palm on the weak underside, where the veins and arteries were. The wanker intended to enjoy this, he was making that clear.

I could feel Ruby's hands, grasping down my back and trying to drag me away from her brother. I could see her pulling at Aralt too, but he wasn't planning to give up his prize that easily.

'Stop this madness.' Ruby's hair was soft against my mug, as she pressed herself between us. 'Both of you desist. You *men*. Please, we can...'

That's when Aralt hit her, backhanding Ruby hard enough to knock her away from us against the wall.

I managed to turn my nut to look at her, but Ruby was staring down at the ground; her cheek was red.

When had Ruby ever looked down?

When I turned back, Aralt noticed my expression and the wanker laughed.

And that laugh? That was the moment. The one when reason returned to me. I was ready.

I might never be a bleeding hero but I could keep my promises. Christ I hoped Alessandro was free now but it was time I freed you, Susan, Ruby and sod it, myself as well.

I would shut down for good that vision of a future world of factory blood without joy or life. And yeah, to hell with it, pay Aralt back for every belting and taunt, for Alessandro's blood on his hands and for every tear you'd shed.

I let the force of Aralt's next clout into my bruised ribs slam me back against the front doors because then the handle was in my hand again. When Aralt advanced on me for the next swing, I hooked my other arm around his waist, dragging him in close. As he decked me across the chin, I turned the handle, letting the force of the blow knock us both out into the sunlight.

I heard Ruby's shocked scream and then saw Aralt scramble for the building's safety. But I linked my arms tighter around the tosser's waist, as I grappled him further into the light, away from the line of shadow cast by the oaks along the pavement.

My retinas were already scorched; it was too bright. A world aflame. I could feel my skin crisping. I held Aralt on top of me, like a shield.

Aralt's howls were deafening. He was ripping at my hands to free himself but he was jerky in his agony and blinded.

Caught off guard, Aralt stumbled. I hurled him far out into the street under the hot sun and this world he'd thirsted to conquer – *let him have it*.

I staggered back under the shade of the oaks. Aralt was shrieking and giving these pathetic little yelps. His eyeballs were scorched out of their sockets; he was grasping the air with his fingers, as if he could somehow find a way out of the darkness. Then he collapsed to his knees, as the skin melted from his body, like a candle's wax. The same as the anatomical man in Florence, with his inner workings on display bloody.

Finally Aralt was nothing but a shuddering mess. There wasn't even that pitiful yelping anymore because his tongue was puddled too. There was nothing but a pool of blood left, like that vast vat in the hold of Radio Komodo, sucking the life from comatose First Lifers. The same stink too.

It's not often you see your own future so vividly illustrated right in front of you.

Then there was no time for thought because I was melting too: there's only so much a few branches can do against a savage sun. The first scream was wrenched from my reluctant throat.

I told you that you never forget the stench of melted skin fused to leather.

I staggered back through the oak's shade to Advance's entrance, banging against the doors. But they wouldn't open. I wrenched on the handle, becoming increasingly frantic, when I realised Ruby had locked me out to face the sun with her brother. Choices and decisions, you see?

It seemed Ruby had made hers.

Ruby stepped closer to the darkened door. She placed her hand to the glass. As our eyes met, I slowly raised my seared palm to hers.

That's when I knew there was no way out of it. I was going to cop it. Soon I'd be no more than a puddle in the sun too. You know what? It was better to be the flame, which burns out bright and fast because wasn't that how I'd always lived?

I turned and fought to hold onto enough of myself just for the final few moments, so I'd go out as me; I didn't want to die like Aralt had - reduced to animalistic terror. I swaggered towards the middle of the empty street, right under the rays of the sun and that pool of congealing blood.

It was agony - a pure and blinding burn - but I wasn't het up. I was calm. It wasn't as if everything was tickety-boo, but rather I was filled with this sense of completion.

With my first death, I'd botched the whole idealistic bollocks, leaving everything behind me in the same bloody mess. I'd lost my life in a stupid, meaningless way. Of course that's the way it goes down for many people. When you're dead, however, it's too late to obsess over it. But if you're elected into Blood Life? You try having centuries of something like that weighing on you. The problem for me, however, was it wasn't a one off. I'd screwed up in the same way regular as clockwork.

This time, however, I'd taken Advance down with me. I'd saved the world. And the biggest surprise of all was I actually gave a damn.

So what if I fried? I'd had a good innings and I'd got to see the sun for the first time in over a hundred years. So I stood there, with my arms out and my peepers turned towards the flaming face of the sun.

And I waited to be burned alive.

See, I still didn't know you well enough, did I? Because then there you were, charging around the corner in your red Mini Cooper. You threw open the side door and then grabbed me by the jacket, dragging me inside.

After everything, it turns out it was you doing the saving.

You didn't need rescuing. I did.

I don't know what you must've thought about the bloody thrashed state of me, the way I huddled instantly under my jacket away from the light, or dragged the picnic rug off the floor and over my nut for protection. You've never told me.

You didn't say anything at all, you simply drove.

It was only when we were out of central London, somewhere north, when city had transformed to suburbs and then fields, hedges and the ridges of countryside, that you pulled off into a rutted lane and turned to me.

That's when I dared to shift my agonised body enough to peer out from my shielding (everything still blurry through my damaged peepers) and realised your stuffed suitcases were crammed onto the backseats: your whole life packed up because you'd known that I'd need you...yet also it'd mean you couldn't go back. Because of me.

At last I built up the bottle to break the final decree - the big one: I told you what I was.

I tore up the rule book into confetti pieces because I was never going to leave you again, which meant you had to know the truth. I trusted you with my secret. And my life.

You might've run from me. Called me *monster*. Kicked me out there and then to melt on the roadside. Yet if we were to spend our lives together, there could be no more masks.

Afterwards, I braced myself, my knuckles white around the rug. I had no right to expect anything but rejection.

The strange thing was, you didn't do any of those things. You merely nodded with a type of detached curiosity, like it was only one more freakish characteristic to add to my long list.

I managed to smile at you tentatively. You looked cute in your sexy scarf, with your new Twiggy cut, which I now appreciated lit up your peepers and lengthened your beautiful neck. 'Have I told you that's a blinding hair do?'

At last you grinned, stroking your bare neck, as if surprised by the feel of it. 'Fancied a change.'

Then you leant over and kissed me dead gentle on my tender lips.

Christ had I missed that.

'You and me both.'

You revved the Mini Cooper. Then we roared off into the light of day. Together.

14

You had to stand still for a bloody long time if you didn't want the photograph to come out blurred. If you moved, it'd look like you were a ghost, hazy at the edges. Sometimes whole families turned out that way. But not often because papa was one of the best at his art.

Papa employed every trick of the photographers' trade: hidden props to tuck behind folk's necks or covers to stick over a mama's head to render them invisible, whilst at the same time stopping their babes from kicking up a shine because they feared they'd been abandoned.

If you know what you're looking for, you can make out these spooks in the pictures.

Papa was always inventing some better process, lens or plate. His excitement was like a little kid's. It was bloody infectious. Mama would sigh and leave us to the dark room, my sisters clinging to her apron, because I was of the same kidney: there was nothing more blinding than this weird new science.

I was obsessed by the way you could capture one moment. I knew it wasn't forever. Photographs faded. Yet it was still someone's squirming Soul laid in the palm of your hand. Power over the natural world, without trickery or magic. I understood it and (young as I was), papa respected me enough to share the voyage of discovery.

'Photography's derived from the Greek for light and writing,' papa once told me. 'We write with light.'

Mama and papa arrived in Watford along with the whistling squeal of the London and Birmingham Railway in 1837, as part of the influx from the inner city, which transformed the old shops with their tiny windows and dim interiors, into bright new stores - like papa's photographic studio.

See, here's the thing, where there'd been just one long street with foul alleyways rising from the River Colne to Cassiobury Park, it transformed around me as I grew too, into a new world of the printing industry and shops as good as any in the City (and that's not simply my pride speaking). Then there was Cassiobury House: a romantic, gothic pile, to which posh birds and famous bleeders gallivanted back and forth from London - and had their portraits taken by papa.

We also returned to London on quests for supplies, equipment or to hang out with other photographers in studios or coffeehouses. Bloody hell, the powerful aroma of coffee was like something exploding right on the back of my tongue. It was the smell of *adventure*. It always will be for me. Very quickly, I came to be viewed as papa's partner in crime.

And London? Christ it was alive, expanding ever further and busier every time we visited, bustling like a banjo, as much with death as with life, both cheek by jowl: a chimneysweep's boy (younger than me), choking up blood, as he staggered by us, black head to foot, a crawler in the shadow of a doorway, twitching under scarlet rags, nothing but a bag of bones, a blue-smocked butcher whistling, laden with a tray, which groaned under fresh joints of lamb and an abandoned newborn, grey and alien, rotting on a dungheap, ignored by everything but the flies that teemed over it.

Before we'd head back to the hiss and screech of the train, papa would take me to stand on the western parapet of London Bridge, amidst sailors in red and blue flannel shirts or nor'westers and the stink of smoke, to peer over at the tugboats, steamers and paddleboats, which were sailing in and out, on the great silver tongue of the Thames.

Papa would point out which were for passengers and which cargo, listing - as if they were no different to the chemicals we experimented with - what were in their holds: spices, tea, sugar, indigo, rum, wool, French wine or my beloved coffee.

Then I'd imagine the faraway lands they'd come from (or were sailing to). And that I was travelling with them.

It was, however, more than simply envisioning.

I felt it in my gut: this burning need to *escape*...I didn't know what...all right then, my own skin. It was too tight. Something in me wanted to blaze brighter.

I knew the world was too large to leave it there in darkness.

One cold morning, I'd settled myself on the Oriental rug in front of the spitting fire in our small drawing room, whilst Nora and Polly played with their doll, which papa had made out of wood and wool. My sisters' shrill little voices were a starling-like chattering.

I lay on my elbows, flicking through the heavy account books, which I'd discovered at the back of the studio.

Papa had never banned me from touching anything; he was eccentric like that. He'd say the *world's for exploring because that's when discoveries are made* and *rules crush natural curiosity*.

I loved him for that.

You spoil that boy, mama was fond of saying. But she didn't stop him, and I saw the way her peepers danced when she said it.

I had papa's books laid out in front of me like a precious find, with this fast heartbeat, which I always had when I'd unearthed something new to be examined. I loved the numbers, which were in neat rows in papa's slanting handwriting: money in, money out, names and dates.

All right then, so there was another reason I spent every hour I could lurking at the back of the studio, sniffing the toxic chemicals, which papa mixed in our night-time experiments or listening to the inane yakking of the ladies and gentlemen, when they came to collect the finished product.

I was desperate to understand why my brain worked the way it did.

If a perfect photograph was a scientific possibility through writing with light, then I wasn't cursed, demon possessed or set for Bedlam (and I'd lain trembling in bed terrified of all three possibilities). If there was a rational explanation for how an image could be caught like that, then I wasn't a freak.

When I heard the door open, I glanced up.

It was a surprise to see papa frowning; he usually looked like an excited kid, or so deep in thought that he was wandering through another world. 'Why are you reading those?'

'I like the numbers, sir.'

At last Papa smiled, as he ruffled my hair. 'Then read away.'

Papa collapsed into the upholstered armchair, dragging the broadsheet, with a crisp shake of the pages, in front of his nose.

I slammed the account book closed. 'All finished.'

Papa peered at me over the top of the *Times*, as he reached for his clay pipe. 'Finished, Thomas?'

'But...are the two columns not meant to balance? There's a discrepancy of nine guineas on page five, no amount entered for Mrs Doubleday on page 14 and on page 27 a shortfall of 16 guineas and seven shillings...' Papa crumpled the *Times* into his lap and stared at me. Nora and Polly stopped playing at the sound, gazing over at us with their large peepers. When Papa held out his hand, I passed over the book to show him. 'There are more...'

Bloody hell, I'd done it now. The camouflage had slipped; my true form was revealed. What would any of them do now the freak within had been unmasked? My pulse beat so hard I thought my heart would explode.

Papa was flicking through the pages, running his finger down the numbers to tote them up.

That's my problem right there: I never got when to keep my gob shut.

I watched each action closely, flinching at the *bang*, as finally papa shut the book and placed it down. He threw the *Times* aside. When papa pushed himself up, for the first time he felt to me like a towering god of justice, poised to give me a thorough slating, rather than my fellow pioneer in this world.

I scrambled up - my nut down - unable to meet his eye.

So, this was it then.

I was surprised to feel papa's warm hand on my shoulder, as he said softly, 'You are a miracle. A human camera. My little Light.'

When I looked up into papa's peepers, they were flaming with pride.

As if they'd sensed but not understood the tension and had now been jolted out of it, my sisters sprang up. They clasped hands and danced round, like they were playing "Ring a Ring o'Roses", whilst they chanted *little Light, little Light*.

I collapsed in a giggling pile of relief: it was going to be all right.

Then papa was laughing too and the quiet drawing room was filled with our hullabaloo. It felt like we could take on anything. Mama stuck her nut round the door in astonishment at the uproar.

You don't get many moments in life like that: pure and perfect joy. In my First Life that was my only one. Yet because I was a *human camera* I captured it with perfect clarity. I could return to it many times over, which was a good thing. Because I bloody needed to.

Six weeks after that, I was playing behind the house with Nora and Polly under the shade of the weeping willow because mama had told me to keep an eye.

I'd positioned my sisters, like sentinels, with these shining silver halfcrowns, which I'd liberated from papa's study for the experiment.

The girls were normally only permitted to learn music and art, like their wanker of a tutor insisted, and I wanted to share with them the wonders, which I was discovering and yet they were barred from. If I wasn't careful, they'd turn into right ninnies...unless they had my help.

My sisters held on dead tight to those halfcrowns, almost hopping on the spot with expectation because this was grown up stuff, until they got the angle right. Then the sun hit the halfcrowns and reflected.

The light was so bright, it got Polly in the peepers first. She looked like she was going to blubber. I dashed to her, shushing her, before shoving her across until – *bam* – the ray bounced between the coins and onto the trailing branches of the weeping willow, where it danced and flitted like a fairy.

Then my sisters gasped, laughing at the light.

That's when mama stumbled into the garden, her face all screwed up.

I knew straightaway something had happened to papa.

It's like you hate yourself for knowing but a wolf awakes deep in your gut and growls at the danger, so you just know, all right?

Papa was dead - killed cold - struck down by a hansom cab, which had been transporting one of those posh fellas to Cassiobury House. It'd been driven by a drunken bastard, too soaked in gin to realise (or care), what he'd done.

The banks swooped in and took the studio. Because those numbers in the account books? Yeah, I'd been right: the two columns should've balanced.

Me? I was sent away to an orphan school in London. I never saw my mama or sisters again.

Instead, I was worked like a bloody servant by the stuck up boys, whose parents could afford to pay the fees, when I wasn't getting a taste of the birch.

Suddenly rules mattered. Everything was banned. And the world was no longer for exploring but a prison to be endured. The light was dimmed.

I fagged for a sadistic little bastard, who never let me forget I was only there (and not in the workhouse), by the grace of charity. No one ever let me forget that again.

Say thank you, Blickle... As I was kneeling at his feet... *Say thank you, Blickle...* As the birch swished down... *Say thank you, Blickle...* As he held me struggling under his sweaty brute weight and... *Say... No, please, no... I said, say thank you, Blickle...*

I learnt to hide my memory and my mind. I didn't want to be seen as more of an outsider or exhibit to be gawped at than I already was. Any I did risk showing, the teachers sniffed at as *low cunning.* They were soon snarling that I was a *reprobate,* when I took to brawling as the only way to garner some scant regard amongst the other lads, as well as to feed the anger, which balled so tight in me some days I was nothing but a blazing sun of rage.

What never went away, was one simple feeling: to lose everything in a moment. And so to be beholden - entirely at another's mercy.

Powerless doesn't even cover it, love.

It wasn't until I was eighteen that my uncle belatedly remembered his duty and found a junior clerk position for me at Overend, Gurney and Company and well...you know how that ended.

There was one thing, which I could hold onto through my First Life, death and into my Blood Life.

You always asked why I was called Light – said my parents must be *right hippies*?

All right then, so when you're elected you get to choose a new name, like a christening. It's the first initiation into Blood Life. The symbolic shedding of humanity. Or that's how some see it: the cleansing of their First Life and a bloody liberation.

But for me? My naming tied me closer to what had been important.

I'm not alone in that. We use it to bind ourselves to our First Lives, loves and hurts, so we'll never forget what it was to be human. Because we'll never *be* human again. But we can remember the whispered spectre of it. We can fight to hold onto the edges. The taste.

That once we loved and were loved.

So I chose *Light*.

And I remembered.

DECEMBER 1968   YORKSHIRE

The black shadow of Ilkley Moor bled out of the weak evening light. The mists were thick around the hills, swallowing the road; the Mini Cooper's lights blurred. Up ahead the stone, whitewashed walls of your father's house rose up in the dark.

Now look, it hadn't been my idea. In fact, I'd have taken you bleeding anywhere, rather than back to your wanker of a father. But you'd insisted. It seems you believed in *family* more than me. At least in times of need. And yeah, this counted. Of course, your family couldn't be as psychotic or dysfunctional as my Blood Lifer one.

Although from what I'd seen, yours weren't that far behind.

We'd hidden out on quiet country lanes, which had given me time to heal, blacking out the car's windows with rugs, so we could sleep in safety during the day and drive by night because we didn't want to give the old git a heart attack when he saw me. At least, *you* didn't.

First, I'd forced you to take me back to London, although not without days of furious rowing. You were right but you still took me back there: it was non-negotiable.

I had to snatch the Triton, you see, sentimental berk that I am. You get attached to things when you have so little. In a century of living, she was all I had to show for my life. Without my Triton, it was like I was no more than a shade.

When I'd slunk into Advance, it'd felt deserted. There was no noise or movement. No pulsing thrum of my Author, muse and liberator.

Settling back over the Triton, it'd been like having a part of myself back, which I'd only dully sensed had been missing.

You drove towards your father's house in the Mini Cooper, as I roared up on the Triton, weaving between the deep, frozen ruts and fighting to retain control, when the bike skidded over the ice. At least one of the blinding things about leathers is they keep out the cold.

We swung onto the track, pulling up in front of a farmhouse, which was buried in the lower slopes of the moor.

As soon as you knocked on the oak door, I knew something was up.

There came this kind of shambling sound and then an unsteady wrenching, as bolts were dragged back. When the door was hauled open, and the dim light puddled out, the hulking outline of your father was silhouetted. But he was swaying, as if he was at sea: he was sodding plastered.

Your father's trousers were stained. His braces hung loose and his shirtsleeves were rolled back. He squinted out at us. 'Kathy?'

You barged past your father into the sitting room, where brass horseshoes hung from the white walls above the two frayed armchairs, whilst a wood fire spat embers.

When I sloped after you, your father twisted and blocked us in. His bleary peepers darted from me to you and then back again.

'What's,' your father tossed his nut at me, 'doin' here?'

'He's with me.'

'Aye.'

They stared at each other. You fidgeted. 'We need... Can we stay here? Just for...a bit.'

Your father snorted. 'What dus't a reckon?'

I could've wrung your father's wrinkled old neck. I hurled myself down into his worn armchair, allowing the warmth of the burning logs to thaw me, as I stared up boldly at him. I raised my eyebrow. Your father glared at me but didn't move.

'I reckon,' Kathy took one step towards her father, 'after everything mother and me--'

'Don't thee talk to me about thine mother--'

'Why not?' A flash of rage; you flamed with it. 'Nowt wrong with our family was there? Nowt wrong with you?'

'Thee'll get a right belt in a--'

'Why hide anymore? We're all unmasked here.'

Your father stumbled towards you. I didn't stop him. You didn't need rescuing. Not like that. If anything, *he* did. 'Thee fair touched lass?'

When you laughed, it was like something had been knocked loose. I'd never heard you sound like that before: it was haunting. And it was all my fault. *Buggering hell, I'd broken you.*

Was this why we kept the existence of Blood Lifers secret, except to the elect? Because First Lifers couldn't cope with the shock of this knowledge?

You shoved closer to your father. Your hand pressed hard to his chest, where his heart would be pumping the blood pounding through him. 'I want to see the monster. You're no man, are you?'

I flung myself out of the chair. I grasped your arm, hauling you away from your father.

Coming here had been a mistake. Why had I let you persuade me? See here's the thing, when have I ever been able to convince you out of anything?

'Time to go, luv?'

Your father, however, confused and rat-arsed as he was, had now cottoned on to your insults and was pissed. His mug had deepened to a mottled purple, as he stomped nearer, forcing our backs to the fire and roasting our coolers on the flames. 'Thee are nowt but a mardy scrubber. Just like thine mother--'

That's when you cracked him. I hadn't even seen the brass poker in your hand.

Then your father fell.

Interesting how the giant of a bloke only took one hit to kill, like smashing an egg.

Your father sprawled there - his skull caved in - scarlet seeping onto the stone flags.

In my hunger, all I could think about was the waste, not of life but of sodding blood. If you hadn't been in the room, I'd have scrabbled on all fours licking it up. The hunger was now at such a pitch, it was like I'd shrapnel in my guts.

You didn't scream, cry or even blink. You simply stood there, hand flexing around the poker. Then you said, in this strange, flat voice, 'We need a spade.'

You've always been practical like that.

At last, something I could do for you, which few other blokes would've understood or had the balls to stand shoulder by shoulder with you on.

Finally, you needed me.

In this new world, I'd botched every attempt to demonstrate my love, whether with jewellery or words: a freak in your world. But this? Burying the father, who you'd murdered, in order to save you the pain of doing it yourself?

That was right down my alley.

I waited until night was darkest, before carrying your father's heavy weight out onto the moors, through the fluffy white tufts of cotton grasses, to damper ground. I buried him deep, where the bogs sucked him deeper, and he'd never be found. One less nightmare to haunt you. Or so I'd thought. Now, however, when I see you rocking and wailing at things, which aren't there..?

Maybe nothing can be buried that easily.

Bleeding frozen, I darted back through the bracken and sharp patches of bramble, which tore at me in the black. I was all het up, not bothering how scratched I became. I was more rent inside, not knowing what I'd find when I got back. Because to a First Lifer killing..? It's no predatory necessity (like it is to us Blood Lifers), as natural as breathing. I remembered the taste of enough humanity to know it wasn't pukka to knock off your old man. Dealing with the corpse was only the business end.

When I climbed the stairs of the farmhouse, however, I found you unpacking your suitcase in what must've been your old room: I could tell by the glamorous posters of The Shirelles, who glimmered in gauzy mauve gowns and clippings of the The Shangri-Las. Dresses, boots, bags, make-up and false hair were spread out like a shop, whilst you were humming, cross-legged in the midst of it all, as you dragged out another piece of your life.

You grinned up at me.

I so hadn't bloody expected this, that I stopped short.

'All right?' You asked.

I nodded. 'Sorted.'

You jumped up, pulling me further into the room.

I'd done something right at last; it burnt me hot inside.

I'll tell you now, I'd never have guessed this is how First Lifers courted today. Sod conventions, rules and petty boxed boundaries.

I don't reckon you'd ever have been content with another First Lifer. You were always too close to Blood Life, even though you never knew it.

'Look what I found.' You pushed me towards a dusty Dansette record player, which was buried under a pile of old records. 'It was my mother's. We'd listen to...everything. You left something at mine. I packed it because...'

You glanced at me with a mixture of shy embarrassment and the same expression, which a kid wears when it's about to produce a present. You rummaged in your suitcase, emerging with my Billy Fury and THE FOUR JAYS LP. I was flooded with an irrational joy because I told you what it's like when the only things you possess are the clothes on your back and a motorbike.

'Nice one!' I swung you round in my arms: you were a blur of blue peepers and laughter. I never wanted to let go. 'Now for the first time in too bloody long, I'm gonna dance.'

When I placed the needle down, the vinyl crackled to life, and there was the rhythm, familiar as my own heartbeat, along with that fragile raw voice.

I clasped you round the waist, curling so close that our bodies and breaths were one; our cheeks touched.

Then we danced. Yeah, we bloody danced.

15

Lemon-scented fern – I spread the fronds in a vase by your bed this morning. You know, the one you haggled for, in the mountain village in Beirut, back in 1971? I picked the fern last night on my wanderings. I reckoned then you could at least smell it, even though now you haven't the strength to turn your nut to see.

I think you can still smell... I wish you could tell me. I've heard it said, however, that it's the last sense to go, when we fade. Ghosted. When you do, you'll remember those nights we'd lie cocooned in the lemon aroma, staring at the map of the sky and plotting our lives. When everything was still open to us, and we seemed to have such a long time together...

The snows are melted now.

That daft bint Wednesday says it's officially spring because the flowers are pushing their heads up to the sun. It is warmer. The track's not so bleeding impassable; the butcher's getting the piss poor pigs' blood through more easily, so I won't have to get munchey on my tosser list, you'll be pleased to know: Wednesday's safe a little longer. I don't need the blankets anymore down in my hidey-hole in the garage either. I remember when you were always fussing over that.

It's been a long time, however, since anyone's fussed over me. I'll have to get used to that, won't I?

And you? Where are you? Every time I look at you in that white bed I...

Don't go thinking I'm some kind of nancy boy, but I've taken to sleeping with your ivory scarf during the day when we're apart, curling it close to my cheek, so I can breathe in your scent.

Wednesday pushed more leaflets under my nose again yesterday. This time there was a new one: *Hospice*, this one read. Then she patted me on the shoulder, giving this little, sympathetic smile, which on her looked plain wrong.

Before you get pissed, you can cool it because the leaflets are binned. Never leave you, right? I made that promise. And I meant it. I won't ever break it again.

Not after what you gave up for me. Not after what you lost. And not when you saved me.

I know I'm losing you. But you'll never lose me.

MARCH 1970   YORKSHIRE

I've always needed something to drive the thrill, buzz and the danger: to dive through the roaring fire.

What? You reckon I was castrated because I fell in love with a First Lifer? My bollocks sliced off neat? That the world sang quieter, my skin didn't tingle like I was ready to combust, or the hunger pulsed less fiercely?

Don't flatter yourself.

Love might have led me by the dick but it didn't control anything else.

Loving doesn't change who you are, only what you choose to do. I came to discover that. Transformation isn't fairy-dust quick. This is no Hollywood namby-pamby fairy-tale.

I struggled, every minute of every day, trapped in that farmhouse. Strike that, every sodding second. I was a predator, who caged myself for you. But I was still a predator. No matter the reasons behind my blood abstention, the impulses and throbbing urges never quietened and the cost didn't lessen. You never asked me how I managed it: maybe not knowing was the only way you could let yourself love me back.

I found these systems of caves, which were dark and cold, especially in high winds.

Before I'd discovered them, I'd spend nights booting the energy out of me at the Twelve Apostles: the remains of a ring of engraved stones on the east of the moors. The stones had fallen amongst the heather; I reckon they were once used for observing the moon. It made me feel closer to the night, jumping from stone to stone, kicking against the millstone grit, cracking my toes and howling at the black. Until you got cross at the state, in which I'd come home.

Then I'd hike all the way to the moor's precipitous north edge, on the gritstone lip, staring out at the tiny lights of Ilkley and Lower Wharfedale, like they were sodding Jerusalem because we were so remote and lonely.

You never seemed to notice. After all, this is where you'd grown up. This was home.

Me? I'd been birthed in the shadow of London. And after my second birth, I'd roamed the delights of the world's greatest cities. I'd known remote but that had been like a penance, after the horrors of the Great War.

Then, of course, you had the day and the other First Lifers, who inhabited it.

You'd told folks your father had gone to London to stay with your cousin and they'd believed you.

In fact Susan was now safely lodging with her mates in Manchester and was the only soul you wrote to, whilst your father rotted under the dark earth. Those were more innocent, less suspicious times.

Bollocks - people just kept their dirty secrets and lives to themselves because if they went digging in someone else's, then maybe someone would go digging in theirs.

The problem was we hadn't got the balance right. It wasn't easy, when only one of us was nocturnal and had been ripped from the Blood Lifer world. Two cultures - day and night - and somehow we were trying to force them together.

It wasn't simply a matter of blood. It was much more basic. Biological. I wanted to claw at the world and tear it to shreds. Yet I couldn't say a word to you because how would you've looked at me then?

Even free from Ruby, the twins, Advance and every other Blood Lifer, I couldn't be free from myself. There was no place for me in the First Lifer world. No role or fulfilment. I was still one of the Lost. I itched with the desperation for excitement. Stimulation. *Something...*

Which is why I was so bloody relieved when I discovered those caves. Then it was like every night

I found a new challenge to satisfy the Blood Lifer I am.

At first, I climbed by hand alone, feeling for footholds and grips... *Left, then right...* I worked out routes dead quick as I hung there, fingers aching and biceps stretching. My fear of heights transmuted to thrill. The adrenaline rush, when I nearly wasn't able to reach far enough and I felt myself slipping...before finally making it, was intoxicating. The next time I'd find a harder route, go higher and further.

I soon became more adventurous.

I sent you out with a shopping list, which you gawped at, like I'd lost my mind. It took you weeks to find everything from specialist places, as I grew increasingly impatient and took greater risks by hand. I wanted to climb higher and higher, deeper and deeper into the caves.

You laid out the equipment on our bed (yeah, it was *our* bed now, and it was blinding we were calling it that): sharp metal pitons, hammers to drive the piton spikes into cracks in the rock, carabiners to attach to the rings and climbing ropes.

You were suddenly all questions, bristling with excitement, as you threaded each one in turn through your fingers, like they were part of some type of elaborate foreplay. That shut me up for a moment because it got me imagining. You stopped, staring at me hopefully.

I realised you wanted to share this secret thrill of the night with me.

I don't reckon you've ever understood what it meant that you didn't want to teach or mould me. Instead you were happy to share in something, which blazed me with passion. I hadn't seen it before in you and no one had shown it to me, in either First or Blood Life.

That's when I truly got what you meant by wanting us both to be free together.

The problem was that the moors weren't safe at night for you. All right then, safe enough for our little excursions together and nookie in the heather. But not to cross the whole thing, when you didn't have my nocturnal vision. That's why we worked out this trick, which became our treat to ourselves, where the caves transformed into our personal, night-time playground.

I'd get there just before dawn, descending deep enough that I wouldn't melt. Then I'd spend the day setting up, before I'd settle back and zonk out. I'd surprise the occasional climber, who'd shake me awake with comic urgency, terrified I'd fallen. It was always fun to see their different responses, when I'd give them the diver's signal for A-ok and then say *cheers*, as I'd settle back for a kip.

When the sun had set, and the last of the climbers had found their way out of the caves, you'd drive down the road up to the quarry. You'd wait until you were alone, before you'd tool up: ropes looped over your shoulder and a helmet with a lamp on your nut.

It wasn't long before you were as good...buggering hell, all right...a *better* climber than me.

We pushed onto harder routes, hammering pitons into new seams. We supported each other when it became tough. Shagged each other on the damp cave floors when we got too turned on.

Funny the burst of extra courage a bloke gets when his bird's watching him. It's even greater when his bird's the one right behind him, shadowing his every move. I wasn't going to back down from a cave wall. And that was the buzz. I was never closer to life, than when I was touching the face of death.

One night, we'd just descended from a bugger of a climb, which had been as exhilarating as hell.

You wrapped your arms tight around me, shivering in the night's cold at the cave's entrance. Then you snogged me hard and long, before drawing back. 'Ready to go? I'm fair starved.'

I shook my nut. 'I want one more shot at it.' I ran my finger down your cheek. 'Eat and get warm.'

You smiled. 'Don't forget the dawn.'

That'd become your singsong catchphrase every night, like I could ever bloody well forget the searing heat of the boiling sun. Yet since I'd had to tell you what'd happened to Aralt... Only under duress, mind you. You'd forced it out of me, whilst I was still smoking in a scorched state on the seat of your car.

Anyway, how I figure it, you deserved the truth, since you were the one, who'd managed to scrub the melted skin from my leather jacket.

It would have done me in to lose that coat.

Well, you'd been anxious since then, every time the sun first started to dye the horizon with light. Look, I don't blame you. What happened was enough to give me sodding pause. So you said, *don't forget the dawn.* And I loved you even more for it.

I watched you back out of the quarry in a trail of dust, before I ducked down into the labyrinth of caverns.

I'd taken my first grip on the rock face, when I knew something was wrong.

That smell - *her* smell.

You never forget the call to blood. But it was too late. Even though every muscle tensed, as I swung my shoulders, the rock still connected with

273

my temple, hard enough to force me stumbling to my knees.

Black crashed over me, like a curtain swishing shut at the flicks. *Show over.*

As my peepers closed, I saw the sweep of red silk.

At last my peepers fluttered open again, blurred and confused.

Christ did my head hurt.

Then panic, twisting into fear, because my wrists and ankles were bound tightly with my own climbing ropes.

As I struggled, my skin crawled with cold and the dawning realisation howled through my muddled brain that I was starkers, stretched across a rock in the caves, like a sacrificial offering.

Bollocks.

I thrashed from side to side wildly – hollering - but the ropes only bit deeper. I could feel the dull, heavy throb of bruises and the sticky trickle of blood.

'Prithee peace. Be still,' Ruby bent over me, her red hair stroking my exposed skin. Her pendant rubbed against my lips, as if expecting a deferential kiss. 'Your brazen-faced First Lifer has gone. We are alone.'

'Why?' I tried to slow my heart and remember I was the predator and not the prey.

But this was Ruby: my Author, muse... Sod it, not my liberator. She'd never been that. But habits bred over a century are difficult to break.

Ruby slapped me hard across the mush; her nails raked my flesh. 'Why? You traitorous wretch. You murdered my brother.'

'He murdered Alessandro. He was gonna murder the world.'

When Ruby drew back, I saw the slightest shard of doubt in her. 'We were going to build a new one.'

'You mean Aralt was? One in his own image?'

'He was a Plantagenet. A slave like you will not speak of him. Not when you left me for a First Lifer bawd.'

Ruby was wrapping a rag around a thick stick, dipping it in something, which stank of...*paraffin.*

Ruby didn't look up at me but her hands were shaking. 'Plantagenet was a bastard son, with no family in a time when that was shameful indeed. When his Author, one of the Magnificoes, elected him, all he wanted was to create a family. A family, which would be his legacy and blot out that beginning. His Author was...foolish, like you. He believed in a time of intolerance that some First Lifers could be trusted. Instead, they mistook him to be the devil. He could have saved himself but to hide the existence of Plantagenet and his family, he let himself burn.' Ruby turned to me: her peepers were hollows. 'We watched him scream and did nothing, as he blackened to ash. We are not one of us safe in this First Lifer world. Pray, do you believe they would willingly share it with us? Love you, if they knew what you are...and what you'd truly done?' I shifted my gaze away from Ruby. This is what I hadn't allowed myself to think. Couldn't think. 'As we hid in the shadows, watching the flames dance, the lesson seeded well.' Ruby paced closer, holding up my gold lighter in her other hand. Then she smiled. As she flicked the lighter and it sparked, I twigged what she was planning. Christ in heaven, those are the moments you wish you were still in the dark. Ruby dipped the paraffin into the flame. The torch roared to life, casting grotesque shadows. I strained against the ropes, but they only cut my skin. Again. 'I could smell you,' Ruby trailed her hand down the length of me, caressing the inside of my thighs and then my tackle. She painted spirals on my chest with her nails. 'I could taste your blood calling.'

'And what was it saying?' I trapped Ruby's gaze with mine. 'Sod off?'

Ruby's hand stopped mid-pattern. Then I was howling with pain, unable to move away - held down by the ropes – and absorbing every ounce of agony, as Ruby shoved the torch against my naked gut. At last she pulled away, leaving my skin seared and blistered.

Right, so the bitch intended to cook me slowly.

Ruby had her back to me now, as if she was watching the shadow puppets cast by the torch. 'Do you remember this, darling Light? My little games?'

'Your games. Not mine.'

Ruby twisted back to me – blazing - the queen she'd always been. She flew at me, burning my right shoulder this time, until it blackened.

I screamed, not because I reckoned somebody would hear but because the pain had to go somewhere, or my nut would explode with it. The reek of my own roasting coated my nostrils.

I panted, as Ruby studied me, before gently wiping the tears from my cheek with her trembling finger. 'Nay,' Ruby agreed softly, 'you were all about the kill.'

And Ruby was right. Who was I kidding? Like I was any better? Any *different*? I've never been one for heroics. We'd hunted the world together and drained it dry, so who knew me better than Ruby? That's what I was: one of the Lost. What was the point in trying to deny that to my own Author?

I was a Plantagenet too.

When Ruby leaned closer, I tensed. Ruby, however, merely kissed my cheek, like a mama would their own kid. It'd been so long since anyone had given me that little gesture: it broke something inside.

I wanted to curl into Ruby again and be lost in her deadly safety, as I had for so long. I craved to let her cradle me close and forget how she'd betrayed me for her addiction to bloodlust and power. As our foreheads touched, I swore I saw a glimmer of my old Ruby. The one from before the taint of Advance, which she'd kept just for me, when we were two flames free in the world to dance in its ashes.

Then I remembered: the First Lifers strung on the walls of Radio Komodo, looped with tubes of blood and chemicals and the barren world, which Ruby would've left as her legacy, out of love for a brother, who'd hurt, controlled and battered, until there'd been nothing good left.

The fires were put out. And I was cold again.

Ruby nuzzled my neck. 'Dearest prince, why did you foreswear me?'

'You left me. For him.'

'You were jealous?'

When Ruby sat up, gazing down at me steadily, I read something in her peepers. My hands clenched. 'It was a bloody game? You and Aralt?'

Ruby laughed. 'Love's always a game.'

Maybe I'd been flamed to a crisp but even that was, for a moment, washed out of my shuddering body by a wave of lava hot fury. Those long months of torture and loss. Smelling Aralt on Ruby. Watching her share blood. Everything that had happened since - and all because Ruby had been pulling my strings in some twisted idea of romance, or adding spice, more out of skew even than my own..?

Remember I said that some Blood Lifers come back wrong but there's no such thing as wrong, rather emotions amplified?

What must Ruby have been like in life? How screwed up by her father and husband to play with a bloke like that?

Yet even then I couldn't hate my red-haired devil. That's the thing with your Author. There's a blood bond. And yeah, don't strop, but our love had blazed through the decades and across continents.

But a *game*?

'Not to me,' I said softly, 'it wasn't a game to me.'

Ruby balanced the torch between my bare feet, sprawling over the rock next to me. When she rubbed her body against mine, the fire was back in the blistering burns.

I gritted my teeth.

Ruby pressed her knockers against my chest. 'We played the world together. Ate it ripe. Do not tell me now that you're tamed?' Ruby's long tongue licked against my lips.

'No,' Ruby's tongue retracted, like a snake back into its hole, when I smiled. 'I'm *happy*.'

Ruby sat bolt upright, staring down at me. Then she snatched up the torch, holding it against the sole of my right foot. She always knew how to hurt, Ruby did.

Through the haze of pain, I managed to hiss, 'This world it's...' When Ruby eased off for a moment, I suddenly realised I was desperate not only to stop her burning me again, but for her to understand, so I could return to that feeling of wholeness, like when Ruby had kissed my cheek. 'We get the night; the day's not our due. First Lifers aren't there to crush or conquer, exterminate or enslave, like they're animals. Or we're animals. We're not. None of us. You'd have seen it too if you'd not been bound to the blood, your brother and this desperate desire never to be controlled again. And what am I? Just something for you to mould as dark as you and keep you warm in the shadows? Don't you want something more? We don't need to kill...'

Ruby bayed with laugher then, shocking in its sudden loudness. 'A Blood Lifer who will not kill? Your shyness was not odd when you were first elected. But now?' Her peepers quivered with tears. 'That First Lifer has broken you.'

I managed to smile through the agony, which was hitting me in dizzying waves. 'No. She's freed me.'

Ruby didn't talk to me after that. Instead she made her point with pain and she was bloody good with that. She knew how long to leave it between blows, so you didn't grow numb or fall into shock because you want the bloke to feel it. To build up the anticipation, which is part of the whole deal: the waiting. Pain had always been Ruby's thing. Not mine.

I discovered Ruby knew tricks, which she'd never loosed on me, from an age long before; I guess she'd been playing gentle with me over the years after all.

I told you Ruby remembered the Inquisition from first time around, didn't I?

I began to feel like I was floating, lifted by such expertly dealt agony that there were no coherent thoughts left in me. That's when I knew I was going to cop it. It was only a matter of boredom now - it always was with Ruby.

It was when light was creeping into the upper caves (because Ruby wasn't a climber, she hadn't taken me deep), that we reached that point.

I was coughing, spluttering for breath. My body felt like a thousand different parts, each one screaming, mewling, weeping and each unique in its own hell. Then I saw through my eyelashes, which were thick with matted blood, Ruby picking up a hooked knife – that fitted the sacrificial picture all right. Then her shadow was dark over me.

So, this was it then.

I tensed muscles too sore to tighten and stretch.

How many First Lifers had I plunged down this dark tunnel? I could hear the echo of them ghostly, chanting my name and slow clapping. They were watching for the delicious moment when the light faded from my peepers too.

Then what? No one knows what's for dessert, do they? And right at that moment, *that's* what terrified me, even though it'd never scared me before.

I closed my peepers, waiting for the slice before the spurt, as Ruby cut my throat clean through at the jugular, like a poor bloody lamb.

I groaned in shock, when instead Ruby thrust the knife deep into my chest.

Sodding hell, was that my heart?

My heart was still pumping. I was aware of its beating, as well as the ebb and flow of arteries and veins around my thrashed body, in a heightened way, more than a Blood Lifer does every moment of existence. Then Ruby was cutting in grinding slices around that organ, and I knew - bugger it all, did I know - that she was going to cut my still beating heart from my body and hold it, warm in her hands, before my peepers. Whilst I died.

How's that for a break up?

Ruby's voice was cold with accusation. 'I gifted you Blood Life.'

'No, you robbed me of my death.'

'Then let me return it.' Ruby pushed the knife deeper, and I arched, waiting for it to be over.

There was this sudden look of surprise on Ruby's mush.

The knife loosened in Ruby's fingers, before clattering from them. She looked down.

When I did too, I saw a blossoming burgundy, deeper red than Ruby's dress. It was staining her chest, where her heart was. I smelt her blood.

Then Ruby was falling.

I could see the steel piton buried in Ruby's back. She clutched at me, curling round me as she died, as if she wanted to cradle me, like she always had. Because after half a millennium, the second death had found her.

That's when you saved me – again.

I wish you could remember that: you didn't simply save me once. But twice.

The next thing I saw was your face, gazing down into my swollen peepers, as you wept and repeated over and over, 'The dawn came and you weren't there. The dawn came and you weren't...'

Today I lie here with you, in those quiet hours before dawn breaks, writing this and I know you don't remember me.

Truth, right? It's all I have left.

My First Life died, and now my second life - with you - is fading so fast I can't keep up.

I've lost you, I bloody know that now.

But our love? It exists in these pages and maybe (a bloke can hope can't he?), somewhere buried in that darkly blinding brain of yours.

Did I leave out the poetry? Because at the end, that's all there is: the bleeding words.

When I slept earlier, I dreamt we were strolling down Carnaby Street together in the sun, under the swags of Union Jack flags, by boutiques blaring music and spilling out Mods. You were young again, like me. An unchanging waxwork.

When I awoke, I was suddenly very tired.

Now I study the wisps of white hair, which are caught down your lined cheek. It'd be so easy to live in the memory. To hide nice and safe there, holding the photograph in my palm.

But bugger that.

You once cried salty tears, turning away from me, disgusted by your own ageing body, whilst I remained forever young. You tried to cover your stomach, knockers, muff and then your mug.

Some Blood Lifers pick the ripe before they can wither. All they want to see is mirrored perfection, stretching on for eternity. But that's the Plantagenets of this world. I may bear their name and blood but I'm my own man: no one's ever going to dictate my choices because of family.

The real fun starts with the flaws.

Because here's the thing I've come to realise: First Lifers are meant to decay. Your cells degrade and die every day. But your Souls don't. I still see yours shining bright.

The shell?

One day soon it'll be in the ground, where mine should've been by rights a long time ago. Then I'll bury it and I'll weep. But I'll live because that's all I can do.

I remain the Lost.

I've seen more of this world than I could've ever imagined, even in my dreams, when I stood on London Bridge with my papa. More than I sodding wish I had too. I can't say I've come to a higher understanding.

Blood Lifers shouldn't be revered. That's the greatest bollocks myth of them all. If there's a god, we're damned. But if there's a devil? Then I didn't sign no sodding contract.

Are you happy now you've forgotten me? What's it like not to remember?

I used to reckon that my memory was a blessing. A *miracle* of the *human camera.*

I was wrong.

It's a curse having to relive such nightmares with the clarity of a photograph. If only some of them had moved and blurred to ghosts.

I hope you're happy, my love.

Most of all, I want you to die a mortal death – natural - as you've lived. A First Lifer always. And when you're gone?

You once said that the darkness consumes us all eventually; it swallows us like tasty little titbits, one by one.

Bollocks to that.

If the dark comes, I'll nut it to oblivion. I was never one to conform me. But you know what? You may be lost, and I may be alone, but after all the *nasties and wankery,* I never left you. We're together at the end.

Now *that's* bloody life.

✳✳✳✳

Blood Dragons over too soon? If you enjoyed *Rebel Vampires Volume 1*, you'll love the next book in the series, *Rebel Vampires Volume 2: Blood Shackles*.

Prepare yourself for the secret world of the Blood Club. Read on for an exclusive excerpt.

EXCERPT

REBEL VAMPIRES 2: BLOOD SHACKLES

As M.C. worked on tying me down, the Doctor was busy laying onto the coffee table his grisly work tools: curved extraction forceps, brushed satin stainless steel scissors, orthodontia pliers, an ominously large pile of gauze and a pair of steel dental retractors...

I shuddered, struggling to control my shallow, panted breathing. But I'd been through this once and nothing that'd been done to me had touched this sacrilege: fangs are a Blood Lifer's proof of evolution.

At last I understood why M.C. had made bloody sure you weren't here to witness this abuse.

I couldn't help the tears forming.

The Doctor soothed his hand over my forehead, as if I was his patient, rather than his victim. 'Now, now, come on, be brave; there's a good chap. It'll soon be over. You know the drill: open your mouth.'

I considered keeping my lips clamped shut, but that'd only earn me another dose of the wankering tracker. Reluctantly, I opened my gob. The Doctor shoved in the retractors, winding until my jaw ached. 'Has he been a good enough boy for anaesthetic...this time?' The Doctor gave a bright smile, which didn't reach his peepers.

I stared up at M.C., as if at an executioner. Her expression was hungry and hard. It didn't surprise me, when she shook her nut.

'Shame,' the Doctor purred. Then he spread green plastic sheeting over me and the chair because God forbid my blood stain the furniture, before he selected the steel forceps. He tested them a few times - *the sadistic tosser*. Finally he was all I could see, as he stood close, tapping my canine. 'Fangs out.'

I could feel my fangs shrivelling back inside my gums, like a bloke's goolies when he sees a mate taking a boot to the privates. My half-formed fangs shot out, as the Doctor grabbed me by the hair with one hand and gripped the first fang with the forceps, ready to wrench. I closed my peepers. I tried to hold still but I was shivering.

'What the frig are you doing?' *You*. My saviour. My Sun Girl. *Thank you, thank you, thank you...* And you were dead pissed. 'I said...'

The Doctor didn't even remove the forceps from my fang. In fact, he twisted.

I let out a distorted holler.

Before I knew what was what, the Doctor was sprawled face first on the wooden floorboards, his tools clattered with him.

'Out,' you barked. 'Get your damn asses out of here. Both of you.'

M.C., for the first time, appeared flustered. 'Sis, the Doc's safe. He's gotta remove the liccle leech's fangs before--'

'Get the hell out of my apartment.'

M.C. nodded. 'Alright. But I be telling dad dat you ain't following care instructions. You reckon he be letting you keep an untrained bitch with all its fangs?' The Doctor shuffled – limping - out of the apartment, casting obsequious, apologetic glances at you. M.C., however, threw back, before she slammed the front door, 'When it be mine, I'll do more than defang it, you feel me?'

Then you were a blur: flinging the plastic sheeting off me, unwinding the ropes around the chair, ripping at the knots over my chest, arms and wrists and then dropping to your knees next to me. You rubbed my bruised wrists, which were encircled by a deep purple line, before lifting each to your lips and tenderly kissing them in turn.

I held dead still in case somehow I broke the spell.

My fangs were out, for the first time since they'd last been ripped from my gob. It felt blinding. Yet I also knew how you felt about my Blood Lifer status: this *parasite*.

I began to pull my fangs into my gums, but when you knelt up and gently removed the dental retractor, you didn't recoil.

Gasping with pain, I stretched my jaw. I was still only half a Blood Lifer: my venom wouldn't function until the fangs were fully regrown. But you hadn't let the Blood Club take them again.

You'd saved me.

Now I had to save the others.

You were stroking the back of my hand. 'I...decided I wanted to be here tonight more than work.' Your peepers were bright with tears. 'What if

I'd chosen work..?' Those tears were for me. Deny it all you like. Call it a non-date. I don't sodding care: you couldn't let them do that to me because...*we both know why*. 'Tell me,' you begged, 'everything they did to you.'

Finally, I retracted my fangs and then, even though my wrists throbbed, I took your hand because you looked so bloody defeated. 'Nosey bugger you are. I thought you were reading my journal?'

'The truth.'

'It is the truth.'

'I need...the worst.'

'It's not enough?'

You examined me with an intense gaze. '*Family*? *Promises*? There's a whole notha buried story going on. And I wanna know.'

I tensed. *You're no daft bint, are you*? 'If I tell you...will you let me go?'

You snatched your hand back from mine in shock. 'You wanna leave me?'

I shoved up from the chair, still unsteady but unable to stop my agitated pacing. 'I want to be free, sweetheart.'

'Then *no*, Light,' your voice had hardened, as you too pushed yourself up, your arms firmly crossed. 'If freeing you means I lose you, then frickin' no.'

I was breathing too rapidly. 'OK then, how about this: loan me out...just for...buggering hell...for a bit? I've got business, right?'

'Business?' You stared at me blankly.

'I'll write it. The worst of it. What I've promised and left behind. I write it. You read it. Then you'll understand why you need to let me go. Even if I have to come back to you.'

✳✳✳✳

Want to find out what happens next in *Rebel Vampires Volume 2: Blood Shackles*?

Pre-order it today on Amazon.

Blood Shackles is released November 2016. Then sit back and experience the secret world of the Blood Club...

DID YOU LIKE THIS BOOK?

Let everyone know by posting a review on Amazon and Goodreads.

Remember, please feed this author reviews – they're better than chocolate (and Rosemary *loves* chocolate...)

Love Reading Gripping Fantasy?

If so, sign up to Rosemary A John's VIP Email List to be notified of new promotions and never miss out on hot new releases.

Indulge yourself, grab a coffee and then dive into a Fantasy Rebel book – they're fantasy for rebels.

Plus you'll also receive Rosemary's FREE and exclusive short story "All the Tin Soldiers".

It's our gift to you.

Visit Rosemary's website to subscribe: rosemaryajohns.com

ABOUT THE AUTHOR

ROSEMARY A JOHNS wrote her first fantasy novel at the age of ten, when she discovered the weird worlds inside her head were more exciting than double swimming. Teachers called her parents, concerned about the 'strange fantasy and science fiction books' she was avidly reading. Her parents were rather proud of that. Since then she's studied history at Oxford University, run a theatre company (her critically acclaimed plays have been described as 'uncomfortable, unsettling and uneasily true to life') and worked with disability charities. She believes everyone is different. An individual. When Rosemary's not falling in love with the rebels fighting their way onto the page, she heads the Oxford writing group Dreaming Spires. She can also be found listening to Nirvana. At full volume. Or not found at all. When she's dived into her secret world again.

Hooked on *Rebel Vampires*?

Let the world know. Go to Amazon and Goodreads to leave a review today. Remember, reviews are better than chocolate - and Rosemary *loves* chocolate...

Reward yourself with another enthralling book by Rosemary A Johns. Pre-order *Rebel Vampires Volume 2: Blood Shackles* now on Amazon.

Discover Rosemary's dark scribblings online:
rosemaryajohns.com
www.facebook.com/RosemaryAnnJohns
www.twitter.com/RosemaryAJohns
https://uk.pinterest.com/rosemaryjohns1
https://uk.linkedin.com/in/rosemary-johns-488603121

Questions? Comments? Random thoughts? Rosemary would love to hear from you.

Go ahead and drop Rosemary a line at:
rosemary.johns1@btinternet.com

Member of a Book Club?

Share *Blood Dragons* with your group and delve into the free Reading Group Notes at rosemaryajohns.com

18461627R00173

Printed in Great Britain
by Amazon